The
Pieces of
Ourselves

The Pieces of Ourselves

MAGGIE HARCOURT

USBORNE

For my mother, who would have said "I told you so".

(And yes. She did.)

First published in the UK in 2020 by Usborne Publishing Ltd., Usborne House, 83-85 Saffron Hill, London EC1N 8RT, England. www.usborne.com

Text © Maggie Harcourt 2020

The right of Maggie Harcourt to be identified as the author of this work has been asserted by her in accordance with the Copyright, Designs and Patents Act, 1988.

Author photograph © Lou Abercrombie

Close up surface floating water with ripples © MP_Foto/Shutterstock; Lonely girl sitting in front of lake © Sirle Kabanen/Shutterstock; Green sea water in calm © Joe Besure/Shutterstock; Autumn Tree Reflecting in Ripple in Creek © Michael Warwick/Shutterstock

The name Usborne and the devices ♀ ⊕ USBORNE are Trade Marks of Usborne Publishing Ltd.

A CIP catalogue record for this book is available from the British Library.

ISBN 9781474940696   04702/1   FMAMJJASOND/20

Printed and bound in Great Britain by CPI Group (UK) Ltd, Croydon, CR0 4YY

"What's past is prologue."
William Shakespeare, *The Tempest*

One

I have picked the worst possible moment to be standing on the pavement outside the village shop: the *exact* moment the bus to the sixth-form college goes past on its last morning run of the term.

If only I hadn't agreed to pick up my brother's parcel from the post office counter before work.

If only Mr Parkins and his stupid package to Australia hadn't been ahead of me in the queue.

If only I hadn't told my friend Mira that I'd meet her and we could walk back up to the hotel to start our housekeeping shifts together.

If.

Only.

But here I am, and here's the bus, and as it stops to let Mr Parkins cross the road with agonizing slowness, every single face behind the bus windows turns to look at me – and I am fixed to the spot as firmly and definitively as if someone had driven iron spikes through my shoes.

Everything stops: time, my heart, the movement of the Earth through space. *Everything.* I am trapped in this moment, pinned like a butterfly on a board. Me on one side of the windows; the people I used to go to school with, the people I used to know – the people I *used to be friends with* – staring at me from the other.

And then Mr Parkins has made it to the other side of the street and, just like that, the world is moving again and the bus is gone. I step off the pavement to watch it disappear from view between the hedges and the green overhanging branches of trees.

There goes the life I could have had.

Almost did have.

A strange, horrible screeching sound fills my head, drowning everything else out – and at first I wonder if it's just in my head or whether it's me and I'm doing it out loud…and then I realize that Mrs Rolfe from the Old Vicarage has stopped in the middle of the pavement and is staring at me, and the screech stops and there's a new noise. One that sounds a bit like…like a car horn.

A car horn coming from behind me.

I'm in the middle of the road, aren't I? That screech was brakes.

Slowly, I turn around.

It's an old green car – one of those vintage things that looks like a squashed frog.

More blasts on the horn, sharp and angry, then long. One-two-three-*fooooooouuuurrrr*.

Sweat prickles along the back of my neck, along the lines of my palms.

Is everybody looking? Has anyone else seen? Are people peering from behind their curtains to see what all the noise is in this tiny little nothing village at this time of the morning?

No big deal – just Flora Sutherland, standing in the middle of the road.

I make myself take a step sideways, back to the safety of the pavement, and hope that's enough. I wish the car would go, that the ground could swallow me, that nobody has noticed or shaken their heads and thought, *Well, what do you expect from someone like her?* But the driver's door swings open with a creak.

"What the hell are you doing? I almost hit you!"

Red hair, sunglasses above a dark T-shirt, and a face bleached pale with shock.

"Are you *crazy*? Hello? HELLO?!"

The word "crazy" hits me harder than the car could ever have done. I flinch – then panic in case he saw, but he whisks straight past me and drops into a crouch in front of the car.

He's checking it for damage. Buffing at the paint with the palm of his hand.

He doesn't care whether he nearly hit me. He cares

whether I somehow dinged his paint job.

I take a deep breath, hugging Charlie's parcel tighter to my chest like a shield.

Is this a balanced reaction?

Satisfied I haven't magically dented his paintwork, he turns back to me and sees me watching him.

"What the hell do you think you're doing, just standing there in the road? Have you got some kind of death wish?" He pulls the sunglasses off his face and waves them around him like he's conducting the orchestra at an outrage concert. "If I hadn't looked up right then..." he starts – then stops himself.

"Maybe," I say quietly, "you should look where you're going." I almost add, "Instead of calling other people crazy..." but decide it's better if I don't.

"Maybe," he snaps back, "you shouldn't stand in traffic." He's younger than someone with that kind of car should be. My age, maybe a couple of years older. Eighteen? Nineteen? His eyes are a washed-out shade somewhere between blue and green, and he squints against the bright sunshine.

"Yes. Traffic. There's so much of it round here," I mutter, turning my face away again and letting his gaze slide off me.

I hear him open his mouth to speak, but there's no other sound.

Just go. Get in your car and go. Leave me alone.

He still hasn't moved. Why won't he go?

"Look, seriously, are you okay?" He says it gently now – there's real concern in his voice. "Do you need me to call some—"

"I'm fine," I snap. "You can go now. Really." The edges of the parcel dig into my ribs, and there's a pounding in my ears – I can't tell if it's my heart or my brain that's thumping, but something is. Maybe it's both of them.

"Can you just leave? Please?"

"Wow. Okay." He leans away, his eyes as wide as if I'd slapped him. "Fine. Whatever. I mean… Jesus. I was just trying to find this hotel…"

His lips keep moving, but it doesn't matter; I can't hear a word.

He's a *guest*.

He's talking about Hopwood Home Hotel. There are no other hotels for miles around. There's *nothing else at all* for miles around, not out here.

Oh god, he's a guest he's a guest he's a guest.

Get it together, Flora.

He reaches into the car, pulling a sheet of paper from the dashboard. The sheet of paper he must have been looking at when he nearly hit me. He holds it out. "I don't suppose you know where it is, do you? It's not on my satnav and there's *no* phone reception out here."

"I work there." It falls out of my mouth before I can stop it. I end up half-swallowing the last part of "there" and feel stupid. He, however, brightens.

"Oh, amazing. I'm so lost. Totally, totally lost." Running a hand back through his hair, he looks around – as though to say that the only reason he'd be anywhere near a village like Hopwood-in-the-Hollows is to pass through it on the way to somewhere else. With that kind of car, and dressed the way he is – carefully, neatly, probably expensively – it seems about right.

And if he's staying at the Hopwood, and I've been stupid enough to let slip that I work there, the last thing I need is him complaining about the super-unhelpful staff member standing in the road on his way to check in.

Get it together, Flora. The sooner he gets directions, the sooner he'll be gone.

"You're going the wrong way."

"I am?" He squints along the road, the same way the bus went, then turns around to look behind him. "But…"

"You need to turn around then go back through the village, past the pub and take a right. Go past the farm with the ice-cream sign shaped like a cow, then keep going until the road gets narrow and forks off to the left. Take the left fork, and there'll be a metal gate with a gatehouse and an intercom. That's the hotel."

There's a long silence, then: "So that was a left at the farm?"

"Do you have a pen?"

He hands me the paper, and reaches back into the car to pull out a biro with a chewed end. I slide the parcel under one arm, and sketch out a quick map. It's not good, and I realize it was a mistake to try and make the cow-shaped sign actually cow-shaped so I label it "cow", but at least it should get him to the Hopwood. And away from me.

I pass the paper back and he takes it, nodding. "Thanks," he says – and hesitates. "You sure you're okay?"

Am I sure I'm okay?

Ask me that a year ago.

"Fine. Thanks." I slide the parcel back around to my chest and look down at the floor. "Please just go?"

The almost-smile on his face disappears behind a frown. "No problem. Thanks for…whatever."

I wince as he slams his door, starting the engine with a loud roar…and just like that, he's driving away.

And there – coming up the street with perfect timing – is Mira, rounding the corner from her house with her bag over her shoulder, sunglasses pulled down over her eyes and her housekeeping uniform looking like she slept in it. She raises her head and smiles when she sees me, stuffing the envelope she's carrying into her pocket.

"What's that?" She nods at the package in my arms.

"Charlie's anniversary present for Felix. He asked me to pick it up for him." And on every level possible, I wish I'd said I couldn't.

Mira makes a thoughtful noise as – tyres screeching – the green car goes past the other way, vanishing around the corner behind the village primary school with its row of sunflowers along the front wall.

"What happened to your uniform?" I ask, but Mira just shakes her head.

"No asking questions, thank you," she mutters – and when I open my mouth to do exactly that, she growls something in Polish at me. My Polish is non-existent, but this being Mira, I'm willing to bet that what she said is very, very rude.

See? Everything's normal. Everything's *fine*.

Except she's eyeing me suspiciously. "You're not right."

"I'm perfectly right, thanks."

"Also a terrible liar. What's wrong?"

"Nothing's wrong. Honestly."

"No. Really." She peers at me over her sunglasses. "You had one of your mad head things?"

"Can we not call them that?" I drop my bag from my shoulder and squeeze the parcel into it, forcing the zip of my backpack shut over the top.

"But that's what you called them!"

Which is true, because how else was I meant to explain the stuff that goes on in my head to my best friend? Charlie knows all the proper words for it, and what they all mean, because he's my big brother. I know all the proper words for it and what they all *feel* like because…well, it's my head. But how do you explain the inside of your mind to somebody else – particularly when it doesn't work quite the way it's meant to? Besides, nothing seemed to do the job of describing the anxiety or the swings between crazy energy and slow heavy despair better than "a mad head thing". Trying to describe what my brain is doing at any given point to someone who isn't inside it is kind of like…trying to explain the point of an octopus to an apple.

"You're okay, yes?"

You're okay, Flora. You're okay. Be okay.

"I'm okay."

"Good, because…you know. Tick tock." She waves her wrist in front of my face, trying to make a point about the time.

"Your watch is on upside down."

More Polish swearing, but at least she's laughing as she switches it round. "Upside down or not, we're going to be late. Tell me whatever it is bothering you on the way. And you've got your parcel, so?"

I sling my bag back up onto my shoulder, wondering if becoming friends with Mira was some kind of cosmic trade-off for losing everything else. I nod. "So. Let's go."

We take the usual shortcut round the back of the village and head for the grounds of the hotel, clambering over a stile and cutting through a field. The tall grass is splashed with patches of red poppies, and swifts screech and wheel overhead as I tell Mira about the bus and about the guy with the green car. She nods, and even though I know she can't completely understand *why* it's set me so much on edge, she understands that it has – and that's all I need.

When I get to the bit about the guy turning out to be a guest, she winces. When I admit that I told him I work at the Hopwood, she laughs as we climb over the low wooden fence marking the Hopwood estate boundary into the woods.

"But you know he will already have forgotten you, right? Staff don't have faces to them. We're just...part of the furniture."

"Them" being the kind of people who come to stay at Hopwood Home. And she's right. Nobody notices us.

Which is one of the reasons I came here.

The hotel grounds unspool over miles of gardens, woods, fields, river, deer park – even estate cottages for some of the staff, like the one I live in. Hopwood Home used to be one of those big wealthy family mansions before the First World War, but now it's a hotel: one of, according to the brochure, the top thirty-five boutique country house hotels in the country. Which has always sounded like a bit of a weird number to me, but I don't write the marketing material. All I have to do is clean the rooms.

Also, not be late.

After working here for nine months full-time, and a whole year of weekend and summer hours before that, I'm still struggling with that second one.

I try a change of subject. "What was that post you had?"

Even from behind her sunglasses, I can feel her blinking at me. "Post?"

"When you were coming up the road earlier."

"No?"

"That envelope you put in your pocket – I mean, god, I'm just trying to make conversation."

"Oh. Junk mail." She straightens her sunglasses and sniffs. To anyone who doesn't know Mira like I do, it might seem like she's kind of grumpy – but I do know Mira, and that's not it at all. If she was really grumpy or prickly, she wouldn't be so patient. She wouldn't be the one who crosses her arms and tells me I've got into "one of those bad thinking circles" when my thoughts start spiralling down into the darkness, or that I'm being an idiot when my mania kicks in – because that's what it looks like from outside. The thing about Mira is that mostly she's just not good at mornings – which I guess is a bit problematic when your job is all about mornings.

The woods give way to the gardens: mown and rolled lawns spread out like green velvet around the gravelled drive, still sparkling with dew, and the sun makes the front of the hotel looks like it's glowing. We walk round to the staff entrance at the side, down the narrow stone steps and along the corridor to the locker room. Already in her uniform, all Mira has to do is throw her bag and sunglasses in her locker, leaving me to cram my backpack into my own with one hand while yanking out my uniform on its hanger with the other. Miraculously, I manage to change into my dress and apron, kick off my trainers and shove my feet into my work plimsolls *and* make it into the staff room a full five seconds before Mrs Tilney walks in with the worksheets for the day.

If only I wasn't so out of breath, she might have thought I'd actually been there ages.

She hands out the day's room lists, checking off our names on her clipboard as she goes, and giving Mira a very long hard look as she passes, one eyebrow raised. Mira tries to smooth some of the creases out of her dress with her hand. It doesn't work. Between us, we've got six rooms to do – all changeovers, needing a full clean and fresh sheets and towels ahead of new arrivals – and something on the list that I've not seen before. A room marked with a green star.

When Mrs Tilney asks if there are questions, I raise my hand. "Mrs T? What's the mark next to room fifteen?"

"Hmm?"

"The star. Is it important?"

"Oh, number fifteen. Yes. I wanted to talk to you and Mira about that one." She looks over her shoulder at the rest of the staff – three of them today, all pretty new. "The rest of you can go make a start," she says, before turning back to us. "Room fifteen. It's a long-stay booking – ten nights – so it needs a few extras."

"Ten nights?" Mira says it, but I'm thinking it too. Ten nights here is a long time – nobody ever stays for ten nights. Two or three, sure. Four at the very most. But *ten*? Out here? Being in the middle of nowhere is one of the things Hopwood Home sells itself on – other than a handful of villages and a couple of National Trust houses, there's nothing but fields and trees for miles around. No big towns, no cities, nothing.

The perfect place to escape from absolutely everything. The kind of place to run away to.

And whatever the reason they're coming, a ten-night stay means they're obviously *loaded*.

Two

Room fifteen is up on the second floor of the hotel, overlooking the gardens at the front. For guests, it's lovely because it's reached by the grand staircase in the lobby, then by another secret, narrow, wooden one hidden behind a bookcase at the end of the first-floor landing. Checking in and being led up the stairs for the first time must be pretty magical. For housekeeping staff, however, who have to get a laundry trolley up there, the journey is slightly less magical because it involves the ancient freight lift, which can only take one person and a trolley and always sticks between the basement and the ground floor. I draw the short straw and get lumbered with the trolley, so by the time I get to the room Mira is already waiting, the key in her hand. She tosses it to me, then knocks on the door. We both wait.

"Who do you think it is coming? Somebody famous?"

"Why would somebody famous – who could go *literally*

anywhere – come here?" With no answer from the room, I fumble with the keys until the lock clicks and the door swings open.

We've just finished stripping the bed and straightening the mess left by the last guest when a scraping noise drifts up through the open window, along with faint whistling. Someone's working on the flower bed below.

Charlie.

His parcel! The parcel I promised I'd drop off with him before I started my shift!

Mira hears him at the same time I do. "You didn't give it to him, did you?"

"I completely forgot. With the bus, and the car, and then being late…"

"It can't wait until we've got a break?"

"No. It's…" I lower my voice, just in case. "It's their anniversary *today*."

"He forgot?" Mira's eyes widen.

"*Again*. Felix will kill him."

"Go."

"Two minutes," I promise, backing out of the room. "I'll be quick."

I make it down to the locker room, grab the parcel and run out to Charlie in record time. He leans on his rake as he watches me sprint round the corner from the staff entrance, his wavy hair pushed back from his face by a green bandana that matches his gardener's uniform.

"Did you get it?"

"Here," I pant, holding it out to him.

"I owe you one. I don't think Felix would forgive me if I forgot again this year." My older brother winces, taking the box and tucking it into his wheelbarrow.

"What is it, anyway? It better be worth it." I decide not to tell him any more about my morning – despite the quizzical look he shoots me – and point at the parcel in the wheelbarrow. "It's not another T-shirt, is it? Tell me it's not another T-shirt." Felix's collection of Metallica shirts is already out of control.

Charlie beams. "Original nineties *Burn your fingers* design. He's wanted one for years."

"Oh." As presents for Felix go, that one's pretty much perfect.

Charlie studies me carefully. "What's wrong?"

Obviously my attempt at misdirection has not worked.

Above us, Mira sticks her head out of the window of room fifteen. "Tell him."

"Mira!" I hiss back up at her – but it's too late. The damage is done, and Charlie's expression has already changed from interest to concern.

"Tell me what?"

"It's nothing."

"Tell me."

"I said it's nothing. It was just the school bus, that's all. It went past. No big deal." I shrug and try to wave the question away, wave the whole memory away…but it hovers above me like a stubborn wasp.

"Flora."

"And then there was this guy with a car, and…" I pause to choose the right words; ones that won't make Charlie freak out and tell me to go through the checklist. "And it was…fine?" This comes out less confidently than I had hoped – mostly because as soon as I even start thinking about the bus and that guest with the car, my stomach turns cold and fills with acid and twists itself into a tangle.

It all replays inside my head, scene by scene in bright colours and extreme close-up. The faces inside the bus. The car hooting. The guest getting out of his car. Oh, god. Was I all right? I told him to leave, didn't I? Is he going to arrive at the hotel and tell them how awful I was?

The questions form a staircase, each step lower than the one before and leading me down, down, down inside my mind.

Is this a balanced reaction?

Charlie leans his rake against the barrow. "You know you're meant to tell me if something—"

"I said I'm *FINE!*" I snap.

Charlie just blinks slowly at me, his expression carefully neutral. Waiting.

"I was coming out of the post office, okay? And the bus

23

was there, and it stopped, and I saw a bunch of people from school, and they saw me. And they were staring, and basically it sucked. Okay? And I didn't want to have to come running to you and talk about it, *because* it sucked."

"I understand that. Have you gone through your checklist?"

"I don't need the checklist."

"It's part of the deal. Anything that upsets you, you're supposed to go through the checklist and decide whether you're reacting to it…" He hesitates – then stops altogether.

I finish his sentence for him. "Like a not-crazy person?"

"I was going to say, like someone who has a more balanced view of the world. But sure…" He smiles at me. "Not-crazy works too."

"I said I don't need the checklist." This is so *humiliating*.

"Part of the deal."

"Well, the deal sucks too."

"Flora…"

"And it's not like you're Dad or anything…"

"So stop making me have to behave like I am!" he groans.

I look at my shoes, feeling a stab of guilt. Charlie's nothing like our dad. He's still here, for a start, and he's probably the closest thing to a proper father I've ever known. Our *actual* father decided that he didn't really want to do the parent thing again when I came along ten years after my brother – an accident apparently – so he left.

I wouldn't have taken it personally, except he set up a whole new family pretty quickly after that, one we've never met. So I guess it wasn't that he didn't want to do the parent thing again – he just didn't want to do it for us. For me.

"Sorry," I mumble.

Charlie pulls his bandana off his head and his hair flops across his face.

"I don't want to have to nag you. Christ, I'm not the life police. You're entitled to do your own thing, have your own space – but you know the rules. You don't want to get ill again."

No. I don't. That's why I'm here, isn't it? Because everything out there is…too much.

"And a bus full of the kids you used to go to school with – who were all there – I think that counts as something you should mention, don't you?"

"Yes, Charlie." I make a circle in the dusty gravel of the path with my shoe. "Sorry, Charlie."

"And you can drop that attitude while you're at it." He shakes his head in frustration, suddenly sounding a lot more than ten years older than me. "I just want you to be all right. You've been doing so well lately – you've been so stable. I promised Mum when she moved… I promised her that Felix and I would make sure you were okay…"

"You promised you wouldn't let me spiral up *or* down, I know. Look, I'm not going to totally lose my mind in the next fifteen minutes. That's not how it works."

25

"That's not what I meant."

I can see the tension in his face – in the set of his jaw and the little vertical lines above the bridge of his nose. He gets them every time we have to talk about my condition – even more so if the "Incident" comes up. It's not like I ever want to talk about it either, or even think about it – all it does is remind me of another life. *My* other life. A life with messages and phone calls, with cinema trips in a group all sharing popcorn and going to get food and to dissect every minute of it afterwards; with shopping, with music and gigs and shouting across the seats of the bus and…

"I'm fine. It was just a lot. Especially with suddenly having a total stranger in my face and being a nightmare."

"You're sure?"

"Which one of us is living in my head?" I snap back. "Me or you?"

"Flora…"

"Me. Exactly. So which one of us is likely to know whether I'm fine or not?"

He doesn't respond. All I can hear is the cry of the swifts overhead and a sudden clatter of crockery from the breakfast room nearby.

Finally, he scrubs a hand back and forth across his face. "You know the answer to that," he says softly.

And however much I hate it, and hate him for saying it – maybe even hate him more for knowing it – he's right. It's not me.

* * *

There was an Incident – *The* Incident. Halfway through my GCSEs. Halfway through an actual paper, in fact. I don't really remember it. I don't really remember much for weeks before it either, other than the constant trickle of pre-exam stress – an ever-present prickle of panic under the top layer of my mind... And then suddenly it all went away. I wasn't stressed any more, wasn't panicked about my exams or revising or any of it – I just knew I could do it. Better than that, I wasn't just going to pass, I was going to pass *amazingly*. Of course I was. It all suddenly made sense, like someone had switched on a light in a dark room, or opened a magical door that had *everything* behind it. The world was brighter, louder and sharper. Everything was clearer – so clear that I wanted to run down the street shaking people and telling them to *look*...

And then it all went wrong.

I went wrong.

Actually, that's not true. It wasn't me that went wrong, it was my wiring, the switches, the tiny little invisible lights that come on and go off inside my brain which broke. And when they stopped working properly, they took me, Flora Sutherland, down with them.

I've tried to piece it all back together from what Charlie's told me, from what the doctor and Sanjay, my therapist, have said. It's not easy because even the things I remember feel wrong, like I'm looking at the memories underwater – the edges of them are too sharp and too shiny, and they don't feel like they happened to me at all.

I know I was revising beforehand. I didn't sleep much – a couple of hours a night at most – but I wasn't tired. At all. I sat my first few exams and I was fine. More than fine. I had so much energy, and everything seemed so easy all of a sudden. I was even the first one to finish, by a long way. Like, an *hour* early. In a two-hour paper.

The morning it happened, I got up and went to school – like I had done every other day. I sat down and waited for the exam to start – like I had done every other day. I started writing – like I had done every other day.

And just like that, "every other day" became something that only *used* to happen.

After that, there were waiting rooms – I remember that much. Blue plastic chairs and wall-mounted bottles of antibacterial handwash.

And then there were pills: a prescription from the GP, who handed the slip over with a smile and a "Let's see how you do with these."

He referred me to Sanjay, in his little office in the corner of the surgery building, where the blinds were always drawn. "Mania," he called it, this thing that had stripped me away from myself. It was mania that took "every other day" away. It was mania that meant I wouldn't – couldn't – be on that bus with everyone else who had sat those exams. I thought too quickly, spoke too quickly, jumped from idea to idea *way* too quickly. My brain had got stuck in high gear and nobody could keep up with it – not even me.

And everyone, everyone I knew…they all saw it.

I didn't care at the time. I was moving too fast and burning too brightly. In my head, I was a superhero. I was a genius. I was a comet, a sun, a shooting star…

But even suns burn out, and shooting stars fall to earth, and comets are nothing but exploding ice; enormous dirty snowballs crashing through space. And so after the high came the low, and the weeks when even breathing hurt; where every thought felt like it was wrapped in mud and all I wanted to do was sleep and sleep and sleep. To lie face down on the floor and never get up again. Ever.

So. Back to the doctor.

"Mmm. Everything you're telling me – the heaviness, the slowness, the exhaustion – sounds like a classic depressive episode," he said, nodding at me. "Mania *and* depression in a cycle like this?" He typed something into his computer. "I think we're looking at bipolar disorder here. Bipolar II."

There was another prescription. There were more pills. There was more Sanjay.

Suddenly Flora's Craziness was real. It wasn't just in my

head – even if it sort of was. It had a label and a name. Even if I didn't recognize it, couldn't figure out what it meant or whether I was supposed to just live with it now…or why it had landed on *me*.

One thing never changed. I might have had a head full of crazy, but I also had Charlie.

It was Charlie who sorted out the mess with school, who tried to get me to go back and resit. Charlie who drove me from appointment to appointment in his old Land Rover that makes you feel like your bones are being shaken loose. Charlie (and Felix) who moved me into the spare room in the cottage in the Hopwood grounds when Mum said her job was being relocated up north, and wouldn't it be better for me to stay here, somewhere familiar? I remember hearing the fight between Mum and Charlie from my old bedroom and I've never heard him as angry as he was then, accusing her of running away. I don't blame her. I'd have run away from me too if I could. I ran away from everything else.

It was Charlie and Felix who put me back together. Charlie sat on the floor of my room and read to me when all I could do was stare at the ceiling; he held my hair back when the medication I'd been given to help flatten out the roller coaster in my head made me sick for twenty-four hours straight. Felix dragged me out of the house and along with him on his regular tours of the estate – pointing out trees and badger setts and rabbit tracks, calling out bird songs as he heard them, making me hear them too.

Together, they made me remember who I am – who I *really* am, rather than the ball of misfiring mental wires that looked a little like me. They gave the world shape again. They gave *me* shape again. Because roller-coaster Flora wasn't quite me – she was just a fraction of me, a faction of me.

So now I *am* me again. But I'm just…not always good at holding on to the actual me. And that's what this is about – Charlie and his deal, the checklists, the constant self-analysis and self-editing. It's about holding my shape, keeping me together. Stopping another Incident, even though that's what being bipolar is: a cycle, a roller coaster, a constant orbit around my very own axis. I just wish I could do that without all the questions I have to ask myself every time I feel *anything* – good or bad: *is this a balanced reaction? Does my mood match the moment?*

Finally, Charlie reties his bandana round his head, and looks me up and down. "Okay," he says.

"Okay?" I blink at him. "No checklist?"

"You say you're all right. I don't have much choice except to believe you, do I?"

I shrug. "I just got a bit…flustered. That's all. Look, I have to get back to work." I turn back to the hotel and mutter: "And also kill Mira for making me tell you."

"You leave Mira be," Charlie calls after me. "She's looking out for you. We all are."

At a jog, I shove through the glass front door into the lobby – it'll be far quicker than taking the staff entrance, and I need to get back up to the second floor before Mrs Tilney does her first round of the day – but halfway across the polished wooden floor, I freeze.

A new arrival is standing beside the soft velvet sofas by the window; an expensive looking leather bag and a smart backpack stacked on top of each other by his feet, a bundle of papers on the low coffee table in front of him.

Red hair, sunglasses pushed up onto the top of his head.

Oh no.

With a sinking feeling, I step back from the door and lean out into the sunlight to check the drive. There it is: the squashed-frog car.

When I creep back into the lobby, he has pulled off his sunglasses and is watching me. His gaze is direct, unflinching.

He recognizes me.

Oh *god.*

"Mr Waverley? I'm Barney, the general manager. Welcome to Hopwood Home…"

The voice comes from behind me as Barney strides across the lobby from his office. He passes me, shoes clicking against the polished floor and walks up to the guy, holding out his hand to shake. I dart for the staff door behind the check-in desk, but even when the door has closed behind me, I can still feel those pale eyes on me.

Upstairs, Mira has already finished room fifteen and is packing all our cleaning stuff back into the trolley. "Quick, you said," she snorts, throwing a towel at me as I walk in through the open door.

"And I would have been, if you hadn't dropped me in it with Charlie."

She pouts, looking about as unapologetic as it's possible to be when something is technically your fault. "He needed to know."

"Did he, though? I mean, *did* he?" I wave the plug of the vacuum cleaner at her.

"Yes." She pouts some more, and I sigh.

"How can I disagree with an argument like that?"

She throws another towel – and it's right when I bend over to pick them both up that Mrs Tilney appears from nowhere in the doorway.

"Flora? Barney would like to see you in his office, please. Now."

Three

The door to Barney's office is firmly closed, the little brass plaque in the middle that reads *Barney Scott, General Manager* gleaming at me like an eye. I straighten my already-straight uniform for the third time and knock.

"Come in."

Barney is sitting at his desk, stacks of paperwork piled up across the wooden top in front of him, his back to a big window that overlooks the drive and gardens. He looks up and smiles as I close the door. Which is a more promising start than I'd expected.

"Flora. Take a seat." He gestures to the old leather chair in front of his desk and shoves one of the paper stacks aside.

"Mrs Tilney said you wanted to see me?" The chair makes an alarming creak as I sit down.

"I did. It's about a guest who checked in this morning."

Of course it is. *He's complained. I knew he looked like a complainer.*

I stare at the edge of Barney's desk, waiting.

He reaches into one of the drawers, pulling out a stapled form and turning the pages to read them. I catch a glimpse of my own handwriting – or at least, my handwriting from a couple of years ago, when I applied for the Saturday job here.

Overthinking things is what I do, but having your boss pull your job application form out of his desk is *probably* not good.

"There we go – that's what I thought," he says, more to himself than to me. "On your form, there's a section for awards and achievements, and you've put *winner of regional school history competition.*" He lowers the papers and looks at me over the top. "Maybe you could tell me a bit more about that?"

"Umm…"

What is there to say? That my history teacher had cornered me at the end of class one day and told me I should enter – that it was something she thought I'd be interested in, and good at? And I was. Out of all the projects submitted, from all the schools in the whole south-west, mine won. I spent weeks working on it, researching it, drawing little maps, putting together the perfect project on all the places Jane Austen lived in Bath. I remember how much I loved doing it…but maybe that was just a little light mania and I didn't know it. Maybe every time I've thought I've been good at something, I've actually just been mad. Maybe it was the mad bit of me who won.

Barney takes pity on me and smiles again, dropping the application form on the desk and folding his hands on top of it.

"It's fine, Flora. You're not in trouble. Whatever it is you've done that you think I know about, I don't know about it yet." He pauses, then adds: "*Is* there anything?"

"No! No, no. I was just…" I shake my head, picking at the edge of a fingernail. "I didn't want to be in trouble." I sound like a kid.

"It's not that at all – as a matter of fact, it's something you can help me with. Well," he says, "not me, exactly. A guest."

I'm not sure I like where this is going.

"We've got a new guest, who's staying with us for a while in room fifteen…"

The long stay. With a sinking feeling, I connect the dots.

This morning's guy in the lobby
who obviously recognized me

+

long-staying guest who is clearly said guy

=

so much for Mira confidently saying
he'd forget about me.

"…and he's doing some kind of research – a personal project. He could use a little help, and I thought with your

36

interest…" Barney picks up the form again and waves it.

"You want me to help a guest with research?"

"I've already spoken to Mrs Tilney about it, and she's cleared your shifts from the rota…"

"You can't take my shifts!" It comes out in a panicked blurt before I can stop it. I can hear how desperate I sound – but I can't help it, because if I'm not here, not at the hotel and working and cleaning and *busy*…what else is there?

Barney leans back in his chair and steeples his fingers together, studying me over the top of them. He does it for a very, very long time, but when he speaks his voice is soft and warm, his Dublin accent stronger than usual.

"I'm not taking your shifts, don't worry. You're still down for the same hours and the same pay. You'll just be doing different work, that's all."

"What kind of work?" I focus very, very hard on a red paper clip by his elbow.

"Research, reading, cataloguing. Sorting through papers. Whatever Mr Waverley needs help with."

"I'm not really a researcher, though. What if I do it wrong?"

"I think you're underestimating yourself. Besides, I don't think any of it will be too complicated."

I open my mouth to say something else, but he shakes his head and continues. "Just think about it. Please. As I was about to say, this could be good for the hotel. A bit of publicity, maybe? We can always do with that, and whatever it is Mr Waverley is looking for, it's brought him here. You know we have a lot of old papers in the attics, don't you?"

I do. It's one of the first things Mrs Tilney told me when I started: the top floor of the hotel is divided in two; one half is storerooms, the other is the old attics. And the old attics are completely off-limits to housekeeping staff because of all the old boxes left in there, dumped after the Second World War. Nobody is *ever* allowed in the attics. Which was annoying, because after hearing about them, they were the first place I wanted to go.

"He's going into the attics?"

"No. I've arranged to have some of the boxes up there brought down to the library for him – to begin with, at least."

"Oh." I don't even bother hiding my disappointment. For a minute there, this almost sounded like it might be interesting.

"It's good business, Flora – he's an important client. His family own the Waverley Hotels group…"

"So he's not so much a client as the competition?"

Barney laughs. "While he's staying here, he's a client. Whatever else he is too. Although," he adds, "I can tell you, his father Eddie is a grade-A, weaponized *arse*." He grins conspiratorially. "Luckily for us, the son doesn't seem quite so bad."

Great, I guess?

"So I just…help him sort through papers? That's all?"

"More or less. I'm sure he'll explain in person."

Outside, one of the waiters is sprinting across the drive, his shoes kicking up gravel, his tie clutched in one hand. Realizing he's in sight of Barney's window, he slows to an invisible-staff kind of walk...then, blatantly thinking he's in the clear, speeds up again as he heads for the staff entrance.

Barney chuckles, shaking his head. "Daft fecker thinks I can only see him when he's dead in front of me." He stares out of the window for a moment, then turns back to me. "So what do you say?"

"I think..."

I think what? That I don't exactly have much of a choice; that if this is what I'm being told to do, it's what I have to do. Barney's been pretty good about, well, *me* and I don't want to make a fuss so...mostly I think that I should just keep quiet and nod, and deal with all this later.

I take a deep breath. "When do you need me?"

"You'll do it? Great. I knew I could rely on you, Flora." He taps his knuckles lightly on his desk – then he's out of his chair, striding around the desk and across the office to open the door. "Nine o'clock tomorrow should do it, in the library. I'm sure you'll be an enormous help to him." He pauses to usher me over the threshold, then adds: "And a great asset to the hotel."

And with a smile, he gently closes the door.

* * *

By the time Barney has finished with me, Mira's already cleaned another room. I catch up with her halfway along the first floor, wiping dried toothpaste out of a sink.

"What was that?" she asks, barely even looking round when I walk in.

"Barney wants me to help a guest with a project."

"What project? What guest?"

"The one who was asking directions in the village."

She looks at me blankly.

"Keep up. The guy who checked in this morning? What is *with* you today?"

With perfect timing, she yawns. "I was up late. Studying."

"Studying?" I did *not* expect that. "Studying what?"

Mira waves a hand vaguely at the mirror, but just for a second her eyes widen. "Nothing, nothing. A course." She gives the gleaming sink tap one more brisk rub with a cloth. "You look like bad news. It's a bad thing, helping him?"

"I think I might have been a bit rude to him. But then he *did* nearly run me over…"

Mira's eyes meet mine in the mirror. "In his defence, you were in the middle of the road."

"Please don't take his side – this is grim enough already. He's doing some research about… I don't actually know. But Barney says he's asked for help, and I got volunteered. I'll tell you more tomorrow – when I figure out what I've been signed up for. Other than having to sit in the library with a total stranger who thinks I'm…oh god, who even

40

knows what he thinks." I'm not sure I want to know anything else about him at all, actually. I know his name, and that's probably as close to him as I want to get, thanks.

The same uneasy feeling stays with me through the rest of my shift, and all the way back out of the staff entrance that afternoon. The idea of having to spend time with a stranger, doing…whatever it is he's trying to do…makes my teeth jangle and the inside of my skin itch. It's not what I'm here for. I tip my head back and stare upwards.

"It's not part of the deal!" I tell the empty sky – but it doesn't answer, so I carry on heading home. Unlike most of the other staff, I don't have to walk all the way back down into the village or down the long, sweeping drive to the bus stop – because Felix's house is part of the Hopwood Home estate, right in the middle of the hotel grounds. So I get to cross the gardens around the old hedge maze, then take the little bridge over the end of the lake and wander out through the deer park…and there, at the end of an avenue of chestnut trees, is Charlie and Felix's cottage. Home. It's ridiculously pretty, considering it's just an old gardener's cottage. It was a bit tatty and run-down when Felix took it over five years ago, but apparently he went through the whole house with a hammer and a crowbar and just… ripped everything out. By the time my brother moved in with him, there were floors and *occasionally* working plumbing, but it was Charlie who fixed the chaos Felix had made – even down to the rambling roses and the honeysuckle he planted either side of the front door. They climb up the walls and around the windows, and when my bedroom window's open in the summer, the scent of flowers drifts in on the warm air. It was Charlie who made it home.

Felix is already in when I kick the door shut behind me, his feet up on the table in front of the unlit stove.

He glances up from the tool catalogue he's reading, and grins at me. "D'you reckon I can convince Barney we need a new trailer for the estate?"

Before I met Felix, if anyone had asked me to describe the kind of guy my brother would fall for, I probably would have described someone a lot like Barney, with his combed-back hair and his suits. Despite being our boss, he's only a year older than Charlie – they're actually pretty good friends. But then one day I came home from school and it was like someone had lit a lamp inside my brother, and he told me he'd met someone. The One. Which turned out to be Felix, with his questionable taste in T-shirts, arms covered in tattoos, his eyebrow ring and hair that looks like he's been through seven hedges backwards in a high wind… And as soon as I met him, I realized the thought of Charlie being with anyone else was just impossible.

I shake my head and drop onto the sofa beside him.

"How was your shift?" he asks.

"It was."

42

He waits for more, then – realizing that was the entire sentence – peers at me. "Charlie told me about the bus."

"I'm fine. It's not that."

The catalogue drops to the floor with a thump and Felix folds his arms across his chest, fixing me with an expectant look.

I hold out as long as I can, but there's just something about Felix's face that makes him impossible to ignore. "Barney's told me I've got to help this guest," I mumble, picking up the single ancient scatter cushion that lives wedged in the corner of the sofa and turning it over and over on my lap. "He's got some historical research project and apparently because I put my history prize on my job application, I'm supposed to be useful."

"That doesn't sound so bad. Makes a change from cleaning rooms, doesn't it?"

"Yes, but…"

"But what?"

"I don't know him!"

"You don't need to know him! Besides, if he was that awful, Barney wouldn't ask you to help him out."

"Wouldn't he?" I rub at a worn patch on the edge of the cushion. "Anyway, he's people, and I don't *do* people," I add.

"Mmm." He gives me a long and meaningful look.

"Look, I don't want to talk about it. Happy anniversary, by the way." I lever myself off the sofa and head for the shower. As if today's not been rubbish enough, I've got to

43

go back in later and do the turn-down shift tonight too.

Felix's voice bounces up the narrow stairs: "You should give this thing a chance. You never know – you might actually enjoy it!"

I close the bathroom door and lean against it. Then I crank the shower up as hot as it will go and step into the stream of water, letting it pour over me and wash other people's dust and dirt away and down the drain.

Shower done, I hop across the landing and into my room. The mid-afternoon sunlight floods in, filling it with warmth and making the posters pinned up on the white walls glow orange. Sometimes, I wonder if they're really "me" any more. I put them up out of habit when I moved in, because I felt like I should – the giant *Grand Budapest Hotel* poster that Mira thinks is so funny (I guess it kind of is given the hotel thing) and the blow-up of Teleman's *Brilliant Sanity* artwork that I got at one of their gigs at Thekla in Bristol. But maybe they're just relics of where I was, who I used to be.

Looking out of my window, I can just make out the roof of Hopwood Home through the trees of the deer park and gardens. It's peaceful. It's familiar. It's safe and it's stable.

I know where I am *now*, and that's all I need.

Knock-knock-knock.

Pause.

I already wish I hadn't agreed to do the turn-downs. The hotel at night is different – there are too many people drifting through the lobby or wafting gently up and down the stairs. Too many eyes not to catch, too many polite and semi-invisible smiles to make.

Today has apparently been full of bad choices – and all of them have conspired to drop me outside room fifteen.

Knock-knock-knock.

Pause.

Just keep it together. Pretend everything's normal. Pretend you're normal.

"Good evening? Housekeeping?"

Pause.

Knock-knock-knock.

"Housekeeping? Turn-down service?"

There's a scraping sound from the other side of the door, then something like papers shuffling...then footsteps. "Just a minute..." The door cracks open, and a familiar face peers around it at me.

"Sorry to disturb you. Did you want the turn-down service this evening?"

Beyond him, the room is an explosion of paper. Even through the narrow gap between the door and the frame, I can see sheets of it covering every flat surface. Desk, bed, chair, floor. *Everywhere.* There are little Post-it notes stuck to the walls.

"Turn-down service?" He frowns, staring at me. There's a flicker of something behind his eyes.

"Fresh towels? Turn down the corner of the sheets?" I lift the arm holding the towels a little, trying to keep my own eyes fixed on a spot in the middle of the doorknob. "Some guests say they find it welcoming."

"I know what a turn-down service is, thanks. And I think I can manage to get into bed without you making it welcoming..." He stops suddenly and his eyes widen as he mentally plays back what he just said, getting redder with every passing second. "Oh. God. No. That didn't... I didn't mean... That came out..." He stops again and sighs. "I'm so sorry."

I shake my head, trying to keep a straight face. "Right. You don't need the turn-down." I go to walk away but something stops me. I turn back to face him. "Do you want the chocolate anyway?" I rummage in my pocket and pull out what I'm relatively sure is a chocolate and not a soap – because they do look pretty similar, whatever Mrs Tilney says – holding it out to him. "Here."

"Oh. Thanks. Thank you." He takes it. "And...you know. Sorry. Again."

"No problem. Goodnight." I want to go. I do. But I... *can't*.

The door doesn't close. I can hear it creaking, like he's leaning on it, waiting for something. "This morning – it was you, wasn't it? In the village."

"Me? Oh. Yes."

A pause. "Thanks. For the directions." Another pause. "Look, I'm sorry – I should have…" He sighs and bites his lip.

There's an awkward silence and then: "By the way, I'm Hal. Henry. Hal – Hal Waverley." He smiles, and it changes everything about him. His face, which was long and almost too angular, brightens and warms.

"Flora," I say in return. "Welcome to Hopwood Home. Have a good night." I step back from the door, but as it starts to close I glance back over my shoulder and, in the narrowing gap, I see him thoughtfully turning the square of chocolate over in his fingers.

The latch clicks.

Goodnight.

Four

The Hopwood Home hotel library is supposed to look just as it would have done when this place was a house. There's a polished wooden floor scattered with antique rugs, a handful of enormous sofas and armchairs upholstered in velvet and leather, a big stone fireplace with an open grate and a row of French windows opening onto the terrace and gardens at the side of the hotel. There are lamps everywhere: little ones with old-fashioned glass shades on side tables, wood and brass floor lamps in the corners, and a row of old library lamps down the centre of the huge, dark, burnished oak table that fills the middle of the room. And – of course – there are the bookcases. They line the walls, stretching up to the ceiling, heavy shelves groaning with books. Some of those are antiques, covered in cracked red leather, some are newer, and some, tucked carefully behind the door and mostly out of sight, are the books left behind by guests.

"Here we are!" Barney says brightly, clapping his hands

as we walk in together at nine o'clock. The room swallows the sound. At the far end of the big table, bending over a pile of folders and notebooks, is Hal Waverley. His red hair gleams as he leans into a shaft of sunlight cutting in through the window. He straightens and looks round at us – seeing first Barney, then me. There's a flash of surprise, and then his face does something complicated – like a mask slamming down across it in that second when he saw me. Obviously he didn't know it was *me* helping him – and maybe he could hide it last night outside his room, but in here…there's no disguising the fact he hates the idea of crazy, rude Flora helping him with this. Whatever it is.

"Flora, this is Hal Waverley, who's looking into the history of…" Barney's voice slides into white noise and I'm back on the pavement in the village, the car stopped in the middle of the road. The look on his face when I asked him to just go. That "Whatever" as he got back into the car. The screech of tyres as he tried to get away as fast as possible. And now here he is, stuck with me.

"…this is Flora Sutherland, who'll be helping you," Barney says, holding a hand out to indicate me.

Eyes the colour of faded denim look straight at me… then, almost as quickly, they look away.

"We've met," says Hal Waverley quietly.

"You have?" Barney's question is loaded, but before I can say anything Hal cuts in.

"I stopped to ask directions to the hotel, and the person

49

who gave them to me was…" There's the faintest break in his words, then: "Flora," he finishes.

"Oh. Well. Good." Barney's already giving Hal his best management smile. "Flora's part of the housekeeping team – she's been with us almost a year now – but she's a local and she has a little experience with historical research, so she'll be delighted to help you with anything you need."

Hal nods. I look at a spot in the middle of the table, waiting for him to mention my standing in the road, or how he's glad I'm not as rude now as I was then, or whether I'm – you know – *okay*.

What would Barney do then? Send me back to Mrs Tilney? Pull a face and lower his voice, whispering something about me having had "a difficult time" lately? The sensible bit of me says that Barney would never think that, let alone say it out loud. The less-sensible bit of me, the bit that I have to square with the looks on those faces through the bus windows, is less confident.

There is an awkward silence that stretches on and on and on.

"I'll…ah, leave you to it then, shall I?" Barney says at last, looking from one to the other of us. "Anything you need, just get reception to give me a buzz."

Hal nods again, says thank you…and just like that, Barney's gone and it's me and Hal Waverley alone in the library.

The silence seeps from the shelves, from between the

pages of the books. It slides out and down to the floor, piling up and threatening to bury us. He's just *standing there*. And so am I. But what else am I supposed to do? Barney told me I have to help, so here I am.

"A year?" he says, suddenly.

"Sorry?"

"You've been here a year. Working."

"Oh. Yes. Maybe a bit less, but…" I know it's less than a year – a year ago, at the end of that July, I was still stitching myself back together, figuring out which piece fitted where. I was less person, more puddle. But he doesn't need to know that.

"When I saw you before I thought it was just, sort of, a summer job? You seem pretty young. To be working, you know?" He blurts it all out in a hurry.

I wonder whether he's judging me, weighing me up based on what he's seen so far.

Is this a balanced reaction?

Maybe he's just trying to make conversation.

I shake my head gently, carefully avoiding his gaze. "It counts towards an apprenticeship, so I can work instead of being in sixth-form college."

He considers this. "And helping me with this…" He jerks his head towards the piles of paper on the table. "Does that count too?"

"I doubt it," I mumble, only half-hoping he won't hear me.

The corner of his mouth twitches and he runs his hands back through his hair, brushing it away from his face. It flops right back into his eyes as he slides a sheet of paper out of the folder closest to him and places it gently on the table in front of me.

"Okay. Right. I guess I need to tell you what I'm – we're – doing. So. I'm looking for something. A house. A specific house," he says. "And I think I need someone who knows the area. I asked if there was anyone who could help, and your manager said…" He gestures to the page. It looks old.

"I don't know how much *I* can help, but okay."

I reach for the paper and then stop. Something about it sitting there in the middle of the glossy wood makes it seem vulnerable, fragile. I hesitate, my hand hovering just above it, remembering how carefully he'd handled it. He smiles.

"It's only a photocopy – it's all right. You can pick it up."

The page has been folded and refolded so many times that the paper feels soft. The corners are bashed-up and crumpled, and there are scuff marks and rubbed-out pencil scribbles all around the edges.

Hal watches me examine it. "I'm trying to figure out where somebody came from. A soldier in the First World War. I guess, to start with, I'm trying to work out whether he even existed. I don't exactly have much to go on, just an old story…and this."

"What is it?" I peer at the sheet. The copy's not great –

the original can't have been very clear, because this isn't much more than a ghost, all muddy shades of grey. It's a handwritten letter, I realize, but all I can make out is a line in the middle.

I will not conspire in your ruin, nor in deceiving a family of such good standing.

He doesn't give me a chance to ask more questions. He's too excited about it, the words tumbling from his lips. "It's from a woman – Jane, she signs it – to someone. I've been trying to pick out the address she sent it to. Look." He leans a little closer and plants a fingertip next to a particularly smudgy bit near the top. There's an H, and then a little further along, a D – but the rest of it is too blurry to read. "It's like that in the original," he adds.

I squint at it. He's standing so close. I try to ignore how small the space between our shoulders is and focus on the writing. It's too blurred to be sure of the word.

"If that letter was sent *here*, then it means I'm in the right place. Finally."

"Finally?"

Hal steps away from me with a shrug. "I've been trying to find this house for a while now," he says, turning away. "It's important."

"Important?" If *I* did something like this, Sanjay would give me one of his long, hard looks and ask if I was manic again – and it would be checklist central.

"Personal, then. It's personal."

"A First World War soldier?"

"Yes."

"Why?"

He closes the folder he's been flicking through with a slap. "It doesn't really matter, does it?"

"I guess not." I shrug and slide the photocopied letter back onto the table. "So how does this fit in?"

"It was with some of the other papers I've found while I've been researching. It's the best lead I've got."

"It's not exactly a good one. You said there was a story. Can that help?"

"I don't know. Maybe?" He pulls a chair out for himself and then another one for me, gesturing to it. Nobody's ever done that before, actually pulling a chair out for me.

We both sit.

It's weird.

But…nicely weird.

Perhaps he doesn't think I'm so crazy? Or maybe he's just really good at hiding it. Better than most people, anyway.

He doesn't know the half of it, though, does he? He wouldn't be able to hide it then. Nobody else can.

He's lost in his own thoughts for a moment. "There was a soldier," he says quietly. "He was the only heir to an estate – a big country house, land, the works."

"Like on *Downton Abbey*?" It makes me die a little inside to admit I know *Downton*, but I do. It's one of Felix's favourite things ever. He has the box sets. All of them.

This actually gets a smile. "Like on *Downton*. Except this soldier was killed fighting in the war. When he died, there was no one to take over the estate and the family sold it."

"But in *Downton*…"

"There was another bit of the family who could inherit it, yes – I know. Maybe there wasn't for this estate, or maybe the family couldn't afford to keep it running or… whatever. This one got sold and I want to find it." He drums his fingers on the table. "There were a lot of big houses sold just after the war, either because there was no money left or no more owners."

"And you've been to them all?"

"Some."

"Why?"

"Because." He shrugs.

"It's not much to go on."

Hal looks defensive. "It's brought me this far." He blinks at me from under his fringe. "Look, I have to know."

I stare at the list of bullet points on the Hopwood Home notepad I've "borrowed" from the writing desk in the corner of the library. It's still very short.

As in, it's two points long, even after a couple of hours

of Hal sifting through the first stack of papers, looking up every now and again to frown at the wall or mutter something to himself.

I'm not even sure two points counts as a list.

All this effort, all this trouble and expense, with so little to guide him. I know he said it was personal, but this? It's more heart than head, more soul than sense.

But something about it tugs at me, deep inside. There's a puzzle here waiting to be solved. I can feel it – just enough of it anyway.

Glancing up from the notepad, I try to sneak a look at him. He's staring out of the window. From where I'm sitting, all I can see is the silhouette of his face against the bright light outside. He's so still, it's like watching a statue. One with a straight nose and a high forehead and – I suppose, from this angle – some pretty good cheekbones.

Maybe he feels me watching him, or maybe I have really bad timing – either way, he glances around and his eyes meet mine and hold them. But I can't make out a single thing from his expression. Nothing. I can't tell if he's angry or sad or happy or embarrassed. It's like trying to read stone.

"There has to be more to this." I pick up the pad and balance it on my lap, pushing my chair back from the table. "Tell me the whole story. All of it."

"I already told you. Soldier. War. Died."

"That isn't all of it, though, is it?"

He opens his mouth, then closes it again, narrowing his eyes. "What?"

"Look." I tap my pencil against my pad. "I don't know you and this is really none of my business. But you're saying you've been all over the place looking for one house that used to belong to one soldier's family – based on *this*?" I point at the letter. "I think there's more, and if you don't tell me everything, I *can't* help you."

He takes a deep breath and nods. "That story. It's something my grandfather used to tell me when I was growing up – a story *his* grandfather used to tell him, about a soldier he knew in the war. There was a big country house. Wealthy family, servants…you know, the works. And the heir to the house, this solider, had fallen in love with one of the housemaids."

However much I've tried to avoid it, I have apparently still seen enough *Downton* to know how that goes. "I bet that went down well with the family."

He shakes his head. "They kept it secret. They were going to elope. Run off together, you know?"

"You think that's what the letter's about! Ruin and deception."

He nods. "Exactly. But they never got the chance. The war started, he went off to fight and he never came back."

A shiver runs through me, starting at the top of my head and working its way all the way down to my feet. I was right: it *is* a puzzle. One with forbidden love and tragedy and…stuff. But still a puzzle. And puzzles I can do.

Before…after…when I was recovering, I did a lot of jigsaws. It wasn't exactly a thing I wanted to do, but Sanjay said it might be "a worthwhile exercise", so I did one – and weirdly, I was kind of good at it. There was something about laying out the pieces and slowly filling the empty spaces with picture, connecting one thing to another – it made sense when nothing else did. And it filled hours when I literally couldn't do anything else, because my mind was too busy or too tired or sometimes both at once (I still don't know how that's even possible, but welcome to my brain). But as I came back into focus, since I've been better – or *stable*, at least – I've not even thought about puzzles…until now.

I blow a long breath out between my teeth. "It's not the most *cheerful* bedtime story for a kid, is it?"

Hal doesn't miss a beat. "It wasn't a bedtime story. It was when I used to hang out in his office."

Who hangs out in their grandfather's office? Not that I get the chance to ask, because he's already talking again, his eyes shining and the story rushing out of him. "Like I said, it was something *his* grandfather told *him*, but before that I don't know where it came from. The way he used to tell it, though, it meant something to him. He really wanted it to be true."

"And you think it is?"

Hal pulls a face. "Wouldn't be here if I didn't."

The idea there might be a story like that at Hopwood –

at the place where I live – is intriguing. Exciting, even. But what do I know about this stuff? How can a school project qualify me to be any use at *all*? "You need a historian, somebody who knows about houses, like from the National Trust, or one of those BBC programmes. Not me. I've barely even got two GCSEs – not exactly research-assistant material."

"You think I didn't try? There are a lot of houses that fit the description. They all told me to come back when I had more details, more to work with. They treated me like a kid playing a game. Wasting their time."

"Then ask your grandfather if he can remember anything else—"

"I can't." It's sharp and louder than I was expecting. It's a door being slammed.

In my experience, the faster and harder somebody shuts a door, the more interesting everything behind it is. Or messy. It can go either way.

"But…" I try.

He cuts me off. "He won't be able to help, okay?" Then he sighs, and adds, "And anyway, you live here. If this really is the place, maybe you'll know things other people – historians, researchers from outside – don't."

It feels like he hasn't finished, so I wait. I wait for what feels a long, long time – and then, after an age, his eyes find mine, and this time I can actually see into them.

"Please," he says.

There's more to this than he's telling me. I get it. I'm a stranger – and if anyone can understand holding back from a stranger, it's me.

But that doesn't matter: the letter and the story feel like opposite corners of a jigsaw puzzle and *I* want to see what's in the middle.

Besides, the way he's acting, it doesn't seem like he thinks I'm so bad after all.

And perhaps escaping into somebody else's past, someone else's *head* for a while is just what I need.

Five

"So? How was it? What's he like? What did you do?" Mira jogs up the steps from the staff entrance to the wall where I'm sitting waiting for her.

"Do you want me to answer those all together, or maybe one at a time?"

"Either. Whatever."

We turn onto the gravel path that runs along the side of the hotel towards the gardens, the deer park and home. Through the library windows as we pass them, I can see Hal – his head still bent over his stacks of research and notes, his folders full of dead ends and detours. When my shift ended, I said goodbye, that I'd see him in the morning...but he barely even noticed.

She watches me looking back at him and nudges me.

"And?" Her elbow is surprisingly sharp.

"It's fine."

"What are you doing in there?"

"He's researching the hotel, trying to see if it's a house he's been looking for. It doesn't make much sense. But I think he's been doing it for a while – at least, it sounds like he has." I glance back at the last library window, but all I can see is the reflection of the gardens. "Why would anyone do that?"

"Rich people," Mira snorts, as though that explains everything. "I did some research of my own, though, while you've been busy."

"Is this whatever you were studying the other day? What's that about?"

"Oh." She rubs at one of her ears. "No. I meant, I was finding out about your Mr Waverley."

"You know something?"

"Of course." She gives me a nonchalant smile and keeps on walking, feet crunching on the gravel. "Housekeeping knows everything, no?"

"Go on, then. Prove it."

"Nineteen. And an Aquarius. He's mysterious, but also detached."

"Yeah, he's detached all right. And how do you know that?"

"That he's deta—?"

"No, stupid," I interrupt her, smacking her gently on the arm. "His birthday."

"Oh. The usual. I asked Kate on reception to check the scan of his passport. I told her I needed it for age verification for the room."

"That's genius."

She beams at me.

"Two years older than me – he's the same age as you!"

She nods and purses her lips, pressing a hand dramatically to her chest. "But not a majestic Taurus."

"No. Obviously. And not as broke as you, either. What else did you get?"

"That was all I had time for. Mrs Tilney came to ask what I was doing in reception when I was meant to be vacuuming the stairs."

I'm not sure what I was hoping for exactly – it's not like he was going to have written an essay in the *Reason for visit* box on the check-in form, is it?

Mira's continuing breakdown of just how majestic she and her star sign are takes us most of the way back to the cottage. I half-listen, because she's monologuing like she usually does after a solo shift. As I discovered when I started working full-time at Hopwood and was paired with her, Mira needs someone to talk to. Or at. To begin with, that suited me just fine – I didn't really want to talk anyway, and was happy to let her fill the silence that trailed around after me with whatever she wanted. As the months went by, and I started actually listening to her (some of the time, anyway), I realized I enjoyed being around her – and suddenly we were friends. Real friends. Along with Charlie and Felix – and Barney, because he's the boss – she's the only one here who knows about me. About *The Incident*.

I'm pretty sure everybody else thinks I'm just quiet and maybe kind of difficult – "a bit moody", Mira says – but none of them *know*. Which is exactly how I want to keep it. I don't want people looking at me differently, judging me, wondering whether I'm really as crazy as they think I am…

I already do that enough for all of us, thanks.

By the time we make it through the front door and I kick it shut behind us, Mira has not only covered her astrological profile in minute detail, she's moved on to wondering aloud whether the "high-profile" guest Mrs Tilney announced would be checking into the top-floor suite in a couple of days is Tommy Knight – currently Mira's favourite actor, and filming in Wells.

"Doubtful. Hopwood isn't exactly his style, is it?" I mutter, shoving Felix's muddy boots out of the way as we walk into the kitchen. Charlie's in the middle of setting the table as Felix pulls plates out of the dresser, passing them to him. They both look over as we come in, Mira still daydreaming out loud about what would happen if Tommy Knight walked into the lobby and saw her standing there…

"What, after he asked you to take his bags up to his room?" I laugh. Mira ignores me, instead dropping down into one of the chairs around the battered wooden dining table.

"Nice to see you, Mira. You staying to eat?" Felix asks.

Mira stifles a yawn, then grins at him sheepishly. "It's okay if I do? My housemate ate everything in the fridge again," she adds sadly.

"Of course – you're always welcome." Felix hands another plate to Charlie, his fingers gently touching my brother's.

"How's that project of yours going?" Charlie says.

I shrug. "It's not my project. But it's going."

"What's it about?"

"Houses."

"Houses?"

"Yep."

"Any specific kind of houses? Or just…houses as a concept?"

"Old houses. It's very *Downton*."

Charlie laughs. "Really?" He looks pointedly at Felix.

"I just spent the last two hours looking up and listing every single National Trust house within a twenty-mile radius, just in case there's something at one of them that might, maybe, possibly help. Do you know how many of those there are?"

"Quite a lot, I imagine."

"It's more. However many you imagine, it's *more*."

"And what was all that for?" Charlie pulls a couple of bowls out of the fridge and slides them along the table.

"It's something to do with a soldier who died in the First World War. This guest – Hal – his grandfather told him this story that *his* grandfather told *him*, about some guy who fell in love with a maid, but he was killed in the war." I scoop a tiny tomato out of the bowl closest to me.

"Flora!" Charlie takes a seat, reaching across the table to smack the back of my hand with a serving spoon. "No fingers."

"Sorry."

Felix clears his throat, slipping into his own chair. "Which houses are you looking at?"

"All of them. All." I sigh. He waits. "Umm, fine." I picture the list I ended up with, sitting on the library table alongside the map with a big red circle on it, and my phone's browser with a million internet tabs open. "Apart from here? There's Kingsway Manor Hall, Hillwood, Fallowmill House..."

"Wouldn't be Fallowmill." Felix shakes his head. "I do a bit of freelance tree work for them, and I can tell you that place has its own story. Gives me the creeps. They've got an archive there, though – might be worth a visit."

Charlie swallows a mouthful of potato salad. "And it's definitely not Kingsway," he adds, tapping his fork against his plate. "They're a Thankful."

"A Thankful?" I stare at him blankly.

"All the men who went off to fight in the war came home alive, so it was designated a Thankful Village. There's only about fifty of them in the country – it's on the village sign, right under the name."

"*That's* what that means?" I realize how stupid I sound even as I'm saying it, but it doesn't stop me. "I just thought they were, you know, generally *grateful* for stuff." Next to me, Mira chokes on a piece of cucumber. I kick her ankle under the table.

"Flora." Charlie fixes me with a stern look from the far side of Felix. "Honestly."

"What? I always figured they were just...nice. And I suppose everybody knows that, do they?"

There's a chorus of non-committal noises from around the table.

"Fine, then." I stare down at my plate, feeling my cheeks burn in the silence that descends – one broken only by cutlery on plates and chewing. After a while Charlie picks up his bottle of beer. "Well," he says, taking a swig, "I think it sounds fascinating."

"You do?"

He has stopped looking so amused and is studiously peeling the label off his beer bottle – very much avoiding my eye. "It's good to hear you talking about it. This is exactly the kind of thing you'd have been into a couple of years ago."

"I'm just doing my job."

"Are you?" He glances at me across the table.

Suddenly Mira yawns again, loudly – then clamps her hand over her mouth and looks around with eyes that are almost as wide as her jaws were a second ago.

"All right." I drop my fork on my plate and fold my arms. "What's up with you? And don't –" I unfold my arms again and point a finger at her – "tell me that you had a rough shift, or you didn't sleep well or whatever. The truth."

I refold my arms. It makes me look serious.

Does it? Yes. Yes, I'm sure it does.

Different emotions flicker across her face. Embarrassment, guilt…and finally, something that looks a bit like acceptance. She shrugs. "Okay. I've been studying. For a course." Her eyes lock onto a scratch on the table and don't budge. "I was going to tell you."

"A course? What course?"

"Textiles. I was waiting for the right time, but…" She hesitates, and her voice drops. "I want to apply to UWE. Next year. For their fashion course."

It feels like someone has pulled my chair out from underneath me. The University of the West of England is in *Bristol*. Mira wants to *leave* Hopwood?

Why didn't she say something?

How long has she been planning it?

What will I do if she goes?

Who will I talk to?

"Oh." The letter. That's what it was about. She told me it was junk mail.

I know I'm supposed to say something more. Something positive, something encouraging. The part of my brain that Sanjay trained – the bit that tries to keep tabs on the rest of me – kicks the inside of my skull and tells me to sort myself out… But the rest of it – the bit that wants to react, to feel, not sit down and calmly discuss things – that's the bit in control.

Does my mood match the moment? Is this the right response?

68

Well, yes. Mira's leaving. She's just said she is. She's leaving me here. She doesn't want to be here. She doesn't want to be my friend any more.

Is this a balanced reaction?

Did I do something wrong? Is this because Mira doesn't want to be around *me* any more?

IS THIS A BALANCED REACTION?

Charlie's eyes flick over to Felix, his lips pressed tightly together. Mira, it dawns on me, is still talking. I haven't heard a word since she said she was going to apply to UWE.

"…to study pattern-cutting, but I need to make up the points for entry, so I've been working on it after my shift." She clears her throat. "I didn't tell you. I'm sorry."

There's nothing I can say.

Genuinely.

I have to keep my mouth shut, because if I open it, I don't know what will come out – which bit of me will start speaking. The manic part who talks too fast and says things that I don't mean…or the sad one, who will rain all over her best friend's future? I don't want to be either of them right now.

There's nothing I can say.

Luckily, Felix is way ahead of me – and he beams at Mira. "Good for you. If that's what you want to do, you should go for it."

I stare at my plate.

Between them, Charlie and Mira and Felix fill the

silence – talking about her studies, the course she wants to apply for, work stuff… All of it's just noise. Filling the silence, filling the room, filling the house.

Filling my head.

It's almost a relief when Mira says she has to get home – to do more studying, I guess. She gives me a hug as she grabs her bag from the sofa.

"I shouldn't have kept it secret. I'm sorry. I didn't want to…"

To upset me. I know she didn't. Just like she knows that's why I couldn't say anything when she told me – because what comes out isn't always what I mean. It's not always the me I want to be who speaks; the me I *used* to be. The one who could be a friend, who could go out to see bands, who could go to the cinema, who would lie on the floor of other people's rooms and laugh. The one who won prizes for projects, who could catch the bus and drop into a seat next to someone and just *be*.

Now, there's only Mira.

Soon, there won't even be her.

I stand in the porch and watch her walk across the deer park, her headphones already in, while above her head the swifts wheel and dance against the pale summer sky to a music all of their own.

Six

"Woah."

Overnight, the library has been transformed. When I left it yesterday, it did still *look* like a library. Now, it looks like a hundred filing cabinets have exploded in here. There is paper *everywhere*. Stacks of it on every flat surface, covering the table, piled on the chairs – even sections of the floor have disappeared. Dotted across the room are cardboard archive boxes, piled two or three high…and in the middle of it all is Hal, his back to the door. Hearing me walk in, he turns suddenly – so suddenly that he almost loses his balance. His hair is ruffled, the fringe pushed to one side and the shorter hair on the top of his head sticking up as though he's been running his hands through it over and over again.

"Oh. Umm. Hi." He looks vaguely embarrassed, like I've caught him out somehow.

Instead of my housekeeping uniform, which I just sort

of automatically wore before, I've switched to a pair of denim shorts and a pale blue T-shirt – my present from Charlie last Christmas, with a tiny picture of an old-fashioned film camera printed on the pocket. It's not the smartest T-shirt in the world, but it's the only thing I had left in my wardrobe that was clean.

Clothes aren't a problem Hal has, apparently. He's wearing dark jeans, expensively soft-looking, and a plaid shirt half-open over a black T-shirt. It's funny, because it's similar to Felix's work outfit, but Hal looks like some kind of model in it (rather than a woodsman escaped from a fairy story, the way Felix does) and it only shows how far apart he is from the rest of us.

"You've been busy." It feels like a safe thing to say…but it's obviously not, because he frowns and looks at the chaos around him. I tuck my bag into the nearest leather armchair – and just about the only one not piled up with paper. "What do you need me to do?"

He looks from me to the room, and then back to me again.

Fair enough.

Hal picks his way between boxes to the far end of the table and scoops three separate stacks of stuff into his arms, shifting them all to the floor. But he doesn't just drop them – he lays each one down like they're made of spun sugar. There's now a small space on the table. I guess this is where I'm working today.

"Here. I might have found something while I was sorting through these last night. Would you take a look?"

"Last night? How long were you in here?"

"I'm not sure." He frowns again. "I came back in after dinner, and started looking through the box over there by the fireplace…and I sort of lost track of time." He shrugs. "Five or six hours, maybe?"

"Five or six hours? After dinner?" Seeing as the kitchen doesn't even open for dinner till seven o'clock, he can't have gone to bed any earlier than one in the morning. "This is really a big deal to you, isn't it?" I find a path to the clear end of the table and I'm about to pull a chair out when I realize he's beaten me to it. With a sweep of his arm, he offers me the seat. Feeling self-conscious, I sit – and as I do, Hal smoothly slides the chair in under me. There's something about the way he does it – just like the way he put the papers on the floor – that seems *kind*. Gentle.

He pulls up the chair next to mine and as he moves, the faintest scent of lemons and something green-tinted and fresh fills the air around us. It reminds me of the woods in the spring, but it's only there for a moment and then it's gone, lost under the familiar smell of dust.

"These were in one of the boxes. I think they've been moved from somewhere else. Just dumped and forgotten about. There's no order, and they look like they've all been mixed together." He slides the nearest, smallest, stack of papers into the empty space, fanning them out. Some of

73

them are upside down, some of them are sideways, some of them have got crumpled and folded together.

"Like they were in a drawer, maybe? Or a desk? And someone's tipped everything into the box?"

He nods. "That's what I thought. I wasn't sure they'd be worth the time, but there was something…" His voice fades as he peers at the pages, sifting through them. Some are scraps of paper with notes scribbled on them, some are printed leaflets and fliers. There's a page from an old newspaper from 14th July 1953, next to a shopping list for some kind of building work and a scribbled-out menu from 1987.

"Here it is."

Even before he's smoothed it out on the table, I can tell why it caught his eye.

"It's the same handwriting!" It comes out far louder than I expected and he flinches. "Sorry. But it is. I recognize it."

The sheet of paper is old, faded and crumpled, and part of it has either fallen off or been torn away, but the handwriting that covers what's left is unmistakably the same as on the letter he showed me yesterday.

"I think so too. There's not much more in this one – but there is a name."

"There was a name on the last one, wasn't there? You said it was from somebody called Jane."

"Yes." He glances up at me, as though he's surprised

I remember. I meet his gaze, feeling the back of my eyes prickling, until he looks away again. "But this time, it's who the letter was *to*. Somebody who must have lived *here*."

His finger moves across line after blurry line of grey handwriting, all the way to the top. And there it is.

My dearest Issy,

"Issy? Who's that?" I look up from the letter. I can't ignore the rising feeling of excitement buzzing along my fingers, itching its way into my hands.

"I don't know. I'm hoping the answer's somewhere in here." He waves at the room.

"That's a lot of somewhere to go through." I peer at the letter. "I can't even read most of it, can you?"

"Not much." He squints at it, wrinkling his nose as he tries to read the faded letters. "Something about the weather…about a cake, maybe?" His lips move silently as he pieces together fragments of words, fractions of sentences, and then: "Albie."

"Albie?"

"There's something here." He taps a finger on a line right at the bottom of the page, directly above the tear. "I'm sure that's an A – you see it?

I don't. Even when I squint.

"Look." He holds his index finger above the page like a pen. His hands are perfectly long and slender – except for the way this one finger is crooked, the tip at a distinct angle to the rest of it. It's so out of line that I find myself staring, and, of course, he notices.

"What?" But he knows, instinctively curling his hand into a ball.

"What happened to your finger?"

"Nothing. It got broken." He clears his throat uncomfortably, his eyes darting from the table to the door and back again.

"Ah." I nod. "It just looks like my brother's, that's all."

He stares at me blankly.

"My brother, Charlie. He's a gardener. His finger does that exact same thing, from where he broke it moving some rocks a couple of years ago. One fell and trapped his hand. You weren't moving rocks, were you?" The words come out like a landslide.

Slow down, Flora.

Be normal.

"I wasn't." Hal shakes his head…but he uncurls his hand.

"Figures. Because why would you be landscaping, right?"

You need to stop now.

I gulp down the urge to keep talking, to let Manic Flora run her mouth – my mouth – and I swallow all the words piling up on my tongue. The silence between us stretches so thin I can see straight through it…and then, finally, he presses his hand against the page again, tracing the shapes of the letters he thinks he sees.

"Here. A...L...B...I...E."

It all looks like browny-grey smudges to me, but then he sighs and holds out his hand, nodding towards my own where it rests on the table.

"Can I?"

"Umm...?"

And then – slowly, as though he's reaching for a wild animal, something that might bite – he places his hand over mine, lifting it up and straightening my index finger. At first, I nearly pull away, but the gentleness of his touch and the warmth of his fingers make something catch in my stomach as together we trace the loops of the letters.

"A...L...B...I...E," he says again. Reaching the end of the line, he suddenly drops my hand like a dead fish, pulling his own away and folding it under his other hand on the edge of the table.

Did I do something wrong? Is my hand weird? Is it too hot? Too cold? Too clammy?

I kick the chattering, panicked voice inside my head into a mental cupboard, closing my eyes.

When I open them again, Hal is studying me from beneath his fringe, but he immediately pretends he wasn't.

"Sorry. Headache," I mumble. I peer under the table, looking for the notebook I left in here yesterday. There it is, tucked beside one of the legs, just where I left it. Grabbing it,

I let it fall onto the tabletop with a slap.

"So there's a Jane, an Issy and an Albie." I write their names on a blank page.

Now what?

I draw a circle around each name.

Better.

Hal sits back in his seat, making the wood creak. "Jane knows Issy," he says. "She's writing to her."

"And there's this," he says, reaching for something. "I thought it looked interesting."

The book that he puts on the table is – like just about everything else – old and dusty. It's a big journal, bound in leather that has cracked and pulled away in places, leaving tatty old boards visible underneath. It's a murky grey colour – but judging by the clear brownish marks left where he's touched it, that's mostly dirt. It makes a cracking sound as he opens it, and the smell…

"Wow."

Clamping my hand over my face, I realize he's reacted exactly the same way – ducking his nose into the neck of his T-shirt. The book absolutely reeks of mould and dust and…*time*, I guess.

"It must have got damp," I say, peering at it (with my nose still safely covered by my hand). "That's water-staining." I poke at the edge of a page, where a brown swirly mark has seeped across the paper. "Careful when you turn the pages – they're probably stuck together."

Something flickers deep inside my head – a tiny light at the far end of a long tunnel. I remember this. Digging through the past, looking for clues. I remember I liked this. Maybe I actually *was* good at it, not just manic and *thinking* I was good at it – in the same way I'd have thought I could fly, or speak Dutch, or pass my exams, or a hundred other things I literally can't do, but why let a little thing like reality get in the way of a good manic episode?

Hal peels the two pages apart. Just as I thought, they've glued themselves together as they've dried, and they make a sticky tearing sound as they separate. The number *1913* is printed in neat, clear handwriting on the next page.

"Is that a year?"

"I think so." Hal leans closer over the book, then away again as he tries to dodge a fresh waft of that mouldy smell.

He turns another stuck-together page…and the open book in front of us is full of columns in the same tight black ink as the date on the first page. It looks very familiar.

In fact, it looks like Mrs Tilney's shift book.

I think I know what this is.

"This is a housekeeping book. It has to be." I peer at the columns. "It's a housekeeping book from 1913."

"That's what I thought when I found it. These must be staff names." He runs a finger down a column full of different initials. "And this looks like pay."

"And these are their duties – the rooms some of them are assigned to clean." Scanning the pairs of capital letters,

I hit on something. "There's someone with the initial I here." Halfway down the page is a tiny *I.C.* "There should be a staff list or register or something." Without thinking, I grab the book and spin it towards me, leafing through the pages. Luckily, the first few seem to have taken the worst of whatever it was and the smell is nowhere as bad now.

"Are you sure you want to touch that?" Hal asks, watching me riffle through it.

"I've been cleaning other people's hotel rooms for a while now. You'd be amazed at the stuff I've had to touch." I stop and think about this for a second. "And you would definitely be grossed out by it. Here you go."

Triumphantly, I turn the book back towards him. Just where I thought it would be – just like in Mrs Tilney's – right at the back, is a list of the staff's full names. And only one of them begins with the letter I.

"Iris Campbell," Hal says, under his breath. "Look – underneath!" In fainter lettering on the line below: "Goes by 'Issy'." Hal blinks at me. "How did you know to do that?"

I shrug. "I don't know. But that has to be her. Iris Campbell. She was second housemaid." I lean closer to the book, ignoring how close I am to Hal. "And look, here are the family names."

There aren't many on the list, but it takes him a while to see it. Hal's sharp intake of breath tells me when he does.

"Master Albert Holmwood," Hal murmurs softly. His hair falls forward over his face, and for a second I can smell his shampoo, faint against the mustier scent of the book.

"Albert, as in…?"

"As in Albie."

"But the family name is Holmwood. The house is called Hopwood. Wouldn't the house be called the same thing as the family, like Wayne Manor? Or…" My mind blanks. "Other houses named after the people who live in them?"

"The village is Hopwood-in-the-Hollows, though, isn't it?"

"Oh. Yes. Never mind." I bite my lip, feeling stupid. Not that he notices.

"But why would someone be writing to a housemaid—" His voice shakes slightly, even though I can see he's trying to hide it.

"*Second* housemaid."

"*Second* housemaid," he says, "about the…" His eyes widen as he stares at the page. "About the only son of the family that maid is working for?"

I pick up the letter again, holding it carefully in my hand. "I think…maybe you've found your story after all."

Seven

"It can't be that easy." Hal folds his arms across his chest, pushing his spine into the seat back. "It can't."

"Why not? You said you'd been everywhere else. It's like that saying – you always find something in the last place you look."

Hal uncrosses his arms and presses his face into his palms, his voice muffled. "Well, yeah. Because when you find it, you stop looking. So of course it's always in the last place you look."

Which is true, I suppose. But he didn't have to say it like that, did he?

When he drops his hands, he's turned so pale that for a heart-stopping second, I think he's about to faint. Suddenly the freckles I'd barely noticed, but which must have been there all along, stand out so brightly it's like someone drew them on in neon pen.

"Are you feeling okay?"

He doesn't seem to hear me. Instead, he pushes his chair back from the table and stalks off across the library, yanking the door open and disappearing into the lobby without a word.

Not exactly the reaction I was expecting. If it's so important that he finds this story, this *soldier*, and if this is the lead he's been searching for, then why doesn't he look... happy?

I reach for the letter and run my fingertip over the line he pointed out, tracing the writing like he did. My skin prickles at the thought of his hand moving mine and I flex my fingers, trying to shake the feeling off. Maybe it's the dust. There's a *lot* of dust. These boxes have obviously been up in the attics for a long time, forgotten about. Who put them up there? The family, right before they sold the house? Did they pack them up and tuck them under the eaves and then just leave?

The library is absolutely still and silent. Even the lobby is quiet, like the whole of Hopwood is holding its breath. It gets like that sometimes: the weird hush of a hotel when nobody's coming or going, like it forgets what it is. Was it the same back when it was a house, a home, once upon a time? This place had a *before*, a whole different life when there were maids straightening the beds, not housekeeping staff; cooks down in the kitchens making meals for the family instead of for guests; and somebody actually lived here rather than just checking in for a couple of nights.

It never really occurred to me that *every* kind of place has a past – not just the big old buildings that we think about as being "History". They *all* have a story.

Everything, everywhere, everyone. So what's Hal's?

"What happened to your finger?"

"Nothing. It got broken."

That flicker of expression, the pause, the way he hid his hand.

Got broken. Not *I broke it.*

Maybe there's more to *his* story than there seems.

Picking up the letter, I lift it up to the light. The letters spelling out *Albie* are clear now – but if Issy is Iris the housemaid, and Albie is Albert Holmwood, who is Jane? And why is she writing to Iris about him? It doesn't matter how much I squint at the faded squiggles on the page, none of them help. But I can feel the pattern, hiding just below a layer of dirt. I can almost see it – just like I can almost *see* Iris walking in through the library door, the way she must have done over a hundred years ago, and I wish I could beam her out somehow, the same way I used to wish I could hook my head up to a projector and beam out the things I saw in there so they'd make sense to everybody else. So *I'd* make sense. (Apparently, midway through my last manic phase, I told Charlie I actually could. He says I was very convincing about the whole thing.)

A sound from the doorway makes me jump. Hal's there…and the way he's standing, his feet planted square and one hand in a pocket, his head tilted slightly to one side, suggests he's been there a little while.

I slide the letter back onto the table. "I was looking… to see if there was anything…"

Why do I feel guilty? I'm supposed to be helping him, and that's exactly what I was doing. Helping.

"Sorry," he says, taking a step forward and then stopping. "I needed a minute." He comes back over, leaning around me and picking up the letter. "Did you make out anything else in there?" For a second, the air fills with the smell of him. When he steps back, I wish he hadn't.

"No. It's too hard to read." I pick up my notebook. "So what now?"

He doesn't move, just stands there, the page lifted to the light. But his eyes aren't on it – he's looking past it, out into the gardens. As though he can't decide what to say. Or do.

"I don't know." His voice is quiet, and it shakes as he speaks. So does his hand – I can see the paper trembling.

I put my notebook down again. "Are you sure you're feeling okay? I can come back tomorrow?"

"No." He turns away from the window, and his eyes settle on me. I'm so used to being invisible, to *wanting* to be invisible, that it feels very, very strange. But not completely bad. Not from him.

"Can I tell you something?" He slides into the chair next to mine, his voice low as though he's afraid he'll be overheard – although who he thinks is going to overhear him, I don't know.

"Sure." I reach for my pad again – but he shakes his head.

"No. Not…about this." He stops, cocking his head to one side and narrowing his eyes. "Okay, yes. It's still about this…but not." He takes a deep breath, watching me. "My grandfather – I call him Pa, like 'Grandpa'. The one who told me about this stuff. He's…not very well."

"Oh, I'm sorry. Is he in hospital?"

"No. It's not that kind of ill. It's…" And Hal gently taps the side of his head.

I've seen that gesture before. A rapid *tap-tap-tap* to the side of the temple. The international sign for crazy. I've seen it *lots*. But something about the way Hal does it is different – he isn't doing it to make fun of someone. He's doing it because he can't find the words…like he can't bring himself to say it out loud.

Suddenly, I have an idea why this matters so much to him.

"That's why you can't ask him any more about the story, isn't it? You don't want to upset him."

Hal nods, pushing his hands back through his hair again and closing his eyes. "He has trouble remembering. Not all the time, but sometimes. It's like he's looking through a book he's read before, and suddenly there's a page missing. He gets angry."

"And scared?"

Hal's eyes flick open and he looks straight at me, measuring me. "Yes."

Feeling pinned under his gaze, I fidget. "I get it. I've got...someone in my family with mental health stuff."

His stare warms and softens, as though I've passed some kind of test. "Then you know what it's like."

Better than you do.

Hal sighs. "My family's...complicated. Kind of *distant*." From the look on his face I'm not sure that's quite the word he wanted. "Pa's the only one who's never made me feel like I owe him something just for existing, and he's the only one who never treated me like I was a massive pain in the arse when I was growing up."

"Really? My brother still tells me I am one, regularly."

Hal's laugh is as much of a surprise to him as it is to me. "Sorry," he says, a flush creeping across his cheeks.

"No, I'm sorry. I was messing around, and you were saying something important."

"Pa's the important one."

"Which is why...this?" I wave a hand at the stacks of paper.

"Yeah. He always wanted to find out if the story was true. He had this idea about tracking down the guy's family somehow, if there were any of them left, and telling them he hadn't been forgotten." Hal tilts his head back to stare up at the ceiling. "He said that too many things get forgotten

87

about, that people only remember the bad ones, when it's the good memories we should be keeping." This time, his laugh is quiet and sad, and I don't think he's actually talking to me any more. I'm not sure he even remembers I'm here. "So I thought, if I could find out…if I could tell him whether it was true or not, or if it was just some story his grandfather made up…it would be a way of saying thank you. For not making me feel like I was just a…an *inconvenience*. I started looking, and then he started to be…not so good, and now I can't stop."

Then his head tilts forward again, and he looks at me with those pale eyes…and I understand. He's telling me because he can't tell anybody else. I'm never going to cross paths with anyone he knows, let alone his family. They're the kind of people I'm meant to be invisible to, aren't they? Just like in Mrs Tilney's rule book. So what's the harm in him telling me something like this, something quiet and secret? He's never going to see me again after he's figured this out – he might as well go and shout it at the birds.

But he hasn't. He's told me.

Why doesn't he have anyone else he can tell?

The thought drifts quietly through my mind. Does he really not have someone – *anyone* – he can talk to? Watching him sift through the remaining pile, his lips moving silently as he turns the pages over and discards them one by one, I guess not.

"I think we need a better system." His voice pulls me out of thinking about, well, him.

"A better system?"

"Mmm."

"'Better' implies there was one to start with."

"There was!" He jumps up, grabbing the nearest box and hefting it onto the table.

"Right."

A cloud of dust rises into the air as he sweeps a hand across the top of the box, making us both cough. This is not a guy who's used to handling anything dirty. When the dust clears, he seems to have acquired a light grey streak through his red hair – along with a dark smudge across his nose where he's obviously rubbed it.

"You've…ummm…got some dirt." My arm feels like it belongs to somebody else as it sticks straight out, pointing at him. "On your nose."

"Oh. Right. Thanks." He wipes his face with his hand, managing to completely miss the smudge on his nose.

It suits him. The smudge.

You could always wipe it away…

"Okay," I say, quickly turning to the box on the table. "What do you want to do now then?"

"That housekeeping book was dated 1913. We should check the boxes for anything around then. "

"So all we have to do is find the 1913 papers in amongst… this?"

He follows my pointed look around the room. "Things on the table are later. Look – that one's labelled 1932." Already, he's got the next lid off. "This one looks like it's…1915." He twists on the spot, pointing to the next box in the stack. "Try that one. They're the same kind of box, and they look about as dirty as each other – hopefully they're about the same age."

I grab the next box from the pile. It's heavy, but I manage to swing it up onto the table next to Hal's and pull the lid off.

A large spider scuttles out and across the table. It's the size of my hand.

Frozen, we both watch it.

It carries on across the table, down to the floor and sets off over the rug, rounding the door and disappearing from sight.

Hal laughs. "Maybe he wants to talk to Reception about his room."

I sort of hiccup, because: *spider*. And then I glance over at him…and he's looking at me. Heat prickles up my jaw.

"This box looks like it's…" Clearing my throat, I pick up the first thing I see inside: a sheet of heavy notepaper. "Oh. Hang on." When I turn it over, it's covered with flowing handwriting – and topped with an *AEH* monogram. "It's personalized writing paper. Look."

I hold it out to Hal, who is suddenly pressed up against my shoulder. Part of me wants to step away, to keep my distance…but a bigger part of me doesn't. It wants to stay close to the letter, to see what it says at the same time as he does. I want to see the puzzle come together first-hand, to feel the pieces clicking together, and I can't do that from a distance.

Hal slides his palm underneath the old paper to support it. "Careful," he whispers, as though speaking too loudly will make the page fall apart in front of us. "AEH. Like Albert Holmwood?"

"Or Albie." Now I'm whispering too. I can't help it – that's the mood we're going for. (See, Sanjay? I'm matching the mood.)

"Or both."

"Can you read it?" It doesn't make a lot of sense to me – it's that old-fashioned kind of handwriting that makes it look like a quick note took a month to write, and takes just as long to read.

"Some of it. Hang on…" Hal frowns, trying to pick out words, piecing together fragments of ink. This letter is clearer than the other ones – the paper has stood up to time better.

"'It has always struck me as sad, somehow,'" he reads softly, translating the loops and curls aloud, "'that the gardens are at their most beautiful when no one is there to see them. Only the ill-sleepers of the world would ever understand how the mist rises from the streams in the woods and clings to the trees like silk; how the deer move so gently and quietly that often they seem to glide through the bosky grounds like ghosts. How, in the summer, the moon balances on the west chimneys like a globe, and how, when the dew falls on the lawns, it looks like handfuls of diamonds thrown by a fairy queen."'

"Oh, wow."

"Hang on – there's more. 'I thought I was the only one who saw the world at this hour, when I ought to have been asleep. But now I discover you are there too. Perhaps I shall sleep more soundly knowing that someone else, after all, is there to see these things; that they are not just mine. Because what is the point of sights like these if there is no one with whom to share them?'"

My heart is beating faster with every word Hal reads. "Who's this to? Does it say?"

He ignores me, skimming down to the last line of the page. "'And more than any of this, I hope that next time I will see <u>you</u> again.'" He lowers the page, then lifts it again, almost waving it. "Look – he's underlined the 'you'. This is it. It is!" His voice is higher now, louder, the excitement in it matching the faint flush in his cheeks…which matches the pounding in my own chest. It *is* exciting. More exciting than I imagined it could be… Already I can see him, this Albie, walking through the gardens, through the woods and the deer park, as the sky lightens. I can *see* him stopping to watch the deer moving in the rising light…because I've done it too, from my bedroom window. On the nights when

Manic Flora has decided that sleep is for normal people, something so far beneath her as she soars above the rest of the world, I've sat at my window and watched the sun come up on Hopwood.

Because what is the point of sights like these if there is no one with whom to share them?

The words settle on my heart like falling feathers. Of all the things that mania is – in all its terrifying brightness, its loudness, its speed and its dazzling colours – the worst of all is it's *lonely*. How can anyone keep up with a mind moving that fast? How can anyone understand what you're looking at when you see things in a million new colours – colours that don't exist outside your own head?

It's lonely when you're standing in the middle of an exam room, and everyone is looking at you and leaning across the desks, whispering behind their hands... Or when you're standing on the pavement near the college bus, outside looking in... It's lonely when your worst enemy is inside your own head, and nobody else can hear it or see it – and even if you could somehow magically project it outside for the rest of the world to see, what could they do?

I drag my mind back into the room and into the moment.

"So he's an insomniac. He's wandering around in the middle of the night, going for a walk in the gardens – and what? He's seen somebody? Who would be up at that time?"

"One of the maids. The maids were always the first ones up in the morning." Hal is already spreading papers across the only clear bit of the table. "What did the book say Iris Campbell did?"

"Umm…" I leaf back through the pages of the housekeeping book. "Second housemaid."

"Ha!" He brandishes yet another wedge of papers at me, these covered in horrible handwriting. Seeing as I don't think they had biros in 1913, it must be some of his research. "Housemaids lit the fires. That was the first thing they had to do. Early in the morning, they had to clear out the ashes from the night before and light a fresh fire before the family got up."

"I guess it's not all that different to how guests here dump wet towels on their beds and come back to find everything tidied up, and a whole new set of dry ones by the bath," I say, rolling my eyes.

Hal flips a couple of pages in the bundle he's holding, then scribbles something across the top of one of them, not even looking up as he speaks. "That's just how it was back then. It didn't occur to most of the upper class that the fires had to *be* lit, because they just were. I bet half of them didn't even know where the servants' quarters were."

"What, like you know where all the staff rooms are in your hotels?" I don't mean to say anything out loud, let alone that. But it falls out anyway. This *does* make him look at me, one eyebrow arched, even as I wish I could somehow suck the words back into my mouth and parcel them up inside my head, where they were meant to stay all along.

"My family's hotels. Not mine," he says quietly. "Not the same thing."

"Isn't it?"

"No."

"Even if you're the one who's going to take everything over in time? Like a...like an heir?"

"Whether I want to or not? Not every heir wants to inherit the estate. And not all of them carry on the family name." Hal's mouth twists as he says it. "Albert didn't, did he?"

I shake my head. "You don't *think* he did. Until there's actual proof, you can't say that for sure."

"Even though we're standing in his house, and it's a hotel?"

"That doesn't mean anything. It could be a coincidence."

"I don't believe in coincidences." He folds his arms across his chest, like a little kid who's about to stamp his foot.

"Fine, then. I guess we'll have to keep looking, won't we?" I growl back at him, folding my own arms for good measure.

But as he turns away and reaches for yet another box, I'm sure I catch the briefest flash of a smile on his face.

Luckily, with his back to me, he can't see that I'm smiling too.

Eight

Nobody is more surprised than me when I find myself hurrying back to the Hopwood library the next morning. I barely even stop for breakfast – until Charlie flags me down outside the front door, shoving a piece of toast at me. Mira, halfway across the driveway at the front of the hotel, actually does a full double-take when she sees me, waving and shouting my name (after checking over her shoulder, just in case Mrs Tilney appears from nowhere – it's a habit you get into very quickly working here).

"What's the rush?" She reaches for my arm as soon as she gets close.

"No rush – I just want to get back to the research."

"You're not avoiding me?"

"Why would I be avoiding you?"

"You know why."

Of course I know why. I could be avoiding her because I'm upset she's planning on leaving – or I could be avoiding her because I'm upset that she didn't tell me. Or it could be because I'm upset that she thought she couldn't tell me in case it upset me. Even though I'm pretty used to untangling my thoughts, I'm not sure whether that one makes sense.

I stop and look at her. "I wish you'd said something."

"Oh." Mira stares at the ground, rolling a bit of gravel around under her shoe. "I wanted to, I think? I didn't mean to *not* tell you."

I remember her face across the kitchen table. "You were waiting for the right moment."

"Yes? I didn't..." She looks thoughtful, and I know she's trying to pick her way through the minefield that is Talking About Flora's Feelings. "I didn't want you to think it was about you. You understand? You have this way of taking everything and making it personal. Anything bad, anything that makes you sad, it has to be a punishment for something you've done. Like you deserve it. And you hold on to that in your head and you tell it to yourself over and over and over until you believe it. And it's not *true*." Mira sighs. "I didn't want to do that to you, so...I was waiting for a good time to tell you."

"I don't think there ever would have been a good time," I say. "Not with this head."

She puts her arm around my shoulder, gently cuffing the side of my head. "Tell you a secret," she whispers, pulling me alongside her. "I think your head isn't right about you deserving to be sad. You should remember that."

She's right – as usual. But she's still leaving.

We cover the rest of the driveway together, and she changes the subject. "So what is it that's so interesting in the library all of a sudden? Two days ago, you were hating it…"

"I never said I *hated* it, exactly…"

"And now you're here, practically sprinting back to all the boxes." A slow grin spreads across her face. "Or is it not so much the boxes but the *boy*?"

"He's not a boy, Mee."

"Ah! I knew it!" Her elbow digs into my ribs.

"I meant that he's the same age as you, so 'boy' doesn't exactly sound right. And you know it."

"Meh. But it *is* him you're making such a rush for, yes?"

"*No.*"

"No?"

"Can you just drop it? It's not funny." I yank my bag up on my shoulder. Someone has opened the first of the library's French windows. An image of Hal striding across the library and reaching for the handle of the window fills my mind, captured in slow-motion. I can feel the movement of the air as the window opens, see the sunlight flash on his hair, catch the scent of him as he turns back from the window towards me – his hair falling just in front of his eyes, his hand outstretched, reaching for mine, and…

"Hello? Flora?"

Hal's face is replaced by Mira's, her eyebrows raised expectantly at me.

"Sorry – what?"

"I said, what did you find? More houses?"

"No. We think maybe we found the soldier he was looking for after all – *maybe*."

"Good! This means he'll be gone soon, and I get you back. Mrs Tilney keeps pairing me with Ursula on the rota, and she's so boring." Mira drops her voice to a stage-whisper. "And she smears the mirrors."

I take a breath to tell her about the flashes of something I've seen in Hal – the glimpses of whatever it is underneath the surface. But as soon as I open my mouth, there's a shout from behind us, and jogging up the drive from the village is a figure dressed in black-and-white chef's trousers and a red T-shirt, a satchel thrown over his shoulder. Philippe, one of the sous-chefs from the kitchens.

"Hey! How's it going?" He turns his beaming smile on us, looking from me to Mira.

"Oh, you know. It's going." She waves a hand vaguely in the air.

Everything I was about to say to Mira turns to jelly in my mouth, sitting on my tongue and clogging my throat. I shrug, and fiddle with the strap on my backpack. Philippe's arrival has dimmed a bulb in my head. Because however nice he is, he's someone else. Like pretty much the rest of the world. And with him comes the constant scratching feeling under my skin – a reminder that I have to keep up my guard. Don't get manic. Don't get depressed. Keep being normal.

But as the three of us fall into step, Mira and Philippe already moving towards the staff entrance on the left of the drive, me towards the hotel's main entrance ahead, I realize that the entire time I've been in the library, I've not felt like that.

I've known Philippe the whole year I've worked here, and I still feel edgy around him. It's not personal, it's just *people*. But I've known Hal Waverley about five minutes... and I don't feel like that at all.

Maybe it's the stranger thing – just the same as he knew he could tell me something that felt secret. Maybe it's because I know that when he's gone, he's gone. I'll never have to see him again after this.

Then, as the three of us are about to go our separate ways, there's a movement behind the French windows and suddenly Hal appears on the terrace. One hand shades his eyes from the sun, the other is clutching a piece of paper. He scans the driveway and spots me. I feel it. I can see it in the way he straightens, as though a weight has fallen from his back.

He's found more.

Something in my stomach knots and lurches, the way it does at the first drop on a roller coaster.

"Flora! Come on!" The hand that was shielding his eyes is waving now, beckoning; the other holding up the page. "You have to see this!"

With a mumbled, "Got to go – see you," to the others,

I jog towards the terrace steps.

As soon as I make it to the top of the wonky stone steps he clears his throat and starts reading.

"'The ball may only have lasted a few hours, but our dance has continued every night since in my dreams. I hear the music, feel the floor beneath my feet, just as clear and as real as it was that night. The only thing missing is you.'" He looks up from the page expectantly.

"What is that? What ball?"

"You're going to love this – come and see." With a grin, he darts through the open French window into the library.

"Love what?" It takes a second for my eyes to adjust to coming indoors from the bright sunlight. When they do, I see he's cleared most of the papers that were spread out across the table and re-stacked at least half the boxes in neat piles on the far side of the room. Now, three boxes are sitting on the table, lids off, the contents piled in front of each one.

"When did you do this?"

"Oh, last night." He's already grabbing for another piece of paper.

"Don't you ever *sleep*?" I wonder if this is what it's like for Charlie, talking to me?

"Apparently not. Here." He holds the page out to me. Like on most of the other papers from the boxes, the ink has faded over the years, but it's still just about clear enough to know what I'm looking at.

"It's a shopping list. A big one." Bottles of wine, fruit, meat, eggs, flour…and a whole load of things I don't recognize. But whatever they are, there's a lot of them. I look from the page to Hal, and back again. "It's for a party, right?"

"A party or a…?" He waits for me to finish his sentence. Which I would, except I have no idea what he's talking about. After a long, long pause, he bites his lip and looks up at me from beneath his fringe. "No?"

"I have nothing. Sorry."

"A ball. Like there was in the note I just read?"

"*Oh!*" How stupid do I feel? "But if she's a servant, how come they were at a ball together?"

"This is the bit you're going to love. I found this…" He waggles the list, forgetting that it could genuinely fall apart at any second – then remembers and panics, laying it down on the table. He pats it carefully with his fingertips, just to make sure it's okay. "So I went back to the housekeeper's book. And I found *this*."

The book is open to a new place, the pages covered in notes and columns and numbers. But the bit that catches my eye – the bit that Hal has to be talking about – is at the top. "A servants' ball? As in, a ball for the servants?"

"It was a thing they did. Servants had the night off and got to have a big party, dancing – a ball. And the family would come down to their dining hall and dance with them, and sometimes they'd act as their servants…stuff

102

like that. It was the only time they actually got to interact as people. Just for one night."

"How do you know all that?"

Hal wrinkles his nose. It makes him look about eleven years old. "I like history. But look – a ball." He jabs his finger at the paper triumphantly.

"Exactly what a romantic story needs, I guess. And they danced. They *danced*!" The roller-coaster feeling in my stomach is back, and a shiver runs the full length of my spine. I'm not sure if it's because of the story or because a picture of being spun around a ballroom by Hal flashes through my head and is gone again before I can even work out where it came from.

"But this is the best part. You keep saying we need proof?"

"I was talking more about the history of the house, but…"

I stop talking as he slides one more page across the table in front of me.

Thank you for the ribbon you enclosed with your letter, and which gives me cause to hope. I will keep it with me always, to remind me of how it felt to dance with you in a room full of people.

It's addressed to *my Iris*, and signed with an *A*, on the same monogrammed paper.

The roller coaster meets the shiver, and turns into a cloud of furiously fluttering butterflies inside me.

"This is it, right?"

"This is really it, Flora. I told you I don't believe in coincidences. It's them. It's definitely them. It's *real*."

Hal's eyes are blazing, and his voice is full of light and life, and suddenly the room feels both smaller and larger at the same time.

The butterflies in my stomach swirl in formation.

"'To dance with you in a room full of people…'"

"Sorry?" Hal catches my words, even though they were muttered under my breath.

"Oh. Nothing. I was just thinking – that's kind of a weird thing to say, isn't it? Why not just say, 'how it felt to dance with you'? Why the 'room full of people'?"

"Because," he says, finishing my thought for me, "they were used to being together. Just not where anyone could see them."

It makes perfect, perfect sense. "Of course! They aren't *meant* to be together, but they *are*. In secret. He's wealthy, she's the maid…imagine if they got caught! She'd lose her job and be out of the house like *that*." I snap my fingers.

"And nothing would happen to him, obviously, because…"

"Because society only punished women for that kind of thing?" I raise an eyebrow at him.

The faintest tinge of pink passes across his cheeks. "I was just about to say that, actually."

It's very hard not to laugh. Very hard.

Everything feels different this morning: the library, the paperwork, the whole hotel. Hal.

Me.

I feel different. I feel…almost like me again. Like I've been wearing a mask, a shell, a suit of armour – and suddenly I can let it open just a little, because in here it doesn't matter. I don't need it so much. Do I?

The school nurse's shoe squeaks as she leads me down the corridor to the office. Only one shoe – not both. And it suddenly seems so important that she knows this that I want to yell it at her at the top of my voice. I would, too, if my head didn't feel so weird. They don't know what to do with me – should they punish me? Should they call a doctor? They leave me on the little sofa in the office reception while they decide. Outside, a couple of Year Sevens lean around the door to stare at me. "Is she okay?" one of them whispers to the other. I'm about to tell them I'm fine, to get lost, when I realize my face is wet. I'm crying, and I didn't even notice. And now that I know, I can't seem to stop.

I peer into the closest box. "Is the ribbon in there?"

"No. I checked. Maybe it got lost, or fell apart?"

"Or maybe he really *did* keep it with him."

"Maybe." He considers this, his eyes fixed on a spot somewhere halfway up the shelves covering the walls. "There's been nothing of hers, though. Only his. Why?"

"You mean there are no letters *from* her – all these are technically hers, aren't they? He wrote them *to* her. Maybe they got packed up and moved to an archive or something. Maybe the only reason these are here is because they got put away and forgotten, or lost. Maybe she hid them somewhere and then couldn't get to them again?"

"Because it was a secret?" Hal scratches at his eyebrow.

"Exactly! We're always finding stuff in the rooms – things people have hidden and then forgotten. Maybe that's what happened."

This seems to catch his attention, because he folds himself into the nearest chair, stretching his legs out in front of him and looking curiously at me. "Stuff like what?"

"Small things, mostly. Although Mira did find an engagement ring once, shoved under a mattress. It was still in its box." I drop my voice to a whisper. "I'm guessing things didn't go to plan."

"And what about you? What have you found?"

"A pair of shoes."

"Shoes?"

"I know." I lean on the table just along from where he's sitting. "It sounds rubbish. But they were...I don't know. They felt like they were special."

"Shoes?" he says again – but it's the warmth in his voice that I hear.

Even though I found them ages ago, back when this was just a Saturday job, I can still see them. "They were black

106

patent shoes, with a strap across the front – the kind little girls wear to parties. You know the kind I mean?"

"Not personally."

"Well, you get the idea. They were really small, maybe for a six or seven year old? And they were sitting in the cupboard by the bed, all lined up."

Why are you telling him this? Why does he even care about you finding somebody else's shoes in a cupboard two years ago?

I don't know. All I know is that telling him feels…easy.

From his chair, Hal watches me. His expression doesn't change, but his eyes do. They soften and warm, and the colour of them shimmers from faded blue to sea-green. The line of his jaw shifts…and everything about him is a question. A puzzle. A secret.

A secret…

"The letter. The ruin letter – it makes sense now!" The words come out so fast it's like I'm tripping over them and judging by the look on his face, Hal's struggling to keep up with me too. Not that I get the chance to worry about that – it's taking all my energy to rein in my brain, which is bolting for the next idea.

Sanjay's office, and even though the blind is down as always, I can hear the rain outside.

"They're called 'flights of ideas'. It's perfectly normal…"

"Normal? Are you kidding me right now?"

"Normal for this type of condition, Flora."

107

"So, the new normal."

"If that's how you want to see it, yes. When your brain is in a manic phase, it can be harder to stay focused – your thoughts will skip from one thing to the next much faster than usual. You have to learn to pull it back."

"Why? Thinking fast doesn't sound so bad. It's like a superpower."

"Have you ever run on a treadmill?"

"A couple of times."

"What happens if you're running on that treadmill, and I turn up the speed?"

"I run faster."

"And if I keep turning up the speed?"

"I'll probably trip over and land on my face?"

"Yes. Now picture that, but with your brain."

"Oh. So not a superpower then?"

"No, Flora."

"Somebody knew they were together. That's what that first letter you found is about. Somebody knew, and was telling Iris to end it. Before it was too late."

"Jane."

"Maybe we should try and find out who she was?"

"I'll do some digging. You said something about an archive, didn't you?"

I nod. "There's a small local one at Fallowmill. It's another old house, a couple of villages away."

"Maybe there's something there." The Hal who was sitting in the chair listening to me talk about finding shoes slips away. His legs retreat, tucked closer and crossed, one ankle resting on his knee. His back straightens and his shoulders drop and his thoughts are wheeling away. "I'll see if I can call the curator. Now I've got more of a lead, this one might actually let me in."

One by one, the butterflies in my stomach turn to ash. *I* and *me* not *we*. Not *us*. Is that it? As soon as things start to make sense, he doesn't want me here.

That's what happens when you let your brain get ahead of you.
Why would someone like him want you *around?*

Then, quieter, he says: "Maybe you can come back tomorrow – just in case?"

"Tomorrow. No problem."

He leans forward and starts flipping through the papers on the table. The walls of the library push back and the sunlight streaming in through the French windows turns cold... But as I walk out of the door, I'm sure – just for a second – he looks up at me. His voice stops me halfway out. "I'll let you know what I find out, if you like?"

I'd forgotten about Fallowmill until this – the house Felix says gives him the creeps. I made myself forget about it. It's one of those places owned by the National Trust – the kind of place Hopwood could have become if it wasn't a hotel,

I guess, only bigger. *Much* bigger. It's also where my old school's end-of-exams party is always held – in a huge marquee in the grounds by the lake. Jumping in at the end of the night is a tradition, like signing shirts on the last day, and leavers' hoodies with everybody's names on.

"Did you find a dress yet?"

"Nah. There was one, but I think it's too…it's just not me. You know?"

"No. But whatever. Aren't you worried you won't find one? I got mine last month!"

"There's loads of time. I'll get one after the exams."

"There's three weeks, Flora. That's not loads of time – not to find a dress for Fallowmill. You can't just wear any old thing. We're meant to remember this party for the rest *of our lives."*

I never did get my dress. I never got to do any of it.

Because while everyone else was busy having fun at the party, dancing and laughing – and yes, having their photo taken sitting in the water, throwing it around like confetti – I was lying on my bed, watching the ceiling spin, every thought crashing through my head like a spiked ball, and wondering whether this was what dying felt like. Or how, if this was what living felt like, I was meant to keep on doing it day after day after day.

I missed out on the dresses and the laughing and the dancing and the jumping.

I saw it all, though, in tiny little frames on my phone. It was like watching my life – the life I thought I had – through a window, and seeing the world moving on without me. There wasn't even a space for me in it. I might as well have fallen through a gap in the earth. Nobody messaged or called me, nobody emailed. Nobody posted anything on any of my pages or profiles online – and yes, I checked. I checked them over and over and over again until Charlie asked me whether obsessively staring at my phone was really the best thing for me. He was right, I guess. I'm not sure what was worse – scrolling back to the day of The Incident, and seeing all the stuff people wrote on their pages about the weirdo being led out of the exam room after freaking out (that would be me), or the fact that after that they didn't write anything at all. It was like I was erased from existence. I mean, I get it – *now*, anyway. Why would anyone want to be friends with someone like me after *that*? Why shouldn't they keep their distance – afraid that maybe I'd somehow infect them, that madness is catching? Maybe they were embarrassed, maybe they didn't know what to say or how to act around me. Or maybe they knew exactly the same thing that I did, instinctively and unavoidably – that there was something wrong with me, and that I should be ashamed of it. That being broken was my fault, even if I didn't know why.

I scrolled and I scrolled, and I looked for the hole in my friends' feeds where I should have been…and it felt like being left behind – being forgotten – was what I deserved. I wasn't good enough to be remembered, wasn't whole enough to belong.

No wonder they stared at me from the bus. It must have been like seeing a ghost, because that's all I am to them. A ghost, an urban legend. A cautionary tale. "Remember the girl in school who went mad…"

Dismissed by Hal, I head home, my feet dragging through the dusty grass of the deer park. I could have gone down to the break room, but I don't want to talk to anyone right now. Not even Mira. After all, she won't be here long, will she? Not with the course she's applying for. And then it'll just be me left here while everybody else moves on.

Just. Like. A. Ghost.

"Felix?"

Charlie's voice drifts out from the kitchen when I slam the front door.

"No. Just me."

"What are you doing back so soon?" My brother's head peers around the door frame, a pencil tucked behind his ear. He's still working on the planting plans for the new flower border the garden team are putting in next spring.

"I'm surplus to requirements."

He gives me a puzzled look.

"He's going to Fallowmill."

112

"Is that so?" The pencil slips, and Charlie catches it, rolling it between his fingers. "You don't look particularly happy about it."

"It's fine. I'm fine."

"I'm here to listen, if you want."

"Nothing to talk about. I'm going up to my room."

He shouts something after me about whether I should be going back in, whether I'm meant to be *working*-working – but I'm already halfway up the stairs so I just pretend I didn't hear him and close my bedroom door behind me. I ignore my bed, and instead wedge myself onto the tiny shelf under my window that acts as a kind of window seat, my head grazing the low sloping eaves. Taking a deep breath, I pull out my phone.

I'm not a ghost. I don't *want* to be.

But somehow, that's what I've ended up becoming.

A couple of finger-taps and my screen fills with pictures.

Are you sure you want to do this?

Yes.

No.

Maybe?

It somehow feels like the right thing.

Tap-tap-tap, and there's the profile I was looking for. Eoin, the guy on the bus – the first one to see me. I'd almost forgotten his name, forgotten him, until the other morning. Boxed up the memories and put them in a corner of my mind, because everything to do with school means exams means The Incident means…awfulness. But now I remember. He used to sit in front of me in maths. He turned around once and wrote something on my folder. "That's my number, that is," he said, grinning at me. "And?" I'd said, because I was already slipping, already breaking apart. I just didn't know it.

Tap-tap-scroll, rolling back time, and there's the grounds at Fallowmill, a year ago. There they are – everyone I knew. All the friends I thought I had. The friends who left me behind.

That's what happens when people leave. They leave and they don't come back.

Dad, Mum, everybody from school.

Even Mira.

She's leaving me here. She doesn't want to be here. She doesn't want to be my friend any more.

Is this a balanced reaction?

Is this a balanced reaction?

Is this a balanced reaction?

Hal Waverley, turning away.

Sixty-five friends and almost-friends, all of them in dresses and jackets and all of them laughing, smiling, dancing.

The sun setting on the party, on the exams.

On me.

Scoll-scroll-scroll.

But…what if I don't want to be a ghost?

114

Staring at spaces where I should have been and wasn't. Looking for the holes I left behind...

I'm across the room and down the stairs, the front door left swinging and Charlie's voice, startled, following me out into the garden.

"Flora?"

But I'm not stopping.

"Flora!"

Out of breath from running (and speed-walking, because it's actually quite a long way from the cottage to the Hopwood across the grounds) with my T-shirt clammy and my hair sticking to my neck, I race up the steps to the terrace and into the library – scaring the life out of the little old lady browsing the shelf of paperbacks left behind by other guests.

"Sorry..." I mumble, and slip out of the door into the lobby. He's not here. I was sure he'd still be here.

A glance out of the windows at the drive tells me he is in the hotel somewhere. He must be – the squashed-frog car is parked outside. He *could* be out in the gardens, but...

I take the stairs two at a time, and I don't stop until I'm outside the door to room fifteen. It takes a monumental effort not to add "Housekeeping?" to my knock.

I don't want to just walk away from this. I need to see the whole of the puzzle, not just fragments of it, snapshots.

I don't *want* to just glimpse this story the way I've glimpsed the life I could have had. The ghost of the life I thought I was getting.

Hal opens the door and his face immediately changes when he sees me on the other side, quickly shifting through a series of different expressions. He opens his mouth to speak – but I'm faster. Me and my speed-racer brain.

"When you go to Fallowmill…can I come with you?"

Nine

It feels like longer than three days until Tuesday, the day we've agreed to go to Fallowmill to check the archives there. If it were up to me, it wouldn't be so long – I have a couple of days off, but somehow this has stopped feeling like work – but Hal says that's the next time the curator's there. So Tuesday it is and for three whole days, I get to replay the look on Hal's face when I asked to go with him to Fallowmill, over and over and over in my head.

"You want to come?"

"Yes."

A pause, then: "*Why?*"

"Because...I want to know."

The tips of his ears slowly turned pink, the colour seeping down like someone was painting them with watercolours. There was a long, long silence, then: "Okay."

I tried to sound casual. "If there's anything you want to go through before then...maybe Monday?"

"We should probably wait until after Fallowmill. Besides, I have to be somewhere on Monday, so I won't be here for a day or two."

Don't take it personally. It's not about you. Don't make it negative.

I steered my brain away from ninety-eight per cent of the places it wanted to go. "Oh. Then I guess I'll see you Tuesday. My brother's been nagging me about sorting out some stuff at home for ages, so..."

"The one who says you're a pain in the arse?" The faintest glimmer of a smile appeared in his eyes.

He was listening. And he remembered.

"That one." It was my turn to blush, and I could feel it all over my face. "But he mostly only says it when I'm being one. *Mostly*," I added quietly.

He pushed his hair back from his eyes and it fell straight forward again. "Tuesday then. It's nice to have somebody else around for this. All these old papers aren't exactly good company," he said. "Ten o'clock all right? I'll meet you outside the front door of the hotel."

I nodded. "Ten o'clock. I'll be there."

I try not to wake up early. I really try. So when my eyes snap open and my body decides it's morning even though my room is dark, I check the clock.

2 a.m.

Okay.

By 5 a.m., I've gone back to sleep and woken up again three times, and the night has been endless. So I give in and get out of bed, and throw open my curtains. The sun is finally up and the world has turned warm gold, sparkling after the rain that came in over the weekend. Patches of pink-tinted cloud linger across the sky, and a group of deer pick their way across the park in front of the cottage.

By 6.00 a.m., I am dressed and eating a bowl of cereal at the kitchen table – much to Charlie's surprise when he staggers downstairs in an old blue T-shirt and his pyjama bottoms, rubbing his hair and yawning.

"Morning!" I beam at him from behind my spoon.

"Christ!" He twitches so hard it's a miracle he doesn't dislocate his arm. "What are you doing up?"

"It's Tuesday."

"I know it's Tuesday. I've got a stocktake in the glasshouse… Oh, it's *Tuesday*." He peers at the kettle. "You're going off to Fallowmill with your guest, aren't you?"

"Yes." I ignore the weight behind the question.

"And you're sure about this, are you?"

"You're being a dad again."

"I'm not being a dad." He holds the kettle under the tap, although most of the water seems to be going down the side of it rather than into it. "I'm being a responsible adult. You should give it a try sometime."

"I *am* being responsible. I'm fine."

"Mmm."

I try again. "Remember how Sanjay said I should do jigsaw puzzles?"

"I'm still finding some of the pieces down the back of the sofa."

"Well, this is a big jigsaw puzzle."

"And Fallowmill?" Charlie pours water onto a teabag.

"You're being difficult about this on purpose, aren't you?" I drop my bowl and spoon into the sink with a clatter. "You know that, right?"

Still holding the kettle, Charlie hesitates. "I'm not. I'm trying—"

"Yeah, you are," I mutter.

His deep sigh is a pretty good clue that he heard me. "I'm trying to make sure you're thinking clearly. You were upset for days after you missed the party at Fallowmill. It set you back – you know that, and I…"

"You don't want me to get sick again. I know. But I feel like I need to do this – I need to go there and…exorcize it. Or something." It made sense in my head at 4 a.m.

"*Exorcize* it?" He finishes making his tea, pausing just to make sure his incredulity has time to sink in.

"I just really need to do this. I'll be okay – I promise."

At last he nods, and I watch him take a sip of his drink.

I wait.

I wait longer than seems entirely reasonable…and then

it happens. Charlie frowns, looks at his mug, looks at the kettle...and sighs.

"You could have told me I didn't actually boil it, you know."

"What would be the fun in that?"

Still grumbling – about me, about the kettle, about the glasshouses, about *everything* – he empties the mug into the sink and stomps back off upstairs, leaving me alone in the kitchen.

I look at the clock.

6.15 a.m.

Great.

Only three and three-quarter more hours to kill.

I give up trying to pass the time at home and head in to Hopwood, making myself a cup of tea in the still-deserted staff break room. But because it's not even 7 o'clock, nobody's been in here yet and no one's brought the milk in from the main kitchen delivery. I stick my head out into the corridor. Nothing. The only sound from the kitchen is a rhythmic *thump-slap-thump-slap* of dough being kneaded. That means Philippe's in there, but the main breakfast shift – the chefs who start at four or five in the morning – must be getting some fresh air before the rush starts and the kitchen heats up.

I slip across the corridor and in through the kitchen's

steel swing doors. As they swoosh shut behind me, Philippe looks up from the metal counter where he's working a small mountain range of dough. Flour is dusted up his arms, the white standing out starkly against his skin.

"You're in early," he says with a smile. "Still working on all that stuff in the library?"

"Something like that." I point at the nearest of the fridges. "Can I get the milk?"

"Sure – help yourself!" He glances round, then back to me, turning the dough over in his hands. "What's with the apron?"

"The apron?" I stop halfway to the fridge. "What apron?"

He waves a floury hand at me. "That apron."

Then I realize. He means my dress.

He's making fun of you. You look stupid. You are stupid.

Stop. No. Think. Is this the right reaction?

Does my mood match the moment?

I check Philippe's face. He's smiling warmly. His eyes actually twinkle.

He's not making fun of you. He's teasing you. He's just being friendly. If it was Mira, you'd know she was kidding. He's kidding.

"It's a pinafore dress, not an apron." I pull out the big plastic jug of milk for the staff room and close the giant fridge door.

It happens to be a new pinafore dress, too. Well. New-ish. I just haven't had a chance to wear it until now.

122

But I'm definitely not wearing it because of Hal.

Definitely not.

Philippe grins even more widely. "It looks like an apron to me. Good for cleaning."

"It's a nice dress!" Did that sound defensive? I don't *think* it did… "Anyway, nobody could do a full room changeover in this – the straps would catch on everything."

He laughs, rubbing his nose and leaving a stripe of flour across it. "I will never understand fashion. Or women." He shakes his head.

If it was a test, I think I passed. My heart swells with relief, pride, triumph… Do people feel like this all the time? I flourish my milk jug at him in farewell as I turn away…

"Flora!"

"Yes?"

"You're about to walk into the door."

I swerve around the edge of the open door and into the corridor. "Thank you!" I call back, but the only answer I get is the *thump-slap-thump-slap* of him going back to his work.

By the time I get back to my tea, it's overbrewed and bitter. But when I replay the conversation with Philippe in my head – the way I always do with every conversation, however exhausting and miserable that might be – it doesn't seem to matter.

I make another cup of tea and pull out my phone, settling down in a corner to look through other people's

year-old photos. Call it preparation, call it masochism…
but just like going today, it feels like something I have to
do. Something I have to face.

"You're still here," says a familiar voice – Mira, crashing
into the break room with her bag in her hand. "Aren't you
going to—"

"Fallowmill. Yes. In a bit." I cut her off before she asks
why I'm here so early.

Why are you here so early?

Because I couldn't sleep?

And why was that?

Because I'm excited?

Nope.

Because I'm nervous?

Try again. And this time, be honest.

Because I'm scared.

Bingo.

Except, when I look at the clock, it's not early any more.
It's nine o'clock, and somehow I've lost all that time willing
myself into photos I can never be part of. I didn't even
notice the morning rota briefing, even though it must have
happened right next to me.

I lock my phone and drop it into my pocket. "What have
you got in your bag?" Mira's usually neat bag is straining all
along the zip, the seams visibly close to bursting.

"Ah. Coursework." She sets her bag down carefully, as though it's explosive. "For my application. I'm on the lobby and corridor shift today so I brought it to finish before I start."

"Oh. Right. You have to study." Of course. I keep forgetting.

"Are you okay?" She must have seen a change in my face, or maybe my voice is different, because she's looking into my eyes and trying to read them. "You know he's already waiting outside, no?" She winks at me. "Maybe he couldn't wait until ten either."

"He is?"

My stomach flips.

Never mind scared, I think I'm actually *terrified*. And it's not just the thought of going to Fallowmill that's causing it.

"So? You should go."

"I should. Should I? Or should I, you know, wait? It's not even quarter to! He'll think I'm weird or too keen or something. Won't he?"

Mira gives me a withering look. She puts her hands on my shoulders and pushes me towards the door (not exactly gently, either). "Go. Do the thing. Exercise your ghosts, or whatever you call it."

"Exorcize, Mee. *Exorcize*."

With all the running around my head they get to do, I think my ghosts are exercised enough.

* * *

There's a finger smudge on the glass front door to the driveway, and as I step out from the lobby, I wonder, did Hal make that? Like a hair left on a pillow, a twist in the pile of a rug, a fingerprint on a door, we mark our way through the world in the traces we leave behind. Small and insignificant, maybe…

At least to anyone who doesn't know any different.

He's leaning against the side of his car waiting for me, face tilted up towards the sun and legs stretched out. He looks so confident, so sure of himself, and my breath catches in my throat. How can he be so *together*? Is this how life's supposed to be; how I'm supposed to be?

Yeah, right.

Maybe that's just the way things are in his world.

What would that world be like?

Is it the same world where I'm in the group photos at the Fallowmill party? In that world, if I was here and he was waiting for me, would I walk confidently out of the porch and across the drive? And when he heard my feet on the gravel maybe he'd look over at me and smile and take his sunglasses off, and then I'd go to him and I'd be looking into his eyes and he'd be looking back at me and slide his hand around my waist – fingers strong and warm against the small of my back – and he'd pull me close to him and…

Where did that *come from?*

Hal tilts his face down, cocks his head to one side – and looks straight over at the porch. At me.

126

Can he see me from there?

Maybe.

Can he see everything that just went through my head?

He can't. That's not possible.

Nobody can see into someone else's head. There is no *actual* way to project thoughts. No one can tell.

Can they?

No, Flora. They can't. He can't. Now pull yourself together and stop standing here like a loser.

I try to think about something, anything, other than the way he looked just then, in reality and in my daydream.

Think about the flowers at the edge of the drive. The gravel.

Flights of ideas. That's what Sanjay called them. That's all this is – a flight of ideas. My brain skipping along so fast it actually lifts off.

Definitely not thinking about Hal, definitely not his hair and his eyes and the way he's got his arms folded across his chest and…nope.

"Hey," he says – and he pushes himself away from the car, standing upright as I leave the safety of the porch and cross the drive to him.

"Hey!" I say back. And that's it. Just "hey", and then standing there.

This is going well.

"You're early." He turns his car key around in his hand, twirling it and catching it in his palm over and over again, like he needs to do something with his fingers.

"I guess so. I didn't want you to have to wait, but here you are."

"Oh. Yeah, I was early too. I was…I didn't…" He stops, bites his lip. "Shall we go?"

I can feel my heartbeat inside my head. Is that good?

In addition to racing thoughts, some patients display symptoms such as euphoric happiness and a sense of well-being.

I don't think this counts as well-being. Does it?

I shift my weight from one foot to the other and back again.

And back again.

And again. And again.

However, those experiencing hypomania may also find it hard to stay still – moving around unnecessarily and fidgeting uncontrollably.

I stop hopping around.

I don't think he's noticed; he's opening the car door.

"I'm ready if you are."

Why isn't he getting in the car?

He's opened the door. What's he waiting for?

Has he changed his mind?

Did I do something wrong?

What did I do?

My mind races through the last thing I said, the last thing I thought, checking…double-checking…triple-checking…

It's the passenger door.

He's opened the passenger door.

For me.

Oh.

"Sorry. Yes. Sorry." I shuffle up to the car, drop into the seat, and he closes the door gently after me.

Nobody's ever opened a door for me before.

I mean, sure, they've opened a door when I've had my hands full of cleaning equipment or my arms full of towels – but that's just what you do, right? This is different – more like how nobody's ever pulled a chair back for me to sit on. Not before him.

Something under the car creaks alarmingly as he slides into the driver's seat and slams his door. I raise my eyebrows pointedly at him and he waves a hand at the windscreen. "It's fine, don't worry. Just the…umm… Yeah. It's fine. Let's go then."

The gravel crunches under the tyres, and as he turns the car around, I spot Philippe standing at the staff entrance, waving at me as we pass.

I smile back through the window at him and reach for my seat belt.

The engine of the squashed-frog car is noisier than I expected. Somehow I thought Hal's car would be quiet and smooth inside, like his voice, like his clothes. There's no radio or dock, so the only sound – apart from the growl and rattle of the engine – is the world whipping past the open window. The trees lining the drive down to the gate give way to the hedges, to the stone houses of the village... and then to the fields.

"The curator said she'd look through the archives and see if she could find anything that connected to Hopwood. She sounded pretty excited, right up till I told her it wasn't for a TV show."

"Oh. Sorry."

"What are you apologizing for? It's not like it's your fault, is it?"

"No. It's just...well, that must kind of suck."

"It does. But I've got used to it. They normally at least wait to actually see me to be disappointed, though." He slides his sunglasses down his nose and puts on a pinched-sounding voice. "'Oh. Mr Waverley. You're...*younger* than I expected.'" Hal snorts.

"Sorry."

"Seriously, stop apologizing for them."

"Sor—" I snap my mouth shut so quickly that my teeth click together.

"Now you're getting it," he laughs.

Up ahead a sign points to a turning between enormous stone gateposts with an open wrought-iron gate.

"That's it – Fallowmill House." Hal flicks the indicator on and pushes his sunglasses further up the bridge of his nose, hunching over the steering wheel. A screen of trees separates the road from the house ahead as we follow the curve of the drive. "I guess we'll just have to play it by ear… *woah*."

The drive has swept around a patch of woodland, carrying us with it…and suddenly opened up onto a view of the house. "Woah" just about sums it up.

Unlike Hopwood, which is perched on top of a hill that makes it look small at first, Fallowmill wants to impress. It sits squarely at the end of its long, wide drive, an enormous fountain right in front of it, and stares right back at us with rows of glittering windows. Out of the corner of my eye, I spot the lake through the trees.

"Imagine living somewhere like that," Hal mutters, staring at it as it looms towards us.

I peer over my sunglasses at it. It peers back.

When the car creeps to a halt, Hal switches off the ignition…but then he doesn't move.

"Are you okay?"

"Hmm?" For a second, he looks confused to see me there, as though it's hard to pull himself back from wherever he went – but then his eyes clear and he shakes whatever thoughts he was having away. "Yep. Yep, I'm good. I was just…thinking."

"About your grandfather?"

"About lots of things. Maybe I should try not thinking for a bit. Everybody tells me I overthink everything anyway."

He drums his thumbs on the edge of the steering wheel as though he's afraid of what I'll say.

"Me too! Overthink things, I mean. People tell me I do that." I stop. It feels like the best idea.

Sterling work there, Flora.

But if I've bothered him, he doesn't show it. Instead he's climbing out of the car, reaching back to grab his bag stuffed with notebooks and whatever else he carries around with him on this quest of his.

Clambering out of the car, I try to straighten my pinafore, which has somehow managed to twist itself around my lower body. Stupid dress.

The house really feels enormous up close. Most places like this are just glorified big houses, but Fallowmill? Fallowmill is a *proper* stately home. Between the thundering fountain, with its spray drifting across the gravel, and the tall windows along the front, it's built to make anyone standing out here feel small, dwarfed by everything up to the row of carved angels and lions peering down from the roof.

Hal strides across the drive as though he owns the place, bounding up the steps. He stops at the top, turns and looks back towards me, pulling off his sunglasses to see me better. "Are you coming?"

The way he moves his hand, the way his hair falls over his face as his sunglasses come away from his eyes, the way he stands…maybe these could fill in the space where my Fallowmill memories *should* be. I could take all of this, now, and drop it into the gaps in the middle of my puzzle and pretend this was the picture that had been there all along. Maybe it would even work – for a while, anyway.

A woman – older, serious-looking, probably the curator Hal spoke to on the phone – appears in the open front doorway. Hal – still turned towards me – doesn't see the expression on her face, wiped away the instant he turns to face her and replaced by something carefully blank… But I do. It's the look of someone who thinks you can't possibly matter, that you're too unimportant to count. They don't usually bother trying to disguise it for me.

Her face expectant now, she offers her hand to Hal and he takes it, shakes it.

"Mr Waverley."

"Hello." Hal beams at her, but judging by her scowl she's immune to his charm. Maybe she's immune to everyone who arrives without a camera crew.

"If you'd like to follow me?" It's less a question than a command.

Inside, our footsteps echo around the enormous hall. The stairs sweep away up to the first floor in a whirl of carvings; paintings of every size line the walls. There are portraits of the family who lived here, landscapes, horses, still-lifes of piles of fruit and vases full of flowers – all hung on dark walls faded by time. But something else is different here – the feel of the place. Hopwood Home always feels welcoming. Fallowmill is more sombre…as though something broke here, or went missing a long time ago, and was never quite found again.

It feels a bit like a tomb.

Or a prison.

The woman stops outside a small wooden door marked *PRIVATE*, tucked discreetly into a corner – so discreetly, in fact, that I completely miss it, and almost pile into Hal's back. I end up doing a weird sidestep to avoid crashing into him, catching the faintest scent of lemons and green woods as I do.

Judging by the smile Hal's trying to hide, he's either amused, charmed or exasperated by this. "Do you want to come? To the archive?"

I open my mouth to reply, because of course I want to come to the archive…and then behind him, I see her raised eyebrow and pinched mouth. I see the pale white patches either side of her nose. "The papers we store here are very *delicate*. Very *fragile*. Too much exposure to *people* will do them no good at all."

I guess I'm not welcome.

"Then you're probably better off without me to start with – but I'll help you go through anything good?" I say.

"You're sure?"

The curator rests a hand on the doorknob, turning it, opening the door a crack. Beyond it I can see stacks of boxes, rows of cupboards and a couple of narrow desks – the past, lined up and catalogued and inescapable.

I smile, hoping it's enough to cover everything in my head. "Of course. Come find me when you need me."

This is the correct answer as far as the curator is concerned, her mouth unpuckers slightly and she nods. She holds out a small square of laminated card to me. "Why don't you take a look around the house while you wait? This is a guest pass for the house and the grounds. There's no need to pay. Just show this to anyone who asks – and please, keep to the *public* areas?"

Like I don't know what a door marked *private* means...

I pocket the pass and smile at Hal. "I'll be around." He gives me a slightly anxious smile, and before he has a chance to step into the archive, I lay a hand on his arm. He flinches – his eyes flicking down to the spot where I'm touching him – and then smiles at me again, less anxiously this time. A flush creeps up his cheeks. "I hope you find something. Good luck."

Ten

After the curator closes the door behind them, I turn the guest pass around in my pocket. Through the tall windows overlooking the drive, out past the fountain and a formal border of scraggy-looking roses, the lake glints darkly at me.

Baby steps.

I follow the signs that guide visitors around the house, through a chintzy sitting room with a card table set up in the middle, cards laid out as if someone is mid-game. I know the idea is to make the house look like it did when it was still lived in, but the overall effect is creepy, like the players have all left the room at once and could walk back in at any moment. Next is a dining room with a huge table laid with china and crystal and silver. Then there's another sitting room, and then another and one more, which makes me start to wonder exactly how many rooms anyone really needs for just *sitting*. And then a dusty sign points to a door that opens onto a small staircase – I'd know a servants' staircase anywhere. I follow it down to the kitchens, and even though they don't look anything like our modern industrial kitchen back at the hotel – with its stainless steel units and benches, its ovens and walk-in fridges – I can still see the resemblance. Once upon a time, Hopwood must have looked like this too.

Kitchens lead into pantries and storerooms and laundries and other empty, echoing rooms. Just when I feel like I'm never going to find my way out of the basement, there's another staircase leading up and up again and out onto a bright landing and a series of bedrooms. Some of them are made up with four-poster beds. I surreptitiously give the mattress of one a prod as I pass. It creaks alarmingly – Mrs Tilney would *not* be impressed. Finally, there's a nursery with two little beds and a cot, and a narrow single bed in the corner for a nanny. The cot has a threadbare old-fashioned teddy bear lying on the mattress – he's obviously meant to be propped up in the corner, but he's fallen over, and my heart twists because he used to belong to someone. Someone who would have cared that he had fallen down; who would have picked him up and put him right.

"Mum?" I sit up in bed, head splitting, pulse racing, sweat trickling down the back of my neck. "Mum!"

"Flora?" She pushes my bedroom door open, silhouetted against the light from the landing. "What's wrong?"

"There was a fire, and people were screaming. They couldn't

get out, and I was supposed to help them but I couldn't, and they wouldn't stop screaming, and...and..." My voice chokes out as she sits on the end of my bed and pats my hand.

"It was just a dream. The doctor did warn you."

"It was so real. It was so real. I can't go back to sleep. Please don't make me."

"You need to sleep."

"But..."

"It's just a dream. The things in your head can't hurt you, remember? Now, come on. Back to sleep."

She closes the door behind her, cutting off the light.

I reach into the cot to sit the teddy bear up again – but a sudden stern cough from the doorway makes me stop. A middle-aged lady in a cardigan is standing there, scowling at me.

"Please don't touch," she says, still frowning.

I shuffle past her, head down.

Something about the next section of the house feels different. It's a study and a couple of...I don't know, dressing rooms? Rooms for sitting in while you're waiting until it's time to go sit in the downstairs rooms? But there are bars on some of the windows – or the ghosts of them, in places. The doors are thicker too, and carry the scars of extra locks and heavy bolts.

I turn back to the scowling cardigan woman and point to the nearest window. "What are the bars for?"

She nods, looking at the sturdy metal bars bolted to the frame on the other side of the glass. "The house was used as an asylum for a while in the Victorian era, and then again just after the First World War. Shell-shocked soldiers mostly, the ones who were never expected to recover. It's in the guidebook…"

The air curdles and clots around me, suddenly soupy. Menacing. I have a sudden vision of every door slamming, every key turning in every single lock; of bars sprouting from every window sill and trapping me here for ever. I may not have a ton of GCSEs, but even I know that's what happened to people like *me* once upon a time – to people with "conditions" like mine. This. Locked doors and barred windows. Being kept away from the world, not so much so it couldn't damage us, but so we couldn't damage it. Like a broken brain is somehow contagious.

I think perhaps I've had enough of Fallowmill House. I thought coming here would exorcize my ghosts…but now I think it might have given me more.

The library is the only room left. It's twice the size of the one at Hopwood and, like everything else here, it's chilly and deserted. I've done a full loop of the house (or at least the parts I'm allowed to see) and beyond it I can see the hallway where I started. There are no bars on the windows here, just wide open views out onto the drive and the trees. But it doesn't feel like Hopwood at all, and a sudden stab of longing for the woods and the maze and Charlie's borders full of flowers overwhelms me. It's not just that I feel like I belong at Hopwood – I know its rhythms, its routines, its shifts and its timetables – or that it's where my friends are, my family. Hopwood makes me feel protected, makes me feel safe. There are no surprises – not like here, where without warning a bedroom becomes a prison cell and there are bolts on the doors ready to trap you. Hopwood feels like a sanctuary, but the world is full of Fallowmills. Even the books in the library here are kept behind locked mesh doors – what, to keep them safe? But who decides what is safe and what isn't?

What would it take for these doors to slam, for these locks to be turned against me?

No. I keep my own keys. My doors, my locks. My head.

Out in the entrance hall, a door closes and soft footsteps squeak across the floor. A familiar head pokes around the other door to the library – looking the wrong way first, and then turning towards me with a smile. I wipe away everything I was thinking – the bars, the bolts, all of it – before he can see.

So that he won't know.

"Hey!" He lopes over, his face glowing with excitement. My heart skips again.

"How did it go?"

"The archive here is amazing. Really amazing. There's so much – things about the house, about the history of it, everyone who lived here... It's—"

"Amazing?" I finish for him, trying not to laugh.

"Amazing. Exactly. Anyway, I think I found something."

"You did?"

"Come and look."

And he stretches out a hand – almost as though he's about to take mine – before suddenly snatching his fingers back at the last instant, a fraction of a second before they touch me, so close I can actually feel the warmth from his skin before he pulls away. Instead, he tugs his fingers through his hair. "So, umm, yeah. Come on – you have to see it!"

Beyond the small wooden *PRIVATE* door, the archive is exactly as cluttered as it looked from my first glimpse of it. Filing cabinets and stacks of old wooden drawers line the walls, and the whole place smells of dust and stale coffee. A window at the back of the room has been covered with a milky-white film to keep the sun out – and, judging by the stuffy feel of the place, the air too. Not that Hal seems to notice any of that, because he makes a beeline straight for the cluttered old desk in the middle of it all, where the curator is hovering like an exam invigilator.

Footsteps walking, slow and measured, up and down the aisles between the desks...

The steady, endless tick-tick-tick of the clock...

Dozens of pairs of eyes wide, all turned towards me...

The whispering, the sound of papers falling, shuffling...

"This is it." Hal points at a single page, centred in the middle of an old-fashioned desk blotter. I go to pick it up, but the curator makes a squawky disapproving sound in the back of her throat, and Hal ducks around me, lowering his voice to a whisper. "Apparently, we've been doing it all wrong. You have to keep them flat. I never knew that."

"Oh. Right." I peer at the sheet. It looks grubby, surrounded by the pristine white blotting paper, and old. "So how do we turn it over?"

The curator snorts. "*You* don't. I will."

Hal flashes me a look that's somewhere between an eye-roll and a grin. It's conspiratorial – the kind of look shared between friends.

Are we friends?

My heart does a full barrel-roll in my chest. I lean closer to the letter and hope nobody else noticed.

Because it's been kept in an archive, and probably better looked after than all the pages at Hopwood, the ink is less faded and easier to read. The handwriting is nothing like Albie's – it's much spikier, much more untidy. Familiar, though…and realizing whose it is feels like somebody kicking me.

"It's Iris. This is Iris, isn't it?"

"It's Iris. She's signed it. But that's not the best part." Hal is so close that I can feel his hair brushing against mine as he leans over the letter alongside me; I can see the twist in his finger as he points to lines of writing – careful not to actually touch them with the stern curator hovering behind us and peering over our shoulders.

"'To my dearest Jane...'" I can feel the click as my jaw drops. "She's writing back to her!"

"Maybe, or this one might come first. Doesn't matter. She knew someone who lived here and they were writing to each other." He drops his voice to a whisper. "This is where Jane sent her letter from. I didn't even know that."

"Coincidence?"

"I told you, I don't believe in coincidences."

"Neither do I," I whisper back. "So who *is* Jane?"

"If I may?" the curator chips in. "There was a Jane Campbell working in the household here just before the First World War. She was part of the kitchen staff."

"Jane *Campbell*?" My head spins.

Hal nods, and his smile is so wide it more than lights up the room. "She has to be related to Iris. Her sister, I reckon."

I lean even closer over the paper, following the lines of letters.

How can I keep it to myself, when my heart feels like it could burst at any moment? How can I pretend that the world, my world, my life, is the same as it always was, now it has <u>him</u> in it?

"Is she talking about—"

Hal cuts me off with a loud cough and a series of long sniffs. I stare at him.

"The dust," he says, apologizing not to me but to the curator. "Allergies." But as he turns back to the desk, rubbing at the end of his nose, he presses a finger to his lips so only I can see. "Not here," he whispers.

After the tour of the gardens I slipped away from the rest of the party, back to the grotto, and I whispered his name into the water in the River God's cave.

"What does that mean?" I stand up, looking from the letter to the curator. Hal might not want to tell her everything, but she must know what *this* is.

"The grotto? It's part of the landscaping – they were very fashionable when the gardens were laid out in the eighteenth century. It's down by the lake…"

Me, scrolling through other people's photos, looking for the space where I wasn't, water droplets falling like confetti…

She's still talking. "…statue of a nymph and of an unnamed river god – probably inspired by Virgil's—"

"Can we see it?" It's too fast, too high, too desperate. Too manic. "I mean, is it open to the public?"

"Of course." She frowns at me, and a crease appears between her eyes. "The gardens are all open to the public."

"Like in this letter – when she says about touring the gardens?"

"The Russell-Olivers – the family who owned the house – believed in opening the gardens to visitors even while the estate was privately owned. There were regular guided tours for groups. It might seem strange to us, but they saw it as part of their…let's call it civic duty, being part of the upper class. One of the conditions of the sale, when it was agreed, was that the gardens would always remain open. Maybe if this…Iris?…you're looking for knew someone, or had a relative working here, she visited and took a tour."

"Oh! Right."

My feet are itching to leave – even with this letter of Iris's, this piece of her, under my hands. Somehow, it doesn't seem to matter as much as the grotto does; it doesn't seem as big a part of the puzzle. I want to be where she was. I want to listen to the echo of her calling his name into the water. She doesn't even mention his name…but who else could it be?

Albie.

Albie and Iris.

Even the quickest glance across at Hal tells me he feels the same. He wants to be out of the house, looking for *them*. He thanks the curator and shakes her hand, and we both step out into the hallway.

"Told you I found something," he says.

"Why didn't you want…" I check over my shoulder, but the little door has already closed. We head back outside, shrugging off the gloom. "Why didn't you want me to say anything about Albie?"

"Because there's nothing about him in the letter – and I didn't tell her that's what we were looking for. I told her I was researching..." He frowns. "Actually, I don't remember exactly what I told her. I nicked it from the title of a book I saw when my mate at UCL snuck me into the history library there." His face falls even further.

"They snuck you into the library? Why?" Of all the places I could imagine Hal Waverley wanting to be smuggled into, a university library probably wouldn't have been top of the list.

"Oh, long story." He clears his throat and mutters something under his breath. It sounds a lot like "Another life."

My ribs tighten around my heart, squeezing it hard.

He shakes the thought away and brightens again. "Anyway, I didn't want to tell her exactly what we were looking for so I made something up. It seemed to work."

"Okay, but *why*?" Somewhere nearby, there's a sound that could be a plane going over...or could be thunder. The sky that was mostly blue when we arrived is definitely looking a lot less blue now. It is, in fact, the colour of lead.

"Because...I don't know. I thought if she knew, she'd..."

"Try and take over?"

He scrunches up his nose, nodding. "Yeah. That. Does it sound stupid?"

Following him down the steps to the enormous driveway, I open my mouth to tell him that I know exactly how he feels – that I feel the same. That I want to keep this story close, keep it secret.

Keep it *our* secret.

But I can't. And I don't. Instead, I change the subject.

"Anything else interesting in there?"

"How about this?" He spins on his heel, walking backwards down the last couple of steps. "Hopwood wasn't always called Hopwood Home – or even Hopwood House. And it definitely wasn't called that in 1913. There was an old newspaper article in the archive – about the *renaming* of the old Holmwood house after the nearest village."

"Which would be Hopwood! So it *did* change from the family name to the village. It really is the right place – the one you've been looking for!"

"Yep. And then…"

"History happened, and everybody forgot." It takes all my willpower not to jump down the last step. So much energy is buzzing around under my skin that if I don't let it out, I'll split open.

"History happened. I like that," Hal says thoughtfully. A gust of wind catches his hair and ruffles it – and for a second, I can't stop myself from wondering what it feels like.

His hair.

Okay.

A path leads off the side of the drive, dividing into two,

marked with a signpost cut out of a huge lump of tree trunk. One arm of the post points down a long, gentle slope while the other follows the line of a gravelled track, twisting off through the trees. The first one is marked *Grotto*. The second, *Lake*.

In front of them, Hal stops and folds his arms. "Which way do you want to go? They probably join up somewhere, so it doesn't *really* matter, but…"

Lake or grotto.

Which way do I want to go?

Backwards…or forwards?

What's waiting for me on either path – and will I like it? Will it help?

Lake or grotto?

"Grotto. Let's go to the grotto."

"Cool." He takes a step forward – then stops, puzzled. "I forgot – did you say there was something you wanted to do here?" He nods towards the signpost. "We can go down to the lake if you want?"

"Oh. Umm…" The water glistens emptily through the trees at me. "You know what? It doesn't matter."

Another rumble overhead makes us both look up.

"Grotto it is then." And he magics his sunglasses out of his bag then stuffs his hands into his pockets, setting off down the slope, his hair like a beacon.

And I let him lead me away from the house and the lake, and on to the grotto.

* * *

The way down to the grotto winds through trees and big overgrown plants that flump across the path...and then narrows to a tunnel with steep sides and an arching brick roof.

It. Is. Dark.

"This isn't exactly how I pictured it," Hal mutters somewhere ahead of me in the gloom. There's a scuffing sound as he trips on the uneven floor. I'm not even going to risk getting my phone out for light – if I drop it, it'll definitely smash.

I reach a hand out to steady myself against the walls. My fingers sink into cold, damp moss. At least, I hope it's moss. "I was definitely expecting something...prettier."

"Hang on – it's lighter ahead."

And it is. We stumble out of the dark and into a brighter cave, the floor made of big pebbles sunk into the ground in swirling designs, the walls and ceiling lined with hundreds – no, thousands – of shells. I can't tell where the light is coming from, but it's soft and white and beautiful. Not just *pretty*, but flat-out *beautiful*.

"That's more like it."

Hal is crouched down in the corner, so busy peering at the collection of little ferns growing around a poem engraved on the floor that he hasn't even noticed the rest of it.

"Hal. Hal, look."

Nothing.

Slowly, I reach out a hand and touch his shoulder. His head snaps round like a whip. And then he sees.

At the far end of the grotto is a figure emerging from a pool of water, life-sized and carved from stone so white that it glows.

"The River God." My voice comes out as a hoarse whisper. I don't mean it to, but apparently that's how the grotto works.

"This is where she came."

"To whisper his name into the water."

We both walk to the edge of the statue's pool and stare down into the water, as though Albie's name is still in there. Side by side, we stand and we listen – and as we do, the water starts to shine. Brighter and brighter, like it's silver – and then brighter again, until it isn't water at all but liquid light, throwing shimmering patterns across the roof, the walls, *us*. Like it's a sign.

"There must be a light well in the roof somewhere," Hal says, tilting his head back to look for it.

Of course there must be. It's part of the design – a magic trick, an illusion meant to have exactly this effect… But a chill still runs down my spine as the light flickers around us. "Kind of a coincidence, though, isn't it? The sun coming out right now?"

"I don't believe in…oh." He turns around, so close to me that I could count every freckle on his face, count the pale eyelashes lowered over his eyes – and when his eyes meet mine the chill turns warm, sliding into every limb, spreading across every centimetre of my skin.

"I know."

Outside the grotto, there's a low rolling rumble – and there's no way to pretend that isn't thunder.

"And you're going to tell me that's a sign too, are you?" Hal's words echo as we follow the cobbled path back into the dark.

We make it outdoors again, and he follows my gaze up to the sky…right as the first fat raindrop hits my face.

"Yes. It's definitely a sign. A sign we should go."

Another drop. Another. Another and another and the air is suddenly heavy with the thick scent of wet earth and the hissing sound of a million raindrops all coming right for us.

We outrun the rain as far as the slope down from the drive, and then the heavens split completely open. I open my mouth to say that we're not going to make it before we're soaked through, but I don't get that far because quickly, carefully, perfectly *naturally*, his hand closes around mine. He starts running for the car, pulling me into him with one arm, the other holding his bag above our heads like the world's worst umbrella… And all the while the biggest raindrops I've ever seen are hammering down around us and drumming on the ground, on the roof of the car, splashing into the fountain and sending up a dozen tiny echoes of themselves. When we make it to the car and yank the doors open and throw ourselves in, I don't know if I'm more out of breath from the running or the laughing. Or both.

We look at each other and he's grinning, even as he's wiping the rain from his face.

"Let's get out of here," I say, pushing my damp hair out of my eyes.

"You didn't like the house?" He rubs the heels of his hands up and down his face, trying to dry it off. All it does is make his eyebrows stick out.

I don't answer. How can I tell him about the things that bother me about Fallowmill's past without telling him about mine? Instead, I wipe a drip of water off the end of my nose and try to make it look casual.

There's a long silence, and then quietly he says: "I'm glad you came, anyway. I know it sounds kind of selfish…"

I lean back in my seat, studying him. The tips of his ears are turning pink again as he leans over the steering wheel. "You wanted the company. I get it."

It feels like this is going…somewhere. Somewhere I don't quite know how to handle.

Does my mood match the moment?

My hands pick this exact point to start shaking. A lot. I tuck them both under my knees, pressed into the seat.

"It's not just that. I mean, it is that, but…"

But what?

If my heart beats any louder, I'm not going to hear anything he says. I press my lips together.

"It sounded like you really wanted to come, like it was important, and…" He clears his throat, coughs again and scratches at the back of his neck. And then we speak at the same time:

"I was so happy you did, because I didn't really want to do this without you."

"Fallowmill doesn't matter – there was a…a *thing*, but really I think I just wanted to come and do this with you."

Our voices fill the little car with something so much bigger than words. And no sooner have I said it than I'm panicking: what did I just do?

The silence is elastic, stretching tighter and tighter until it snaps.

"You did?" he asks.

I nod.

"*Flora*." The way he says it fills my heart and it rises, like a balloon, like a banner, until it soars up and up and above me and away.

Eleven

The cloudburst is short, and as we drive out of the gates of Fallowmill House, the sky has already started to lighten. Up ahead, there's even the slightest suggestion of a rainbow. Maybe. Half a rainbow, anyway.

Half a rainbow is all I need.

Hal keeps his hands on the wheel, his eyes on the road, but the car feels different. As though something important just happened.

It did. It was.

Sitting in an old car in a downpour, and the way he said my name.

It is.

As he turns back onto the single-lane road, a pheasant takes off out of the hedge, swooping in front of us with a *clatter-clatter-clatter* of wings – and Hal swears under his breath.

I try not to laugh. "They do that a lot. Don't take it personally."

"How do those things even live? They're so stupid. A car comes along and they just...*throw* themselves at it. And anyway, what is *with* these roads?" This, as the whole car bumps sideways into a massive pothole with a splash – and now I can't not laugh. He's getting so cross. "What?" He's still not taking his eyes off the road, but this time I think it's because he's too scared to.

"Nothing."

"You could do better, could you?"

"Oh, I'm not criticizing. I don't actually drive, so."

There's a pause, and he risks a glance away from the windscreen at me.

"You don't drive? How does anyone manage without a car out here?"

"We have these newfangled things called 'buses'. I mean, they only started running a couple of years ago, and it was really confusing at the start. The old people didn't know what to do with them – they'd run in from the street saying there was a monster swallowing people..."

Another pause. Then: "You're mocking me, aren't you?"

"Maybe. Only a bit, though."

"Yeah, all right. I probably deserve it." He laughs back, and it's like I'm hearing the sound his soul makes. It's a lock springing open, a key turning, a door opening. "You said you don't drive – don't or...?"

The question hangs. It's not the first time I've been asked it. Round here, most people have their test booked the day they turn seventeen. It was always a thing at school, another coming-of-age ritual. I always figured it was one I'd go through too, just like everybody else – but that was before the therapy session when Sanjay pointed out that me being in charge of a ton of fast-moving metal while manic might not be the *best* idea. Same went for me being in charge of a ton of fast-moving metal while depressed. So that ruled out the L-plates for me. Just add it to the list.

Hal's gaze flicks over to me and then back again, and all I can hear is the sound of my blood rushing through my head, even over the sound of the engine…and then I'm saved from having to reply because Hal drives us straight into a river.

I mean, it's not a river. Not *technically*. Technically, it's just an old bit of road crossed by a stream – a ford. Which would not normally be a problem, because it's summer and we're in a car and it's all fine.

Except it really did rain a lot over the weekend. And that downpour at Fallowmill might have been quick, but it definitely hasn't helped.

Hal swears and grabs for the gearstick between us, his hand brushing against my knee as he lunges – he snaps it away like I've burned him. "Sorry. Sorry." He splutters out the words, but I can't even tell him it's fine, not to worry, because all of me is quite unexpectedly focused on the tiny spot where his hand grazed me.

There's a horrible mashing sound from the engine, followed by a clonk and a loud scraping as the car jolts backwards and then down at an angle. Whatever he was trying to do, he seems to have found the deepest part of the ford in the form of another pothole.

Hal yanks his sunglasses off his nose, throwing them onto the dashboard and staring at the water streaming past us. "This isn't good."

"It's fine. Just, you know, drive through it."

The engine, clearly hearing me, makes a strangled grating sound, then huffs…then stops.

Hal huffs too.

"Okay. So maybe don't drive through it."

"Nobody could drive through this."

"Charlie never has any trouble with the Land Rover." Beside me, I see Hal open his mouth to reply, then change his mind and close it again. "Hal…"

"*What?*"

"Should my feet be getting wet right now?"

We both look down into my footwell, where the slow drip that started as soon as we drove into the ford has become a steady trickle – and is in serious danger of becoming a gush.

"No, Flora. Your feet should *not* be getting wet."

"Right. Okay. Thought that might be the case." A large

puddle has formed in front of my seat…and it's not getting any smaller.

"Oh," he says. I lean over to peer down at his feet and see water starting to creep in around the pedals too. "This isn't good." He tries the ignition, and there's a crunch and then a click…and then nothing.

He looks at me.

I look at him.

"Any thoughts?" His hands are still resting on the steering wheel – like that's going to help.

"Mostly wondering whether your car does this a lot?"

"It doesn't usually have to drive through rivers." His voice is higher by the end of the sentence. A bit like the water.

"It's not a river – it's a *ford*."

"Ford, river…it's still *wet*, isn't it?"

He sounds so baffled by it that even though I try – I try so hard – I don't quite manage to stop the laugh from bubbling up.

When he looks wounded, I clamp my hands over my mouth. "Sorry," I mumble – but that just makes it worse, and now I really can't stop. His lovely(ish) old car is flooding, and he's just sitting there, and I'm laughing.

And then his frown breaks, and he's laughing too, because how can he not? How can *we* not?

"What the hell do we do now?"

I peer out of my window at the water. "I think we start

by getting above the high water line. You coming?"

"You're not…" He watches me undo my seat belt and open the door – and just like I couldn't hold back my laugh, he can't stop the anguished yelp as more water washes into the car over the door sill.

"Oops. I *may* have miscalculated a little."

I have miscalculated quite a lot, in fact. I thought I was opening the door over a couple of centimetres of water and I could just kind of hop over it to the edge of the ford with no harm done. But not only is there a lot more water out there than I thought, the front wheel of the passenger side of the car is sitting in a pothole – a *deep* one – which means that "a couple of centimetres of water" is actually a massive understatement. Cold water gushes into the footwell over the sill – and the edge of the ford is at least two metres away in any direction.

"Change of plan!" I haul myself up out of the door, moving my feet from the floor to the seat, and then onto the headrest, and then – carefully, because of course I would be wearing a dress for this, wouldn't I? – up again and out onto the roof of the car. The metal clunks under my weight, but nothing disastrous happens – and a minute later, Hal's bag, then his face, then his shoulders appear on the other side of the car and he pulls himself up to join me. I shuffle sideways to make space for him to sit, both of us resting our feet on the bonnet.

"You flooded my car," he says.

"I think you'll find that actually *you* flooded your car by driving into a river."

"I thought you said this was a ford."

"No." I look at the water surrounding us for emphasis. "I think this really does qualify as an actual river."

The current rushes past and around us. Through us, in the case of the car.

"I really didn't think the water was that deep when I opened the door. Sorry."

He snorts and waves my apology away, turning his face to where I can't see. He doesn't actually seem angry. I would be, if I were him.

And then I see his shoulders are shaking.

Oh god. I broke his car and I think I made him cry.

He wipes the back of a hand across his cheek, and I can see the tears. I did. I made him cry. I mean, not that it's really *my* fault, but I do feel kind of responsible…

And then he drops his hands and turns back to me and he *is* crying…because he's laughing so very, very hard. Tears are streaming down his cheeks and his eyes are pink; he's trying to say something, but nothing's coming out of his mouth because he just can't get the words out past the laughter.

Instead, he holds out both his arms in a helpless *look at this* gesture, and his laughter is a river that sweeps us both away.

* * *

It doesn't take long for the sun and the breeze up here to clear the worst of the cloud and dry our rain-damp clothes – and if it wasn't for the fact we have become our own island, it might be hard to believe just how much it poured earlier.

"What do we do now, then?" Hal shades his eyes with his hand, looking up and down the road.

"We can wait for a farmer to come along with his tractor and yell at us for being in the way, and maybe tow us out, or I can phone Charlie." I pull out my phone. The reception's pretty bad, but at least I have some.

"How come you've got reception?" He peers over my shoulder at my screen as though he can't quite believe it.

"Country phone, obviously. Didn't you pick one up at the border?"

"Yeah, all right. I get it." He shakes his head. "I could probably get hold of my breakdown service…"

"What, and sit here for four hours waiting?" (Maybe that's not such a bad thought…) "Charlie's closer."

"Your brother won't mind?"

"Probably. But he's kind of used to me calling him to rescue me."

Hal looks thoughtful. "You don't seem like the kind of person who needs rescuing," he says quietly.

I'm not sure how to answer that. I'm not even sure I'm meant to have heard it. So I make it obvious that I'm concentrating very, very hard on dialling my brother's number (rather than just hitting the favourites button like I normally do).

Charlie answers after a couple of rings. "How's Fallowmill?"

"Oh, fine. Fine, fine. Listen – I need a favour."

"Mmm?"

"Are you out in the Land Rover?"

"Why?"

"We…" I look at Hal. "…slightly broke down."

"You broke down?"

"Yes. In a ford."

"How—?"

I cut him off. "And we really need a lift. And maybe a tow?" Beside me, Hal nods. "Definitely a tow."

"Out of a ford?"

"Please?"

Charlie sighs. "Which one are you in?"

"Umm…the one on the edge of the King farm."

He does not take this particularly well. He puts on his Older Brother Voice. "Flora."

"Yes, yes, I know."

"*Do* you?"

The car roof wobbles ominously as Hal tries to stand up for a better view. There's a loud creaking noise – the sort metal makes when it's really quite unhappy – and he sits down again quickly, wrapping his arms around his shins and pulling his knees up to his chin.

I make an executive decision to ignore everything Older Brother Voice implies. "You told me I'd enjoy this project – and you know what? I am. I really, really am." Before he gets the chance to say anything else, I carry on, because I don't want to have this conversation while I'm sitting on a car roof, and I definitely don't want to have this conversation in front of Hal. "So, you know, you were right and I was wrong and the fact I'm actually saying that means that you have to be supportive now because I'm being self-aware and everything and that's part of the deal. And also, you get to be smug."

There is a very, very deep sigh on the other end of the line. And a bit of swearing.

"In the spirit of *supporting* you, exactly where are you in relation to the ford?"

I peer down at the water bubbling around the wheels of the car.

"Like I said, very, very *in* the ford." The sound on the other end of the line might be laughter, or it might be swearing. It's hard to tell. "Sorry," I add, hoping that's enough.

It must be, because finally my brother says, "All right. I'm on my way. I've got to drop some plants off, and then I'm coming. Five minutes, ten max. Just…stay put."

"Yeah, I don't think we can do anything else."

I put my phone away. "Charlie's coming. He's not very sympathetic, but he's coming."

Hal nods. "You like your brother, don't you?"

I picture Charlie, scowling and swearing in the driver's seat of the Land Rover. "I do, actually. He's a nice person. Not every big brother would have said it was okay for his annoying little sister to move in with him when their mum moved away. Lucky for me he did, really. Lucky for her too."

Hal's look is a question – but one he can obviously tell I won't answer. So he asks a different one. "You couldn't live with your dad?"

"No. He's never been a part of us. Not really. He got married again after he and Mum broke up – apparently I've got a couple of half-brothers and -sisters I've never met. One of them's only just younger than me."

"Oh."

"The way I see it, some people are just very good at compartmentalizing their lives. They finish one thing, they're done with it. They close the door or shut the lid and they move on. My father's one of those people."

Hal doesn't say anything but he nods. Something I've said must make sense.

He's given so little about himself away, beyond what's obvious. The clothes, the car...the hair. The fact he's got money. But other than that, all I know is that he cares about his grandfather. That and he's a city boy. Nothing *real* about his family, nothing about who he *is*. Only pieces of clues, tiny little fragments – like something seen through a keyhole.

Unless this feeling I have about him counts…

This is my chance, isn't it? I mean, we're not going anywhere for a while. So…

"You don't have any brothers or sisters?"

He shakes his head as though he only half-heard me. "Just me," he says – and then in a voice not quite his own, "carrying on the family name, the family business. Whether I want to or not."

"What?" He said something like that before – I thought he was talking about Albie, but maybe not.

"Sorry?" His attention snaps back to me, to here and now. I'm not sure he actually realizes he said something out loud.

I try to see a little more, just a little. "You were saying – it's just you?"

But he's already closed that door. "Mmm. Sorry you didn't get to see much of the gardens and stuff. Or look at all the archive," he says, shuffling a little in his spot on the roof. "I feel bad you wasted your day."

"It's not wasted. It's the *opposite* of wasted."

His hand is splayed on the metal between us, the long fingers outstretched. Slowly, carefully, I reach out and place my own lightly on top of his, matching them, fighting the immediate panic, the urge to snatch them away again.

Should I have done that?

Why did I do it?

He doesn't move his hand. He doesn't move at all.

165

Is this good?

I guess seeing as he hasn't leaped from the roof of the car screaming, that's a yes...?

Try not to go into my head. That's what Charlie said, isn't it? Don't go into my head. Perhaps if I say something...?

"So what do we do now?" *Way to go, Flora. That's the spirit. Not sounding like an idiot at all.* "About the papers, I mean."

Hal thinks about this. "I guess we go back to Hopwood and keep looking. We know Iris and Albie were together – and they weren't meant to be – but there must be more."

"I can ask Barney if we can go check the attics? There's loads of boxes up there."

"That isn't all of them? The stuff in the library?"

"No – he'll have just had the obvious ones brought down for you. There's probably loads more up there. My supervisor, Mrs Tilney, mentioned it when I started at the hotel. Health and safety, or whatever."

"You think he'll let us check them?"

"I don't see why not. If you find something, it's probably good for the hotel. Plus you're happy and he's all about keeping guests happy, so there's that too."

There is the slightest hesitation before he nods...

And then his fingers shift and twist, turning over to close around mine.

He. Is. Holding. On. To. My. Hand.

On *purpose*.

Act normal, Flora. NORMAL.

Do. Not. Freak. Out.

And there we are, sitting on the roof of a car in the middle of a stream and holding hands, when from just around the corner there's the growl of an old Land Rover being driven by someone in a very bad mood.

Midway through edging the Land Rover round the little squashed-frog car, Charlie pauses to peer through his window and raise an eyebrow at me, perched on the roof. "Really?"

"It's not my fault, is it?"

He mutters something under his breath and pulls the Land Rover around in front of us.

I get up as cautiously as anyone standing on the roof of a car would. "Come on."

Hal looks up, watching as I hop down onto the bonnet and lean out to open the back of the Land Rover. Charlie creeps the truck forward so there's space for the door to swing all the way open – but the problem is that this leaves quite a big gap (and more cold water than I'd like to meet today) to get over from one to the other. I take a good, long look at the distance…and jump, my breath knocked from my lungs as I hit the side of the bench seat in the back. Dusting myself off, I look back to see Hal balanced on the very front of his car, his bag slung across his body.

"Come on, it's not too bad – just jump!"

Hal looks over at me. My definition of *not too bad* is obviously a world apart from his…but then I'm not the one whose car has just been given its own interior water feature. His face set with concentration, Hal shifts his weight back and forth a couple of times – and jumps.

I don't know if his foot slips or his shoes don't grip enough or if he's just not had much practice when it comes to jumping into the back of Land Rovers, but even before he leaves the bonnet of the car, I know he's not going to make it.

He might have said I don't look like I need rescuing – but I'm pretty sure one of us does right now…

My hand closes around his wrist in mid-air, and it's the easiest thing to pull him into the safety of the back of the truck, his shoulder crashing into me and his hair in my face and the two of us piled on the cold metal and laughing. Again.

"You two all right back there?" Charlie has one arm draped around the back of the front seats, looking at us as we pick ourselves up. I nod, sliding onto the bench behind me. "What do you want to do about your car? Want a tow?"

Hal smoothes his hair back from his face, peering out at his sad, soggy car sitting in the middle of the ford. "You know, I think it's probably better if I get the breakdown service to pick it up. I'm guessing it's going to need more than just a tow before it'll go again. Will it be a problem if I leave it there for a bit?"

Charlie shakes his head. "It's pretty quiet round here."

"I'll call them when I get back to the hotel."

"Sure?"

Hal nods.

"Okay then. Flora? Door." Charlie straightens up and revs the engine as I lean out of the back to slam the door shut – and Hal's little car is lost behind the bend of the lane.

It's only once the door is closed that we get to collectively appreciate the Land Rover's smell.

I lean over to the driver's seat. "Is that...*sheep* I can smell?"

"Yes. Sorry. Blame Felix."

Our car is forever being used to cart something weird across the estate. It could be worse – in the spring, Charlie was using it to haul horse manure from the stables on the other side of the valley to the gardens and one of the sacks split. Even though we spent ages hosing it out afterwards, the smell stuck around for weeks...so on balance, I'll take the sheep. Hal wrinkles his nose as he perches on the narrow bench, but he's too polite to comment.

The ride back is too rough and too noisy (especially the way Charlie drives) to talk, or even to try – and the overwhelming sheepy smell feels like another passenger sitting in the back with us. But it's only when we pass the Hopwood-in-the-Hollows sign that I realize I don't really care. Not about the smell or about the state of the truck, or any of it.

I could care. I could worry that this guy, this smart and smooth and city-shiny boy, won't understand; I could worry that this life of mine that he's stumbled into will look weird and that he'll judge me by it... But I don't. It's not the outside that bothers me. It's never the outside.

I worry that he'll judge me by my invisible broken places if he sees them, by the cracks and the fissures that skitter across the surface of my mind, by the scars that have hardened over them. Maybe it doesn't even matter that the bolts on the doors at Fallowmill were taken down. Someone still lined them up, still screwed them in place. Still *used* them. In my head, at least, they'll always be there.

Charlie swings the Land Rover around the last curve of the hotel drive, scrunching across the gravel, and pulls up outside the front door. The engine dies with a diesel-y cough and Hal shoves the back open and jumps down.

"Thanks for the lift. I owe you." He smiles awkwardly at Charlie, who laughs, bad mood forgotten. They never last long.

"No problem – and you don't owe me anything," he says, leaning out of the window to watch me hop down onto the drive. "*She* does."

I pull a face at him and he grins, pulling his head back inside.

And Hal turns to me, ruffling his hands back through

his hair then stuffing them into his pockets. He doesn't know what to do with them.

Mine have balled themselves into fists and somehow found their way into the pockets of my dress. I didn't even tell them to.

"So," he says, his pale eyes meeting mine. I wonder what he sees looking back out at him? "That was all...weird."

"It was."

"But...nice?" He makes it a question, not a statement.

"Yes. Nice. No, wait. *Better* than nice."

Hands in pockets, hair in eyes. We are the echo of each other, standing just that little bit too close together for this to all be in my head surely, and that little bit too far apart for it to be more than it already is. He sees it too, and he starts to laugh. Which makes me laugh again, and just like before it's enough to block out the rest of the world, the rest of my head.

It's enough.

And in this moment, *I'm* enough. Just as I am.

Charlie drops a hand out of his window and bangs on the side of his door, calling to me.

"Oi! Come on, Flora. Let's get a move on!"

I shoot him a death-glare which he ignores. Lift or not, I may have to re-evaluate my feelings about my brother.

Hal lowers his gaze, still smiling, and then he turns and walks away from me towards the hotel. As he reaches the porch, he stops and looks back over his shoulder. At me.

Twelve

"You need to go up to the attics as well?" Barney doesn't do as good a job of hiding his surprise as he thinks.

"Yes. Sorry."

"You know it's a disaster up there, don't you? That's why we keep it locked…"

"I know. But Hal's sure there'll be more." I've been over this conversation in my head at least twenty times since getting back from Fallowmill yesterday. I have every angle covered.

"'Hal' now, is it?" Barney's eyebrow arches. "You're getting along all right, then? I hope it's not too difficult."

Every angle except that one.

Umm.

"The project, or getting along with him?"

"All of it." His chair creaks as he shifts his weight behind the desk. "I know you weren't exactly keen on this, so thank you."

"Oh. No. I mean, yes. He's…it's interesting." I swallow the words that almost made it out of my mouth.

Don't start telling the boss how Hal held your hand. He doesn't need to know. You don't need him to know.

Nobody needs to know. Just in case it was all a mistake.

It wasn't a mistake – was it?

"And you're sure you'll be comfortable working up there with him? You're a long way from the rest of the staff, and I don't want to put you in a difficult position." Barney blinks across the desk at me.

Is he kidding?

He blinks again.

He's not kidding.

"It'll be fine. I'll be fine. Does that mean it's okay?"

"Well, if it's okay with you…" He rummages in his desk and pulls out a key ring with a couple of big, old-fashioned keys on it. "Any problems – *any* problems – you know where I am." He holds the keys out across the desk – but when I close my fingers around them, he doesn't let go. "I mean it," he says, fixing me with the kind of look that I thought only Charlie could do.

"I know."

He lets go of the keys. "How's the research going so far then? Found something good?"

"I think so. It's…hard to say. These will help – thanks." The keys jangle when I wave them at him.

"You don't have to thank me. The Waverleys are big

173

names in the trade and if we can help them, it's good business. And speaking of business..." He twists in his chair and slides an envelope out of a different drawer. "You've not forgotten this, have you?"

My heart sinks as he pushes the envelope, with my name written on the front, across the desk to me. I had forgotten. On purpose.

"'All the staff' doesn't include me, though, does it?"

"Yes, Flora. It does. 'All the staff' does indeed include you. Word's come down from on high –" which is how Barney always refers to the Hopwood's owners – "that this anniversary party is going to be a big deal. They've got photographers coming, people from the press... They've even had me bring in caterers and waiting staff, so there's no excuse for any of you to skip it."

"It's an anniversary? What anniversary?"

"Ten years since they bought the hotel – which, in hospitality, is as good as a hundred years – and they want to make a splash."

Barney picks up the envelope again and waggles it at me until I take it.

"You could have just put it in my pigeonhole in the locker room," I mutter, dropping it into my lap.

"Where you could pretend you didn't see it? I don't think so." The corners of his mouth twitch.

"Okay, okay." I gather up the envelope and the keys and haul myself out of my chair.

"Good luck in the attics – let me know if there's anything we can use for marketing, won't you?"

Access to the attics isn't easy; they aren't somewhere a guest could just stumble into. From the second floor, tucked away at the very back of the house and behind a plain white door that looks exactly the same as the service cupboards, a small narrow staircase heads up to the top floor of the Hopwood.

"It must have been the stairs up to the original servants' quarters," Hal says, running a hand along the bare wooden banister. The stairs are plain wood too – not even varnished – and they couldn't feel more different from the sweeping staircase down into the lobby, with its glossy carved banisters and soft carpet. This feels like another world.

Another door at the top of the stairs opens onto a bright, narrow corridor with a window at one end. At the other is a closed door. Hal walks over to it, his hand hesitating over the handle before trying it.

"If you're going to find the rest of Albie's story," I say, reaching around him and slotting an old-fashioned brass key into the lock, "*this* is where it'll be."

There's a click as the lock springs open, and I give the door a push.

The room beyond smells of still air and the warm wood of the roof beams and floorboards. Unless the layer of pale

grey dust counts, there's no carpet, and the walls are bare
– just ancient plaster with the odd lump of horsehair mixed
in, smoothed over narrow strips of wood. Slim shards of
sunlight slip through the wooden shutters on the dormer
windows, puncturing the gloom.

As Hal steps through the door, his feet leaving prints in
the thick dust, there's the faintest suggestion of movement
in the air; a ghost of a breeze on my face. Maybe it's just my
imagination, but I have the strangest sensation the attic
has been holding its breath. Waiting.

For him. For now. For this.

Or maybe it's just that the window frames are old and
warped and draughty – a bit like the one in my bedroom. I
fold back the shutter on the first window and give the
grubby pane a shove – it swings open with an angry creak
and light floods into the room.

"Oh." The sound Hal makes is somewhere between a sigh
and a gasp, interesting enough to make me turn around…

Which is when I see the boxes.

"Oh."

They're stacked up in rows, all along the back wall where
the roof slates meet the stone. Some of them are cardboard
archive boxes like most of the ones in the library. Others
are big wooden tea chests bound with metal bands, some
with their lids half-off. There are metal archive boxes, what
looks like an old filing cabinet and, right at the far end,
a pile of wooden crates.

"That's...a lot of boxes," Hal whispers, staring at them.

"You wanted boxes. Maybe be careful what you wish for." I peer into the nearest of the tea chests. It looks like it's mostly full of straw to me, but it's hard to tell. I give the lid a nudge and it slips off the edge and clatters to the floor, sending up a cloud of dust. Hal coughs pointedly.

"Maybe we start by you not doing that again?" he says, waving the fallout away theatrically. "Some of us have allergies, remember?"

"I thought you were putting that on for the curator! What are you allergic to?" I ignore the urge to sneeze.

"Dust, mostly. And the sun."

"The *sun*? You can't be allergic to the sun."

"Really?" He pulls at a tuft of his hair. "See this? This is the mark of someone who counts the sun as their mortal enemy." He drops the end of his hair. It falls straight into his eyes. "When I was a kid, someone – I don't even remember who – told me that if you're a redhead you've got to watch yourself in the sun because it hates you. So the next day I went out and dyed my hair." He walks over to the next window and unlocks it, swinging the pane open and leaning on the sill to look out over the gardens.

"And how did that go for you?"

"Not well."

I can't help it. I shouldn't laugh, but something about the look on his face – the sheer *disappointment* that he couldn't disguise who he actually is, or change it – is both

177

adorable and very, very funny.

He looks even more wounded when I start laughing, which doesn't help.

"Sorry," I mutter eventually, doodling in the dust with the toe of my shoe. "But now we're here, what's your plan?"

He leans his weight back against the sill and stretches his legs out in front of him, studying the row of boxes. There is a very, very long silence.

"Do you even *have* a plan?"

The sound he makes is high and uncertain.

"You had a plan in the library."

"Yeah, but there wasn't quite so…much." He waves in the general direction of the crates, boxes, cabinets and other items hulking across the attic. "I guess we just pick a box to start with and work our way through from there." Striding from the window, he brushes the dust carefully off the top of the furthest metal box, flipping back the lid and peering inside.

From my spot at the far end of the row, I watch him lean over that box, then the ones either side of him, peering at the lids or labels on the sides like a kid checking the parcels under the tree on Christmas morning, looking for one with their name on it. I try to picture him, little him, eight years old and trying to dye the colour of his hair away.

A feeling I don't quite understand flickers around my heart, as though someone has lit a Catherine wheel inside me, slowly spinning and throwing out sparks. It's not that I don't recognize it – I do – I'm just used to feeling like it's in my *head*, not my heart. It's the same bright, fizzing whirl that comes with mania – the feeling of possibility. That I could *do* anything, that anything could *happen*.

"Hey, Flora!"

He's holding a bundle of old papers. Flakes flutter from the edges, drifting down to the floor like snow.

"Careful, they're breaking apart!" Crouching down beside him, I put my hand beneath the stack to support them. "Should we even be doing this? Remember what that curator was like with her whole, 'You don't touch them, I do' thing?"

"Well, she's not here, is she?" He nudges me, his voice conspiratorial. "Look at this lot. They're names. Names, ages and dates of birth. They're children."

"Why is there a list of children in the attic?"

"They're the bombed babies."

I stare at him. "What the hell is a bombed baby?"

"The curator told me about it at Fallowmill. A couple of the big houses around here were used to house kids who'd been bombed out of their homes in the Second World War." His eyes slide away from the papers and along the row of boxes. "Which would mean these are from the 1940s."

"We want earlier." I lean back. "These boxes are all the same – the metal ones. Maybe we should try a different type?"

179

"That makes sense. The boxes which match were probably all packed up together. Different box, different time. Which ones do we try next then?"

I scramble to my feet, and he does the same – carefully lowering the list of bombed babies back into the box he took it from and sliding the lid back on. I make a mental note to tell Barney what we've found, and move up the row to the wooden tea chests.

"These ones. I think we try these ones next."

"Flora…"

"Mmm?" I half-glance up from the pile of old receipts I've found. The Holmwoods, whoever they were, seemed to really, really like beef broth. At least, I hope they did, because they definitely got through a *lot* of it.

"No, really. Look. Look, it's here. I think…"

Hal's voice skips up an octave – and his hand slides into mine.

"What?"

I don't dare to look down at our hands. I can't. If I look, he might realize and move.

Instead, I look at him, and he looks back, and the hand holding out a piece of writing paper to me trembles.

But all I want is to be with you. Whatever it takes, and whatever it costs.

The writing and the headed notepaper is familiar now, so familiar that I can almost hear Albie in my head as I read. Another of his letters to Iris, hidden away, keeping their secret safe through the years. The light in the attic shifts as a cloud drifts across the sun outside. "Is this what I think it is?"

"Read a bit further down. Near the bottom." Hal tries to point out a line near the end of the page, but his finger is jumping up and down so much that he gives up, folding it away into his palm. "Sorry. It's just…"

"I know. It's a lot." I skim down to the line he was trying to show me and clear my throat. "'All my life, I've been told that I had a role to play, that there was a space in the world I should fill; that I would know it when the time came. Now I do, and that place is beside you, as your husband, if you would do me the honour of having me?'"

"A lot," murmurs Hal. His voice shakes as much as his hand did. "The only thing they could do was elope – there's the ruin and deception Jane was talking about in her letter, right there. If anyone caught them, she'd be finished. No job, no reference – and no Albie."

Does he know how soft his voice has become? How it slides through the attic, carried on the warm dusty air? Maybe, like me, he can feel the change in the atmosphere, in the letters. Hope and fear now sit hand in hand behind Iris and Albie. They have so much at stake. So much to lose.

And we know how the story ends.

* * *

Time slips by in silence, only the shifting shadows on the floor and the moving piles of pages to mark it. The attic air has warmed around us, and filled with something close to static. It makes my skin hum and my hands shake…and I think it's coming from Hal.

Possibility.

Every time he comes near me, sparks flicker up my arms and into my chest. Watching him pore over these letters, half-frowning or moving his lips in an echo of the words on the pages…it makes my heart hurt. But not because I'm sad. The opposite. Something is changing. Something in me is waking up. Something that wants…I don't know. But it's been a long time since I wanted anything, except maybe to be left alone – and now I don't think I want that so much. Or at least I think maybe I do want to be left alone, but alone *with him*.

What would Iris and Albie make of this, of us? Would they mind? Would *I* mind someone reading my letters – my thoughts and hopes and dreams and fears – in a hundred years' time? I don't know. All I know is that it's almost starting to feel like we're *meant* to find them. Sole heir to a family fortune and a housemaid? If it wasn't such a perfect coincidence it would almost be silly. I picture them passing in the hallway of Hopwood, her eyes lowered in case anyone could see them…and then her gaze coming up to meet his. His hand reaching for hers, the slightest, lightest touch and then gone.

"So, she must have agreed to marry him, right? That's what the letter from Jane was about – Iris told her sister, who wrote back and warned her it was a bad idea. What then?" I tip my head back and rub my neck. I've been leaning forward over all these letters, bills and receipts, these pieces of other lives, for so long that it aches when I straighten up.

"They couldn't have just gone. They would have needed a *plan*. Money, somewhere to go. Somewhere they'd be safe, where they could start over without anyone knowing who they were."

Somewhere safe. Somewhere to start over.

Ironic, really – they were running away from the exact place I ran *to*.

"They must have really loved each other. To risk everything – to give everything *up* – just to be together."

"I guess so." Hal's hand rests on the nearest pile of papers, his fingertips almost within touching distance. If I stretched mine out, I could reach them. But I don't, and however much I want him to move his hand towards mine one more time, he doesn't either.

I look at all the papers in front of us. "Do you think it's weird, doing this? Reading their letters? They were here – right here – and now we're looking through the things they wrote, the things they said to each other…? It's like… bringing them back, you know?"

"I guess so. I hadn't really thought about it like that." He brushes a fleck of paper off his knee.

"I mean, it's kind of nice. It's almost like someone finally gets to know their secret. They don't have to hide it any more."

"I'm not sure they did hide it from absolutely everybody in the house, though. That's something else I found." He sifts through one of the piles, spreading out the pages like tarot cards, looking for someone else's future.

Meet tonight usual place GH will come to kitchen door.

"'GH'?"

"I think they had someone helping them. Someone they trusted. They must have done. Think about it – we know they were going to run away, and they must have been meeting up in secret while they were planning it. That can't have been easy, not back then. There's no way they'd have got away with it for long on their own."

"So you think they had someone taking messages for them?"

"Isn't that what *you'd* do?" Hal's eyes move from the sheet of paper to mine, holding them.

"I don't know. *I've* never had a secret relationship."

Hal opens his mouth and closes it a couple of times, like a goldfish. "Nah. Me neither. Or, you know, *any* relationship." His cheeks slowly work through several different shades of pink. "Umm." He clears his throat, scratches his left ear and then apparently becomes very, very, very interested in a splinter of wood sticking up from the floor.

"No. No, right. No."

Me neither.

But maybe…

The words I want just won't come out. They stick to my tongue, they wind around the insides of my ribs like barbed wire.

The attic is suddenly very hot. Very, very hot and filled with the sound of drums, which I think might actually be my heart.

I try to talk over it, just in case he can hear it. "So, is this what you want to do?"

A look of pure panic crosses his face. "Sorry, what?"

Oh.

OH.

"What you want to do. In the future. For a job?" This time, the words all come out in a rush. For once, I'm quite glad.

His face relaxes. "This? You mean research, right?"

"You seem to like it. To be…kind of at home in it." And he does. Not like he belongs in the past, exactly, more like he belongs *with* it. They're comfortable with each other.

I wonder how that feels, being comfortable with the past.

"I guess. Like I said, I spent a lot of time with my

grandfather when I was younger, and he didn't exactly know what to do with a kid. So he took me to museums. Something about the past stuck. I just…like it. I like spending time with it." He pats the nearest stack of papers.

"How come you're not doing it at university?"

It's a mistake – I know it as soon as I've said it, but I don't know *why*. Everything about Hal darkens and closes up again – as though the shell that had almost dropped away has snapped shut around him again. His eyes close, and when they open again there's someone else behind them.

"I wasn't given the choice." Even his voice is darker, heavier.

"To do history?"

"To go to university."

"Oh."

Who would get excited about being smuggled into a university history library? Someone who knew they would never get the chance to be there for real. It can't be the money – someone like Hal Waverley doesn't worry about money. So…why?

He reads the question in my face, and I wish, *I wish*, he hadn't. But he answers anyway.

"Family business, remember?"

Only me to carry on the family name.

"Hang on, you weren't allowed to go to university because of the hotel business?"

"Yep."

"And you're okay with that?"

"It didn't seem to matter either way. And the only person in my family who would have backed me up…"

"Is your grandfather."

"*Was* my grandfather. Once, anyway. Not so much now. I can't ask him to get into the middle of that. Stress isn't good for him." He turns his face away.

"Your dad really didn't give you a choice?"

He looks down at his knees, his hair falling over his face and hiding him from me. "A choice? No. He's not into those. Orders, but not choices. We, uh, don't get along. Which is unfortunate when you think about it, with him being my father *and* my boss. Head of the family, head of the company. He gets the final say on everything." Hal's voice tightens. "*Everything.*"

"What about your mum? Didn't she think it should be your decision?"

I edge closer, hoping to see something familiar behind the curtain of hair.

"She's not around much. She travels a lot – she's the 'company ambassador', which means she gets to be on the payroll for running off and spending as much time away from home as possible. Does a lot of charity events, you know? Drinks a lot of martinis, takes a lot of sedatives. You would too, if you were married to my father."

I leave the space blank, the air empty. His words need it, but I can *feel* there's more here, things under the surface, tucked away in the dark. Things Hal doesn't want to bring out into the light.

I know what it's like to have somebody poking around in your head, trying to know who you are from the inside, not from the outside. I won't force it.

"How about you? You didn't want to go to uni?"

"Ha!" Of course, I didn't mean to make that sound out loud.

Hal raises an eyebrow at me from under his fringe.

"Sorry." I shake my head. "It's complicated. Uni and I are...let's just say we're probably not a good match."

"But you're good at this. Researching."

"Maybe? Kind of. I don't know." I blow out a long, slow breath...and it takes half the dust off the nearest box with it. "I don't think uni would be much use for me, anyway. I always wanted to work in films."

"In films? Doing what?"

"Anything. Working on locations, maybe? I don't know."

I *do* know, because it's what I always used to say when people asked me, before. I wanted to work in films. Always. And I wanted to work in locations – finding them, researching them... I never told anyone, but that was what my prize-winning history project, the one that got me involved in all this, was about. I told myself that if it was good enough, someone would notice. They would see me and think *I* was good enough. I was *convinced*.

Maybe that should have been an early warning.

188

Not that any of it really mattered, because The Future always felt like it was a long way off…and then suddenly it felt like it was the kind of thing that only happened to other people.

"Films," says Hal, thoughtfully. "I wouldn't have guessed that."

"Really?" I fold my arms. "So what would you have said?"

"I don't know," he says – then adds so softly that I almost miss it, "not yet."

Not yet.

It's an invitation – a hand waiting for me to take it. A door held open.

Possibility.

The attic is alive with it.

The sun has moved around from the window. I've got no idea how long we've been up here – my phone is somewhere in my bag on the other side of the attic. All I know is that I don't want to leave right now. If I do, all this possibility might evaporate, slipping through my fingers.

"We should probably call it a day." Hal squints up at the window, then sighs and shuffles the two piles in front of him together, tucking them up against the box.

I don't want to go.

Judging by the speed (or lack of it) that he's moving with, I'm not sure he does either.

His hand reaching for mine.

"Flora…"

"Not yet."

As he tidies the pages of Albie and Iris's story together, I reluctantly pull the window shut and grab my bag…and when I sling it over my shoulder, something flutters down to the floor. Hal scoops it up, holding it out to me. "You dropped this."

"Thanks." I take it, and his fingers brush against mine. He's standing so close – enough to feel the heat of him, breathe in the scent of him, to see the movement of his lips as they part just a little. So close, and still not close enough. Everything in the room blurs, then snaps back into focus, sharper than ever before. "Umm." I force myself to look away and start to scrunch the paper into a ball, but Hal's eyes widen and suddenly he grins.

"Are you going to that?" He points at the page in my hand. I stop crumpling. It's a flier for one of the outdoor film screenings the hotel puts on through the summer.

"I hadn't actually thought about it. Are you?"

"Maybe we should. For, you know, research?"

I look more carefully.

"Oh!"

The flier for tonight's Hopwood Summer Screening is a picture of a horse and a soldier, standing together in front of a blazing summer sunset sky.

War Horse.

"For research," I say, smiling back.

Thirteen

If Mira, eating a hot dog and perched on the wall between the drive and the west lawn, is surprised to spot Hal walking with me towards the part of the gardens where the outdoor screen is set up, she hides it well. At least, she does until he walks past her, his eyes on the garden ahead. Then she gives me a huge grin and a double thumbs-up. One of her thumbs has mustard on it.

I flap a hand at her, signing for her to cut it out before he sees.

"You really think he's even going to notice *me* with you around?" she laughs.

A little way ahead, Hal stops – maybe realizing he's lost me, maybe feeling like someone is talking about him (because we are) – and turns, coming back to where we're standing. He sniffs hungrily at the smell of onions from the vintage hot-dog stand Barney's installed at the edge of the lawn for tonight.

"Hello!" Mira beams at him. Of course, he has literally no idea who she is. I step between them.

"Hal, this is my friend Mira. She's on the housekeeping staff too."

"Hi," he says, but it's me his eyes are watching. Maybe Mira was right. "Are you going to the screening too?"

"Mmm-hmm." She nods, licking the mustard off her fingers. "I was just waiting to see if Fl..." Mira gets halfway through my name, stops and grins even more widely. "... Philippe was coming. Hey, Peep!" she shouts over my shoulder at Philippe, who has just stepped out onto the drive, and jerks her head at the lawn. "You going tonight?"

"Can't," he calls back. "Got an appointment." He shrugs, still walking towards the gates.

I turn back to Mira. "You can sit with us if you want? We thought we'd go for research." Only a tiny, tiny part of me hopes she'll say no.

"*Research?*" Her eyebrows shoot up.

"The First World War."

"Oh. That. *Sure.*" Mira's grin is now so wide that the lower half of her face is entirely smile. "*We?*" she adds, so quietly that Hal doesn't hear. Then, louder, "I think maybe I won't go after all. I'm more tired than I thought..." She stretches her arms ridiculously wide, and pantomimes an enormous yawn.

I snort. "Long day, was it?"

"Yes. Some of us have cleaning to do." She winks.

"Have you got something in your eye, Mee?"

"Hmm?"

"Your eye. It must be sore for you to keep blinking like that."

There's a tiny silence and then she laughs. "No. It's good. I'm good. This is all…" She makes a gesture that is nowhere near as subtle as she thinks, pointing at me and Hal. "*Good.* See you tomorrow!" And still grinning, she pulls out her sunglasses and heads for the shortcut through the woods.

I turn back to Hal, still standing there and probably very confused by Mira's unsubtle comments. "Sorry about her. She's just…Mira."

"Don't apologize. She seemed nice."

"She is. She's really nice."

And leaving soon.

I push the thought away.

The west lawn is already scattered with picnic blankets as people settle in for the evening. The closest cinema is a half-hour away by car (even longer by bus) so even if the film isn't that great, Barney's summer screenings are always busy, with guests, staff and people from the village covering the grass. Another hot-dog stand across the grass is manned by Libby from the kitchens, who gives me a wave. There's a little pop-up bar too, where the barman seems to be making cocktails for a crowd three people deep. Threading their way through the blankets and rugs are a couple of the other restaurant and bar staff, handing out red-and-white striped paper bags full of popcorn.

"Do you want a hot dog?" Hal looks longingly back at the stand behind us. Lunch was a long time ago, thinking about it. In fact, I should let Charlie know I won't be back for dinner – I should have already, but my brother hasn't exactly been taking up much space in my head. I tap out a quick message on my phone and hit send – and immediately get a bland *Okay* back, which probably means he'll want to Talk About This later.

As long as he doesn't want to talk about it *now*, that's okay with me. I turn my phone off and stuff it back in my pocket.

Hal is still gazing at the hot dogs.

"I'll get them." I grab two hot dogs, smiling hello at the waiter who's got lumbered with this shift, and hand one to Hal. He takes it – tucking the bag of popcorn he's managed to get hold of under one arm. "So, we just sit, or...?"

I gulp down a bite of sausage. "Mmmph. No, not here – I know the best spot. Come with me."

Still eating, we follow the line of the drive then veer left into the woods, stepping through dappled patches of shade and buttery late sunlight all the way to the black lattice fence that cuts between the trees.

Hal scrunches up the napkin from his hot dog, stuffing it into the pocket of his jeans. "Are you sure this is the right way?"

"There's a gate up ahead – it's fine. It's just to keep guests from wandering too far into the woods this way and ending up in the sheds."

"The sheds? What do you keep there?"

"My brother, mostly." I wave away a passing cloud of midges. The narrow gate is padlocked, half-hidden by sprawls of collapsed cow parsley and beech branches, but it's there. And thanks to Charlie, I have a key. "If we go through here, round the back of the lawn, there's a great view of the screen from the edge of the woods." The gate creaks as I push it open. Hal steps through, waiting for me to close it behind us.

"I'm guessing not all the guests get this kind of treatment?"

I step into the shadow of the trees, feeling the air cool around me. "Only the good ones."

The place I had in mind is – thankfully – empty. As we came through the woods, I had a horrible image of walking out from the trees and finding Charlie and Felix already sitting there on one of the hotel's big tartan blankets... But when we get there, we have it entirely to ourselves. Right at the edge of the woods, it's partly screened from the lawns by a low hedge of box trees – short enough not to block the view of the screen but tall enough to mostly block the view of us.

It occurs to me, as I grab one of the blankets an enterprising member of the garden team has "borrowed", rolled up and stashed in a bucket by the hedge, that it looks like I've *deliberately* brought us to a secret, secluded place. Did I mean to?

"This is awesome!" Hal beams as he flaps the blanket about, scattering bits of dried grass from the back of it. "How come nobody's already sitting here?"

"Guests never notice it – it's the hedge." I point at the hedge. In case he doesn't know what "hedge" means. "So it's pretty much only the staff who come and sit here – and then they've either got to climb over the hedge or have a key. And not everybody does."

"I'm glad you do," he says, then folds himself down onto the blanket, looking up at me. "Popcorn?" He holds the bag out.

"Thanks." I take a handful, and drop down to sit on the blanket beside him. "I'm glad I do too."

Sitting down, I can hear the quiet chatter of everyone on the lawn, but I can't see them. All I can see is the green of the hedge and the trees above us, the pale sky fading from blue into pink, the gold of the hotel, and the bright white of the screen, waiting to flare into life.

And Hal, fiddling with the ends of his fringe.

I can *feel* him sitting next to me. Even though there's a space between us, every part of me can feel the draw, the pull towards him as he stretches his legs out along the length of the blanket, his face tipped towards the screen. When the projector starts up, I feel him shift, leaning forward as he falls into the film.

And without a single thought, I leave my world – Hopwood and all my history here and everything before it – and fall into it with him.

"Did you see the village?"

The light from the screen fades, and from the other side of the hedge, there's a general packing-up-and-moving noise as everyone gets their stuff together.

"The village?" In the half-light, I can just barely see Hal's frown.

"The village. In the film. It's just down the road!"

"Wasn't it in Devon? I thought…"

"Maybe it was meant to *look* like Devon, but I'm telling you – that was Castle Combe. There, Lacock and Wells – they're used for filming all the time." I tug the blanket, dislodging Hal, and roll it up to stuff back in the bucket. Mostly, I think if I keep moving, I won't actually sound as tearful as I feel. Maybe coming to watch this wasn't the best idea…

"You seem to know a lot about it," he says, and his voice is smiling. I pick my way carefully back towards the gate. There isn't really a path here, and in the twilight it's much harder to tell if the things on the ground in front of me are branches or shadows.

I swing the gate open, holding it for him. "Not really. It's just…okay, where did you grow up?"

"London."

"Exactly. Then there's no way you're going to get it."

"Try me."

I lock the gate behind us, pocketing the key. "You see London in films and shows *all* the time, but when you live somewhere like this…" I wave a hand at the woods, at Hopwood, at the darkness settling in around us. "It's just nice to feel like it's important enough – even if it's actually tiny and insignificant – for somebody to notice."

The thing is, the film made me think – not just about Castle Combe – or about how I could make it look like I was *not* crying at the end – but about Hal and the whole reason he's here. He's looking for someone's story – for *them*, all this time after they lived.

Would anyone bother doing that for me?

Unlikely. I mean, I left school in a mess, and nobody from there came looking for me – not days after, not weeks after…not now. So why would anyone care a hundred years later?

I'll just be gone.

No one would miss you anyway.

Shut up, Flora. Nobody asked you.

What would Albie think, knowing someone cared enough to turn their own life upside down searching for him?

To turn *mine* upside down – because that's what Hal's done.

198

And the thing is…I think that maybe that's been a good thing.

On the driveway, the glow from the windows at the front of the hotel is golden on the gravel and the light from a rising moon tints the gardens silvery grey. We have walked into a painting. We *are* the painting, two figures stopped on the edge of it all, standing almost toe-to-toe.

And neither of us moves.

"I should get back."

Even though I say it, I still don't move.

He doesn't either.

"How are you getting home?"

"The usual – across the deer park."

"In this?" He points at the sky.

"How else am I supposed to get there?"

"But it's dark…?"

"It's fine. I know where I'm going. And some of us are used to no street lamps."

In the light spilling from the windows, the gleam of the moon and the fading dusk, I can see him biting his lip.

"Let me walk you? I mean…can I?"

My heart pinballs off the inside of my chest.

"You don't need to. I don't need you to."

"No, I know." Another pause. "I want to."

"You want to walk me home?"

"Yes. If that's okay?"

Walking me home, holding open doors…sometimes

I wonder whether Hal has escaped from 1913 himself. Nobody I've ever met before acts like he does.

"Pa always told me manners cost nothing," he says, as though he can hear everything I'm thinking.

Can he?

Maybe he can.

What if you said it out loud? What's he going to think of you then? What would he say if you told him everything that goes on in your head?

"Are you sure?"

Please say you're sure. Please.

"It's no problem. And anyway…I'm not ready to go back inside yet."

"You'll have to walk back in the dark, though, and you won't know where you're going."

"I'll manage." His voice is as soft as the sky.

"Okay then."

And the night seems to stretch out and on, just for us. The moon lights a path across the gardens and over the lake, all the way to the park – and when our hands meet, I don't know if it's because I reached for him or he reached for me, and I don't care, because it doesn't matter. I don't have to overthink it – it just *is*.

He just is.

The gardens are quiet; the guests who went to the screening have all headed back indoors and everyone else has gone home. We have the night all to ourselves – the white flicks of rabbits' tails as they scatter, the reflection of the moon caught cleanly in the lake, the stars slipping out from behind the sky…it's ours.

What is the point of sights like these if there is no one with whom to share them?

I step onto the little wooden bridge across the lake. This is what Albie meant, isn't it? Not the seeing, exactly, but the knowing there is someone else seeing the same thing.

The not being alone.

Our footsteps on the bridge vibrate down through the water, rippling out and shaking the moon on the surface – creasing it and folding it until it's nothing more than jumping white lines…before slowly, slowly it finds its way back to its real shape.

I know that feeling. It's the way my mind feels sometimes, the way it felt back *then*. Only I didn't realize it at the time, so I had no idea what was coming when those first ripples hit.

I must have been staring at the lake for a little too long, because suddenly Hal says, "Are you okay?"

"Me? Oh, yeah. I was just…" Just what? Contemplating the complications of my own brain and how it's constantly, *constantly* out to get me? Thinking about how, even though it feels like there are three of me in here sometimes, all wanting different things and there's not enough room for all the feelings and thoughts in my head, it's *lonely*. Because how can I ever be anything but the crazy girl if people don't know who I am – and how can I be who I am without them seeing all of me? "I was just thinking about Albie. And his letter."

"Me too."

"You were?"

"Yeah." His grip on my hand tightens. "I was thinking about him and about what it must have been like. The war," he adds. "Whether it was like the film. And trying to figure out how someone goes from here…" He stares out at the lake. "To there. How they can be in both places and still be *them*."

"Maybe they can't. Maybe places change people?"

"What, like this one?" He laughs, but not at me. His eyes are full of stars and moonlight, and all on me, and when he speaks I can feel every word.

"Why not?" Before I know it, he's spinning me up to him, into him – and suddenly we're face to face in the middle of the bridge, our bodies pressed together. Slowly, I reach up and brush his hair away from his face. It's soft under my fingers and the air suddenly smells of him. "You're telling me you don't feel different here?"

"Maybe that isn't because of the place." He whispers it into my ear, his voice so quiet and his face so close that he must be able to hear my pulse dancing just like I can feel his. He must know that every breath I take is that little bit faster now… He *must*.

His thumb grazes the skin of my cheek gently, carefully, as if he's touching something rare and delicate and doesn't want to damage it, and suddenly everything is sparks and fire as I tilt my face up to meet his… My lips brush his and my veins are full of lightning that crackles under my skin as I lean into him because this, *this* is what I want and I'm sure of it now. His hand moves around me, behind my waist, pulling me nearer still; my hand reaches for the back of his neck, fingers tangling in his hair as his lips press against mine – and everything is quiet and everything is loud and everything is thick velvet darkness and blinding bright light and there is nothing in between – and this time, I am not afraid of either. I welcome them both.

Whether it's him or me who breaks the kiss first, I don't know. I can't tell any more. All I know is that, dizzy and breathless, the feel of his lips on mine stays there even when there's space between us, even as I can see his eyes looking deep into mine, paler than ever in the near-dark.

"Umm."

"Umm."

And then we both laugh at the exact same time – I see the laugh building behind his eyes, and he must see it in me too, and he tilts his forehead to rest against mine. He smells like lemons and the night, like starshine and moonlight and sunset, and his hands holding mine feel like they were always meant to be there.

When the porch light of the cottage comes into view, an eternity away down the line of chestnut trees, it feels like breaking free from orbit, breaking free of gravity.

Walking towards it, stepping up onto the porch, takes everything I have. I turn around so my back is pressed against the door and try to ignore the sound of whatever Charlie and Felix are watching in the front room seeping into the quiet. *Our* quiet.

"So, this is me."

"This is you." His smile is big enough to hold a hundred years.

This, now; the things he said about his family up in the attic. He's letting me see *him*.

And what am I doing? Am I letting him see who I am?

Not exactly. An edited, tidied-up version maybe. One with the sharp edges filed off – because it's the sharp edges that cut. Always. What would I do if they cut him away? If he got too close and they sliced straight into him?

It would be me left with the scars.

"Flora? Is that you?" Charlie's voice is muffled by the door, but I can't ignore it any longer.

"It's me. Just give me a second?" I shout through the door – and then turn back to Hal to say…what?

But there's nothing to say, is there? Not right now.

There's nothing to think, and nothing to do, except just *be*.

And when he leans forward and runs his hand slowly through my hair, letting it slide between his fingers – his other arm slipping around my back to pull me close to him again because he can't help himself and neither can I – the space between us dissolves to nothing. He presses me back against the wall of the house and I pull him with me, wishing I could bring him closer still. His lips burn against mine and my heart is beating so fast inside me that I don't think it will ever slow down again. How can it, after this? My head spins and I never want it to stop. His hands are in my hair and on my face and on my hips, and everywhere he touches I wish there was *more*. The feel of him against me, of him here with me – I could get lost in it.

"Flora? Is everything okay?"

We leap apart at the sound of my brother calling me again.

"Yep. All good. All good," I call back, trying not to laugh, watching Hal's eyes glitter in the light from the porch. "*Really* good, actually," I add – quieter, just for Hal. Above us, the porch light flares and the stars and the moon glow that little bit brighter…and if the way he kissed me on the bridge was a question, this is the answer.

"Goodnight, Flora," he whispers hoarsely, stepping back.

"Goodnight, Hal." Lips numb from his kiss, *for* his kiss, I fumble for the handle, swinging the door open behind me. The familiar smell of the cottage – old woodsmoke, damp boots and dusty wool – floods out, pulling me back to earth… But I keep my eyes on Hal until the second the door closes between us, and I see him murmur my name into the night, and I carry the way it feels into my dreams.

Fourteen

Climbing the stairs up to the attic in the morning, I have no idea what to expect. I mean, I know what to expect from the attic: dust, boxes, paper. But I have no idea what to expect from Hal, not after last night. During my whole walk across the deer park, I've tried to guess how he'll be, what he'll say.

Basically, it's my brain's lucky day.

What if he doesn't say anything? What if he pretends it never happened? That he didn't actually kiss you last night, or that you didn't kiss him back?

What if he does say something? What if he's pleased to see you? What if he's happy?

What if it was a big, huge mistake and now he's pissed because you spoiled everything? You always spoil everything, Flora.

I dig my fingernails into the palms of my hands.

Mira wasn't much use, either – she didn't answer my

messages to her last night, and when I stuck my head around the break-room door on my way in, she was distracted by a folder of coursework and notes.

"Sorry, Flora – I *must* get this finished today, and I'm on a double shift."

"Oh. Okay." Something inside my heart deflated just a little. Part of me had hoped that she would look up and close her folder, seeing that something was different, that something had changed. Something other than her suddenly not having time to listen.

Is this a balanced reaction?

"Hey," she said, resting her pen on her notes. "I want to hear. Really."

"No, it's fine – you're busy. It doesn't matter."

Liar.

"Flora. It *does* matter. I just…" She waved at the spread of notes and doodles on her pad. The whole page was covered in tiny black handwriting and little sketches. It looked like the inside of my head feels half the time: busy. But, looking at it, I think I started to see how much she wants this. Nobody puts in the kind of hours she must be with studying on top of a housekeeping job, not unless they're serious. Or hate sleep.

I shook my head and shook away the shadow that had formed in the corner of my mind. "You're busy. It's okay – you do what you need to do."

"I'll find you later?" She glanced down at her folder and

back up at me with one of her big smiles, and whispered, "And you can tell me *everything*."

I'm not sure what to tell her, especially when I'm not quite sure what "everything" is right now, but I should probably make the most of her still being here. After all, who will I tell when she's gone?

But when I reach the top of the stairs, there he is, sitting on the landing, his back against the door and his feet drawn up. His eyes are closed and he's so lost in his thoughts that he hasn't even heard me coming up the stairs. He looks so himself...so *normal*.

Just like everybody else, but not.

"Hi." I lean on the banister. His eyes open and focus on me – only on me – and they light up.

"Hi." He slides himself upright, still leaning on the door. "Sorry, I was miles away."

"That's okay." I fumble with the key. I seem to be forever unlocking things lately. Doors, gates, histories...my English teacher would have *loved* that. Very symbolic. So would Sanjay.

The attic is just as we left it...but as soon as the door closes behind us, I know that *we* aren't the same as we were when we left it last night. He doesn't say anything, and neither do I, but it hangs between us in the air.

It wasn't a mistake.

He meant it.

And I meant it too.

I press the shutter back into the catch that holds it open, letting sunlight into the room. "You, uh, got back to the hotel okay then?"

"Yeah. And I only put my foot into one rabbit hole and tripped over three big clumps of grass." He grins. "Bit distracted."

"You didn't have to walk me home, you know. It was…" I can't finish the sentence – because actually we both know what it was.

"I did," he says softly, brushing my hair back from my face. "I wanted to."

"I'm glad you did." Now it's my ears turning pink. I can feel them, burning like tiny furnaces stuck to the sides of my head. The way he's looking at me isn't helping either – it makes me want to laugh, to shout and wave my arms around and run as fast as I possibly can…and also to stay right here with him and pull him to me and never let go of him.

A quiet cough from the doorway makes us both jump and leap apart.

Where the hell did he come from?

Barney is standing in the open door, one hand still on the doorknob – and while he's making a big deal of looking at his fingernails, his face says he saw everything. Even what I was thinking.

Nobody can see what you're thinking, stupid.

"Sorry to…interrupt. I just thought I'd pop by and see

how things are going." He takes a cautious step into the attic, and Hal takes an equally cautious one towards the boxes, like he's protecting them.

I want to say "It's only Barney", but I don't, because something tells me it doesn't matter who walked in – Hal's first response is to protect Albie's story. His second is to change completely. I see him do it – another version of himself locks into place around him as his chin lifts and his eyes cool and everything about the way he's standing shifts, until the Hal in front of me is a different one altogether. The way he holds himself says money and power; it's sharp, but it's brittle. I see it all the time in the people who come to stay here – and seeing it on *Hal* is a shock.

Barney either doesn't notice or doesn't care. Probably both. Instead, he glances out of the window and smiles his best manager smile at Hal while I fade into the background. It's what I do best.

"I hope you're finding everything you need up here? I can only apologize for the state of the attic – if you need anything bringing down to the library, I can—"

"No. Thank you." Hal cuts him off with a wave of his hand. "It's absolutely fine."

"And Flora's help has been…?"

"*Invaluable*."

He says it like he means it, and my heart shimmies in my chest.

"Great. Great." Barney claps his hands together in his

standard manager-fashion. "Well, if there's anything you need…"

"This is everything I need. Thank you." Hal fixes a perfectly polite and perfectly chilly smile on his face. "Don't let me keep you."

He basically just told my boss to get out of his own hotel's attic. Even more bizarrely, Barney actually does it. With a smile. And a nod. I'm half-expecting him to back out of the room while bowing.

I wait for his footsteps to reach the bottom of the stairs.

"How did you do that?"

"Do what?"

"You just kicked Barney out. How? Was it magic? Mind control? Because I need to know how to do it. Please teach me?"

Hal laughs, softening again. "You don't want to know."

"No, I do. Seriously. He listened to you. Nobody ever listens to me."

"I was just my dad. That's all." And he turns his face away from me, back towards the boxes.

"Umm." The page is covered in Albie's familiar looping black writing – but something about it is different. It looks rushed; in places the letters have almost pressed through the paper, leaving grazes and scars on the back of the sheet. I turn it round to face Hal.

He reaches for it, and as he takes it from me, my eyes search his as his hand brushes mine. It feels warm and soft, despite all the dust and the grit that seems to have become a second skin to both of us while sorting through the most recent pile of abandoned papers... It feels safe.

"When has anyone ever saying" – I bend the paper back towards me, tilting my head to read the upside-down words – "'I *must* speak with you, come whenever you can, I'll be waiting' been good?"

"When's it from?"

"I don't know. There's no date."

"They're always dated. He *always* dates them, and he *always* signs them."

"Well, apparently he doesn't."

"What's the next one in that pile?"

I shuffle aside what looks like a receipt from a tailor – something about a tunic, dated May 1915 – and suddenly there's nothing but floorboards under my fingers. "This is the last one from that crate, I think."

"Give me a minute." In one fluid move, he's up darting across the floor – away from the window, where we've taken the stack we unpacked this morning for better light – and back to the wooden tea chest that seemed to be absolutely stuffed with Albie's papers. It had felt like a gift when we opened it...but now I'm starting to get a bad feeling about it – the same heavy dread I've had so many times when I've woken up, knowing that all I had ahead of

212

me was another day of pretending everything was fine when it wasn't.

With a sound of splitting wood, Hal levers the loosely-nailed lid off the next crate along and carefully lifts out a bundle tied up with string, carrying it across the attic with one hand underneath, one on the top, as though he's afraid it'll evaporate. Maybe it will. When he lays it down in front of me, carefully undoing the knot and pulling the twine apart, the top letter is face down, unfolded – but when it was sent, it was folded and a single word was written on it.

Iris

Not *My Iris*, or just an initial. Her name. Blotched and smudged as though it's been caught in the rain.

We stare at it, sitting between us like a miniature wrecking ball.

"Are you sure you want to do this?" Hal's hand rests on the edge of the letter, ready to turn it over.

"Are you?"

"We already know how the story ends – we just don't know how it gets there. Don't we owe it to them?"

"Okay then." I put my hand on his, and together we turn the page over.

More than the others, this letter shows its age. The water splodges have bled into the ink, dragging it out of line and into rough grey circles, and it's been unfolded and refolded so many times that the paper is soft along the crease lines and wants to come apart more than it wants to hold together. Albie's writing is still strange, like the last note – smaller than usual, with the letters crushed together as though he's written in a hurry.

I have to go . . .
You know that I can't stay here, doing nothing when everything is happening over there. We must take a stand.

Go where?

It wouldn't be right of me to stay, and if I did, I don't think I would be the man you believed you had given your hand to. I know you will be anxious, maybe even a little angry with me, but I'll be home before you know it. I have your ribbon – the precious ribbon from that night that meant so much to us both and still does, tied around the lock of your hair, and I will keep it with me always.
It will bring me luck, and bring me home to you again from France.

The room suddenly feels cold, even sitting in the middle of the sunlight from the window.

I shan't be alone – George Harbutt from the gardens and Charlie Brewer and Dougie Marton from the village are with me. We're to report to our training officer first thing in the morning. Charlie's a little nervous we'll be found out, but they're as keen as I am to get over there before it's all over and do our bit.

The splodges on the paper come thicker and faster towards the end, and now I understand that they aren't just water or age marks. They're tear stains. Iris's tears. She must have opened this letter and cried when she read it – even if she knew it was coming. *Did* she know?

I carry your ribbon with me, and I leave my heart with you. Keep it safe and wait for me.

Always, your Albie.

I sit back, the letter still in my hand. It feels like someone has hit me, hard – and it must show.

"He left." I flap the page gently at Hal.

"We knew he left. We always knew he left." Carefully he takes the page from between my fingers, running his thumb along the side of my hand, and lays it on the floor. "We always knew he died."

"But *he* doesn't know that. Not when he's writing this."

"Neither does she."

"Yes, she does." I point at the tear marks all over the page. "She knows." I blink back tears from my own eyes. "What does he mean about being 'found out'? He says Charlie…" The name sticks to my tongue, impossible to separate from my own brother; impossible not to imagine him in the middle of a war, even if for a fleeting, heart-stopping second. "He says he's worried they'll be found out. But everyone's going to know they're gone, aren't they?"

"That's not what he means. Hang on." He fishes a small blue notebook out of his back pocket. "I did a bit of research as soon as we had a name." Folding a page open, he holds it out to me – but there's no actual words on it, not as far as I can see. Just a very untidy collection of loops and squiggles.

"Your handwriting's awful." I take the book, turning it round. "Is that even the right way up?"

His cheeks flicker with colour, and then he mutters something under his breath, shakes his head and snatches the book back. "All right, all right. Seeing as you're having so much trouble reading what is perfectly obvious, it says – very clearly, actually, right here – *Albert or Albie Holmwood. Born 1898.*"

"So he'd have been…" I count along on my fingers. Hal watches expectantly. "1915, 1898…he'd have been… seventeen?"

"Give or take, depending on when his birthday was. I think they had to be eighteen or nineteen to join up, and maybe this Charlie Brewer was even younger?"

"They lied about their age?"

He studies his notes, barely even looking up. "Lots of them did, especially early on. Everybody thought the war would be over fast, and they didn't want to miss it."

They didn't want to miss *going to war*.

"But…they're *our* age. *I'm* seventeen. Me. *Now*." I blink at him. Something in my brain has jammed and the cogs won't turn. I shut my eyes. It's not quite enough, so I lie back, flat on the floor. It doesn't feel like a puzzle now, or a story, or some kind of game – and the idea I ever thought that's what it was…it makes the room spin.

There's a rustle of paper, a creak and a scuffling sound and an arm brushes against mine. Hal is lying on the floor beside me. I can hear his breathing, steady and slow. "Hey." His voice sounds a little odd, with him flat on his back, but it's soft; as soft as the touch of his hand against the side of my wrist. "Are you okay?"

"I'm just…it's just…"

"Suddenly a bit real."

"That. I mean, they're…can you imagine being them? Either of them? I thought…I was starting to think…that we're kind of the same, but how can we be? We can't be."

The silence stretches between us. Then suddenly he says, "Maybe they're the same as us, but they're different

217

too. Their world was different, so maybe being seventeen was different. Like, getting married, going to war kind of different." He gulps down a lungful of air. "You know?"

I open my eyes, and there he is beside me, watching me. He rolls onto his back and tucks his hands behind his head, looking up at the ceiling. Without stopping to think about it, I shuffle closer, resting my head on his arm and stare up at the beams and the back of the roof slates above us.

"Okay. But he must have told her he was going to do it."

"What? Join up?"

"It's not the kind of thing you just *do*, is it? Wake up one morning and decide you're going to leave everyone behind."

Hal's eyes take on a faraway, hooded look. "Sometimes people just have to do things, I guess." He shakes his head gently. "Besides, look at the way he's talking. He felt like he *had* to do it. It doesn't read like he feels he's got much of a choice."

"Of course he had a choice!" Because from where I'm sitting, it doesn't sound like he's being called up and forced to go – he's talking about how he *should* go. That's a choice. A choice he *made*; choosing to leave Iris behind. "Do you think she ever saw him again?" The need to know, wild and desperate, climbs up into my throat. I have to know. I *have* to. It – *they* – can't end like this. They loved each other enough to risk everything, didn't they? They had plans. They had a *future*.

If Hal picks up on my desperation, he doesn't respond to it – or maybe I just hide it well. "We'll figure it out. All I... *we*...know now is he was killed somewhere along the line. It all comes from that, or the house wouldn't have been sold and changed its name and ended up being a hotel, would it? But maybe he got leave and came home before that. One last time, you know?"

"And your grandfather never said when he was killed?"

"No. I don't even know if there was any more to the story than he's told me. But if he's joining up in 1915, and he's upper class, he's going to be a junior officer – and if he's in France, he's going to have to make it through the Somme in 1916. And from what I've learned, not many of them did."

Fifteen

Sunlight creeps across the attic floor, the passing of time marked in the dust like a sundial, as piece by piece and letter by letter, we unpack what's left of Albie Holmwood's life.

"What does this mean?" I pick up an envelope – opened like all the others, with the letter tucked carefully back inside – and try to make sense of the pencil marks on the outside: a sequence of letters in an unfamiliar hand. Hal leans over for a better look and his arm brushes mine. The slightest touch makes my skin fizz and, instead of the letter in my hands, all I can see is him standing on my doorstep and all I can hear is him breathing my name. When I pull myself back to now, to the attic, his face is achingly close to mine, his eyes on me.

Somewhere below us, a bedroom door slams, and we both jump. The spell is broken. He runs his hands through his hair, pulling ever so slightly away from me and looking back down at the letter shaking in my hand. I put my other hand around my wrist to try and stop it wobbling. It doesn't help.

"The writing on the envelope?" His voice is low and breathy, and he has to clear his throat before he can speak. "It means it's been censored. To make sure he wasn't saying anything a spy could use. I think most of the letters soldiers sent home were checked. The officers – like him – usually did it, but maybe if he was new, his would have been read too, to begin with."

"Other people read their letters? Isn't that kind of…"

Hal is holding a bundle of letters in his hand. He looks from me to the letters and back again, raising his eyebrows.

"I mean, they were *alive* at the time," I mumble, feeling stupid. "But do you ever think that maybe we're better off not knowing? That maybe it's just too sad?"

Hal tips his head to one side. "When I started, it was more about the story than them. They didn't feel…real. More like characters in a book, and I was just trying to find out if the book actually existed."

I know exactly what he means. It was just another puzzle to solve. But now I've held Albie's letters in my hand, touched the same pages that he touched, seen the marks left by Iris's tears; now I know I'm walking in the same places she walked every single day, even after he left…I'm not so sure.

Hal drops the old newspaper he's been looking at and folds his hands on top of it. "You think we should stop?"

"I don't know."

Because if we leave them here, if we stop, we leave them suspended in this moment and they aren't *finished*. Another thought flickers through my mind – quick and sharp and shiny. They aren't finished, and neither are *we*. Not while Hal's still here.

"We can't change the past, Flora. Nobody can."

"I know, but…"

"So look at it like this. If it was you, if it was…" He swallows, and his voice softens. "…if it was us, wouldn't you want someone to know? If it was *our* story? Wouldn't you want someone to find it? To know that we were here – even if it wasn't for long?"

To know that we were here. That somehow, we left a mark.

Albie and Iris calling through the dark and across the years.

And Hal answered.

If it was me, lost in the dark, would he answer?

I look at him, sitting with his legs half-crossed and a smudge of dust on his cheek, his grey T-shirt flecked with shreds of old paper and dead woodlice and whatever else has been hiding in the bottom of these trunks and boxes for a hundred years… And his eyes meet mine in reply.

Yes.

Yes, he would. He already has.

222

"You do it. My hands are shaking too much." I flap the envelope at him.

Hal takes it and slips the letter out, unfolding it and passing it to me. It's so light, so thin, that it feels like tissue in my hands. But when I actually read it, it's not the beautiful note I was expecting – not the kind of letter I thought Albie would write. It's not much more than a typewritten form with Albie's signature at the bottom.

"Is that it?"

"Two minutes ago you wanted to give up. Now you're disappointed it's not juicy enough?" Hal laughs. "What's the date on it?"

"Uhhh…" I find a handwritten scrawl at the top. "May 1916."

"Then it's probably the standard form soldiers were given to send home to say they'd finished training or moved from one place to another."

"Again, how do you have all this stuff in your head?"

"That's Pa. He liked the Imperial War Museum a lot and it was our thing, you know? Just him and me. So I liked it too. And then I guess I liked it because I liked it." He makes a whistling sound, thinking about the note in my hands. "May 1916."

"Yep."

"The Battle of the Somme started in July 1916. That's where he's headed."

"That's bad, right?"

223

"It's not good."

We both reach for the next letter in the pile at the same time, shuffling closer – and our arms don't just graze one another, they're pressed together. Our shoulders, our hips align, so close we almost occupy the same space. He smiles, wrapping his arm around my waist as I pull out the letter – a real one this time, not just a form or a note. His fingertips brush against the small of my back, trailing sparks behind them.

Albie's handwriting blurs, then flashes a thousand colours as I force my eyes, my mind, my heart and my body to *focus*. And not on Hal…whose hand is still resting at my waist.

"I think this is something."

"Let's have a look?"

"There's none of the censor marks on it – not like most of the others." I skim the paper. No pencil squiggles. "Does that mean nobody read it?"

"Maybe. Could be that he'd learned a way to get it out without being read, or maybe his commanding officer didn't want to censor it. Maybe there were just so many new troops arriving that they didn't check them all? And soldiers got leave sometimes, and were sent home for a few days. Maybe Albie gave it to someone going home on leave and they posted it for him? It wouldn't have been military post, so wouldn't have been checked. There's a dozen possible reasons, and we'll never know for sure. Read it – let's see what it says and just be grateful."

We walked for hours on a long, straight road, flanked at first by trees and fields. A couple of the chaps started singing. We all thought it was a bit of a lark, not so different from summer at home really – but then we heard thunder in the distance. Not a cloud to be seen for miles around, and thunder. Someone said it wasn't thunder, but guns.

The sound of it was enough to split the sky open.

Of course, we officers put our best faces on, but everything stopped feeling quite so jolly after that. The further we walked, the further I felt from home, from Holmwood, from you, until at last we rounded a corner and saw what sort of world we had walked into.

The only way I can explain it, that sight, is to imagine a great blade had come down from the heavens and split the land clean in two – along the very road we walked. On one side there were fields and farmhouses, flowers in the hedgerows and leafy trees, just as there must always have been. But on the other side it was all a twisted vision of the world, like a dark reflection. I think for a moment we believed we had seen hell. I think I still believe it. The earth was churned into peaks and *troughs the like of which I've never seen before, the trees blasted to nothing, and the hedges we had so taken for granted had become monstrous coils of wire. The unending wires, the craters.*

No one spoke. The jokes, the whistles, the songs, they died on our lips and – I fear – in our souls. I have never known silence like it. Not stillness, the kind I have always loved so in the gardens at Holmwood at night, but silence akin to that of a tomb. There was not a single bird in the sky, no sound of one singing nearby. There was nothing for them to sing about.

When I put the letter down, Hal is watching me – carefully, seriously. Everything in my heart after reading Albie's letter must be etched on my face, because he shakes his head gently and twines his fingers through mine.

"I'm glad it's you," he says quietly.

"Glad what's me?"

"Here. This. I'm glad it's all with you. That I'm not doing it on my own."

"It didn't need to be me, though, did it? Anyone would have done. Your grandfather – he'd have been even better, wouldn't he?" I squeeze his hand back.

"Nah." And he smiles. "It had to be you."

The air thickens and fills with a million tiny bolts of lightning – they strike all over me, crackling across my skin. There is lightning in my hair, in my fingertips, running up and down my arms. Hal feels it too – I know he does. It's in his eyes, still locked on mine. It's in the way he tilts his head, in the way his lips soften and part so slightly as, gently, he takes Albie's letter from my hands and sets the past aside on the floor, pulling me to a place where history – Albie's, the hotel's, his, mine – can't reach us. Closer to here and now.

I run to it with open arms.

The more of Albie's letters I read, the more I feel I know him – and the more I like him. There's something easy about him, familiar. Kind. How could Iris *not* fall for him? How could anyone not? Maybe it's just that he's in my head now. After all, he didn't mean these letters for anyone other than Iris (and maybe not even for her, not always – some of them feel like they're more to get the thoughts out of his head, like a diary…or a therapist) but they speak to *me*.

Whatever trick he had to get his letters out, it seems to have worked – most of this batch are uncensored. Reading them is like listening to him speak; I can almost hear his voice if I try. He talks about the soldiers, mostly, what so-and-so said or did, where they're from and who they've left behind. In a few, he describes the horses the senior officers have – the ones they ride or the ones that pull the huge guns ranged around the network of trenches and fields that are the front line. It makes me think of *War Horse*; of seeing that story play out on a big screen in front of a hotel that has another story that can easily match it. And how, of all the people watching on the grass, we were the only ones who knew.

He talks about a little stray dog someone in his unit adopts and feeds scraps to, hoping to keep the rats away. He talks about how suddenly there are birds again – not the swifts he misses so much, but skylarks, barrelling through the sky above the Somme. And he talks about the rain and the strange colour of the sky, the smoke and the silences – and the loss. So much loss. His letters ache with it – friends injured or killed, or simply missing. It feels so fresh, so clear and new, that I want to reach into the past and take Albie's hand and tell him that everything will be all right.

Even though it won't be. Because I know what he doesn't. That his time is running out too.

But through all the letters, the one thing he never talks about is the fear. He never talks about it, but it's there, running through every letter like a seam of coal.

Hal's story isn't just a story any more. The people in it have lives. Friends. Parents. People who loved them. They lived; they even lived *here*. And they died. And I can't square it – how they were just like me and Hal and Mira…

and they went to war. They walked away from this place, from everything they'd ever known, and they went *there* and faced *that*. Guns and bombs and fear and death.

You can't even face yourself. Can't even face the people around you knowing who you really are.

The thought prickles uncomfortably through my brain.

"Look. It's a photo. There's a photo here." Hal's fingers touch my arm.

"A photo?"

"It's him. It's Albie. It has to be."

It had never occurred to me that there might be a photo; that we might somehow be able to see what he really looked like.

The picture Hal's found shows a group of men…are they even men? A couple of them still look like kids – younger than us in their uniforms and caps. There are six of them pictured in fuzzy black-and-white: three sitting on wooden chairs, three standing behind. The photo looks like it's been taken in somebody's garden – there's grass under their feet and leaves from a plant at the side of the frame. A stone wall, half-covered in ivy, is behind them.

They look almost the same in their uniforms, so close that they're practically identical, staring straight into the camera. Or at least they do at first – because the longer I stare at the picture, the more differences I see. The sitter on the right has his feet tucked together in front of him; the one on the far left has his apart. The man seated between them is taller than the others, and it almost looks like he's slouching – trying to not be the tallest, just for once. But standing behind them, the guy in the middle is almost smiling, as though that's what his face naturally wants to do. His tie isn't quite as straight as it should be, and his hat is pushed back a little and it makes him look less intimidating than the others around him. The picture's too blurry, too blotchy to see him as clearly as I'd like…but I'm sure that's him. I point at him.

"That's Albie," I say quietly.

"How do you know?" Hal's voice is equal parts serious and curious.

"He looks like he matches the words. Does that make sense?"

He makes a non-committal sound. "You can't even see him properly."

"I know, but try to picture any of them – all of them in that photo – writing the stuff we've read. He's the only one who fits."

After a long pause, he nods. "Maybe. Or we could just check the letter with it."

"Which one?" I wave at the letters that have spread out around us like a sunburst.

"This one." He picks it up and starts skimming through it. "He says there was a French photographer taking portraits to send home. Somewhere near where he was based, a farm, I think? It's smudged. But he says who the others are, so I guess if we eliminate them, we'll be left with him." Hal frowns over the letter, glancing from it to the photo. "Sitting down, there's Bill Fosse, George Harbutt…"

The name is enough to snap me back to myself. "GH? The gardener?"

Hal nods. "I guess so. Or another coincidence?"

The tall guy, the one trying not to stand out…he was their mystery helper. I stare at him, sitting in the middle of the row in a garden in France – a long way from home.

"And then there's Fred Keane. Oh, and here he says 'either side of me', see? You were right. 'Either side of me are Dougie Marton and Charlie Brewer.'"

I wince at the name as my brother's face flashes before me. Even if it's not him…it could have been.

Hal doesn't notice – he's too deep in the past. He sits back on his heels, staring at the photo.

"So that's them," he says, looking up from the letter. "Bill, George, Fred, Dougie, Charlie…and Albie."

But my brain has latched onto something – or at least part of it has. The fast part, the manic part. The determined, yappy little terrier part of it that can't bear to stop moving.

The puzzle-solving part.

Something about my brother. Something about those initials – GH. George Harbutt.

George Harbutt was a gardener.

GH.

My brother.

GH.

Got it.

I brush the dust off my knees. "Do you want to get out of here for a minute?"

He blinks up at me. Probably wondering why I don't want to stare at the photo some more. After all this, he wants to put a face to the name. A voice to the words that have led us here.

But I want more than that. I don't need to hear Albie's voice – I already know it. I can feel it in every word he writes. I want something more – something that connects them and us, then and now. Somewhere they've left a mark.

And I know just where to find it.

Sixteen

Some people would call it a greenhouse – and *technically*, they'd be right – but that makes it sound small and neat, like something you'd find at the bottom of one of the gardens in the village. That's not what this is. The Hopwood glasshouses are long, broad sheds, but with the walls and roofs made entirely of glass panes held in place by old oak frames. The floor is bare earth, beaten and trampled hard by generations of feet crossing it to reach the wooden workbenches, which stretch most of the length and are loaded with trays of baby plants, or the nursery beds dug straight into the ground. Inside, it smells of damp soil and tomato leaves. Faint traces of mist from the watering system hang in the air.

The door sticks, so I give it a shove, making the hinges squeak and the glass panes rattle. Hal eyes them suspiciously.

"It's okay, they always do that." Reaching back, I slip my hand into his and pull him into the glasshouse, nudging the door shut again with my toe.

"Are we meant to be in here?" His voice is little more than a whisper, swallowed by the green hush filling the glasshouse.

"It's fine. I come in here all the time."

Which is true. This is where I came every time I had a panic attack in those first weeks after The Incident; every time I felt like someone had swapped all the blood in my veins for pure distilled adrenalin and my lungs closed up and my heart screamed at me that it couldn't keep doing this, while quietly, my head told me that this was what I *deserved*. This glasshouse was where I came to breathe in the scent of the plants, to hear the *tick-tick-tick* of the watering hoses, to dig my fingertips into the soil or run my hands along the old benches…to ground myself.

Of course the next piece of the puzzle is hidden here. Of *course* it is.

Drops of water from the humid air settle on Hal's lashes, where they glitter. I can see myself reflected in his eyes – or at least a version of me. Whoever that girl is, surrounded by leaves and plants and flowers. And behind my reflection, I see – what, exactly? Deep in his eyes, I see him. Golden. Dazzling.

Blinding.

But when he smiles and leans into me and his lips press against mine, all of that slips away…and he's just him and I'm just me…

With his forehead resting against mine and his arms around me, I could put down roots here – right here, in the middle of the glasshouse and the plants and the flowers and the misty dew from the watering hoses. A made-up Eden, perfect for someone like me. Someone who needs a safe place.

Maybe even for someone like Hal too.

His breath and mine curl together in the air, and the glasshouse has never felt safer. I wonder whether it felt safe to them too, to Albie and Iris?

I nudge my nose against his. "That wasn't what I brought you here for, you know."

"I know." He grins, and the glasshouse lights up.

"This way."

I lead him deeper into the glasshouse – past the ancient potting bench, dented and battered by generations of gardeners; past the trays of seedlings for the autumn and the frames of baby vegetables for the kitchen gardens; under the sprawling grapevine that dapples the floor beneath it with shade even on the brightest day...and right to the back, to the oldest, gloomiest corner up against the hedge, where Charlie has his garden planning boards set up and keeps his favourite kit. Not even the junior gardeners dare come here looking for tools or seeds in case they mess something up. But I know exactly what I'm looking for – the point where two corners of the roof meet the walls, and the massive oak post that joins them.

"Look there," I say to Hal, and point at the post.

"What?"

"Look. Really look. Or better yet…" I lift his hand and press it against the wood, my hand on top of it, sliding down the beam. "You'll know it when you find it."

Under my hand, he runs his fingertips down the grain of the wood until he reaches a rough patch, and he stops. His whole arm tenses and his eyes open wide. He's found it, and I drop my hand, letting him duck around the post to get a better look.

His nose pressed almost up to the wood, he outlines the letters cut into the post with his fingers. "What *are* they?"

"They're initials." A dozen pairs of them, all in a column. *BP, DF*…and more, up and down the post. And right at the bottom: *GH*. "They're the gardeners. When Charlie started working here, there was a guy on the gardening staff who'd been here basically for ever. He showed him these on his first day – he told him that right before they left, the gardeners who went to fight in the First World War all came here to carve their initials."

"GH has got to be our GH – right? George Harbutt."

I nod. "The one who helped Albie and Iris."

"It fits. It all *fits*, Flora." He tilts his head forward and rests it against the pillar, almost like he rested his head against mine a few minutes ago, and his voice cracks as he says it.

"It fits."

236

The glasshouse is so quiet that I can almost hear the plants growing.

"I can't believe it. I thought maybe I'd find a name or something…but *all this*?"

"I'm glad. I mean, I didn't want you to be…" I take a deep breath. "Disappointed."

In this. In here.

In *me*.

Half in the shadow of the post, Hal slowly shakes his head, his eyes fixed on mine and his lips curving into a smile.

"What possible reason could I have to be disappointed? I came here looking for a story and I found it. And then I found something *much* more interesting."

"What's that?"

"You."

I know exactly what he means, because I didn't even know I was looking for him, either…but suddenly, here we are.

Found.

"Listen," he says as I haul the door closed behind us, keeping the damp air of the glasshouse in and the summer evening air out. "That party in a couple of days. Here."

"The anniversary one?" I brush my hair out of my eyes.

"That's what it's for?" Hal clears his throat and stuffs his hands into his pockets, staring at the gravel path – suddenly awkward.

"It's ten years since Hopwood Home opened. The owners want it to be a big thing – Barney's had to invite the local press and people from all over the place."

"Mmm." He scuffs one of his shoes backwards and forwards on the path. Bits of gravel *ting* off a glass pane. "It's just…I was wondering…would you…I mean, maybe? I thought…did you…?"

I can barely hear what he's saying over the humming of my heart.

He frowns and screws his eyes shut, and his chest rises and falls as he takes the deepest of all possible breaths, and I hope he's breathing for both of us, because I just can't.

"Would you like to go? With me? Umm, what I'm trying to say is – would you like to go to the party with me?" The words rush out of him, and the second they're out, he opens his eyes and I can see everything in them. Everything I've learned about him, everything I've *felt*…and the ground underneath me is just as solid as it's ever been, but the sky is spinning and I could step up into it and *soar*.

"I'd love to."

"Yesss!" Hal punches the air.

I try not to laugh. It's very difficult.

But he shakes his hair out of his eyes and beams at me. "Sorry. It's just…I was really worried you'd say no."

"Why would I say no?"

"Because…" He shrugs, and mumbles something under his breath. It sounds a lot like "I'm me", but why would *he* say that?

I want to tell him so much that of course I want to go with him *because* he's him. That all of this, the attic and the glasshouse and the roof of his car and the deer park under the moon…it's because he's him, and he makes me feel I can be the closest to *me* I've been in a long time. But instead of saying that – or even some of it – I freeze. If I told him that, I'd have to tell him everything.

The version of myself I saw in his eyes isn't all of me, is it? It's the version who treads the line between the darkness and the light, not the Other Flora who couldn't get out of bed, who couldn't even speak or think or breathe without it hurting, who wished more than anything in the whole world that everything would just *stop*… And it's not the Flora who ran full-speed and headlong into the light and left everything behind, even her mind, even *herself*. Sad Flora is the long dark shadow that the blazing light of Mad Flora casts, and both are part of me – but they aren't the parts I've let him see.

How could I? *Should* I? No.

I can't – because what if they're not what he wants to see? What if he saw, and was afraid of them, of me? As afraid as *I've* been? What if he sees them, sees the condition, the label…and that's suddenly *all* he can see?

What if I took this moment, this thing, this glorious all

of it, and just as it was spreading its wings to fly, I knocked it down to earth with a perfect, perfect bombshell?

There are footsteps on the gravel path behind the hedges circling the glasshouse, somewhere near and getting closer, which means I don't have time to think about it. Hal's face says he's been watching me, and he wants to ask something – I can feel it – but he doesn't. Instead, he smiles. "Listen, I really want to go and write all this down. I feel like if I don't get it out of my head and into a notebook, I'm going to forget something – and I want to be able to tell Pa *all* of it."

"Not *all-of-it* all of it, though – right?"

"Okay." His ears turn scarlet. "Maybe not *all* of it. But most of it."

"The important parts."

"No." He shakes his head. "The stuff I wouldn't tell him is just as important." He beams at me again. "Are you okay walking home, or…?"

"While I would absolutely love for you to walk me home again, I get it. You go." I laugh, and shoo him in the direction of the hotel. My heart tugs at me to follow him, like it's a balloon on a string and he's holding the end – but I watch him turn the corner of the path, rounding the hedge and, just for a second, stopping to look back at me. I wave and smile, and then he's gone – leaving me with one searing thought that crowds out all the others.

I need a new dress.

Because Hal Waverley asked *me* to go to the party with him.

He *asked* me.

I hold the thought to me, tucking it tightly around me like a pair of folded wings.

"...know you're just trying to protect her..."

The crunch of feet on gravel is closer and Felix's voice drifts over the hedge.

"Of course I'm trying to protect her!"

That's Charlie.

Charlie and Felix are heading for the glasshouse...and they're talking about me.

"And I understand, I do, but..."

"But what, Fix? What?"

I duck behind a stack of old planters at the side of the glasshouse, pressing myself back into the shadow of the hedge. Whatever they're saying, I want to hear it. Felix, closer now, sighs.

"You want to keep her safe, and make sure she's stable."

"That's my job! I'm her brother, and I promised..."

"You promised your mother, I know. But it's not your job to keep her on the level. That's Sanjay's job – and now she's better at it, it's Flora's. Your job is being her brother." They reach the path right in front of the glasshouse, and I hold my breath. "I want to protect her just as much as you do – I love her too, and that's what I'm trying to say. She needs to be normal, and this place..." He sighs again, banging his hand on the glasshouse frame. The panes rattle even louder than they did earlier and I pray that one doesn't fall out on me. "College, a *life*. Friends. That's what she needs."

"And when she's ready, I'll support her doing that."

"She's ready, Charlie. You *know* she's ready. She's so much better. Think how she's been since that kid turned up with the research project! You said it yourself – it's like seeing her *before*. She's *ready*. And you need to help her see that."

There's silence, except for a quiet scraping sound. My brother's picking loose splinters of wood away from the door frame. He does it when they fight at home sometimes, leaning against the wall or the stairs and *picking*.

But he only ever does it when he knows Felix is right.

The glasshouse door creaks open as Felix speaks. "Listen to me, Charlie. You want what's best for Flora, yes. But she's been treading water – and people can only do that for so long before they sink."

They close the door behind them.

I lean into the hedge, barely daring to breathe in case they notice me, watching their shadows move as they head for the back of the glasshouse, where Hal and I were, what now feels like a lifetime ago.

She's ready.

Ready for what, exactly?

But even as I try to draw the safety, the familiarity of

242

Hopwood closer, something deep inside me – just like Charlie – knows Felix is right.

She's ready.

Does ready mean not being scared?

Because I'm still scared. More scared now than I was before…because I know what can happen. I remember that I didn't see it coming when I broke.

College, a life. Friends. That's what she needs.

A life.

Like the one Mira's making for herself? She knows where she wants to go, and what she needs to do – and she's doing it. She's going. She's leaving me behind, because how can I go anywhere when I don't know where it is I'm meant to be heading? How can I have a life when *life* is the thing I can't seem to handle?

It's like seeing her before.

I'd forgotten what it felt like to be me before. But I think, just maybe, I remember now.

The old me, the Flora I was, who didn't always second-guess and doubt and worry about moving too fast or too slow… The one who just *was*, who didn't need to be afraid that what she felt might not be real or right. She just felt it.

Suddenly I think I might have been more like her again than I realized – ever since Hal arrived. Not because he's some kind of handsome prince, riding in to rescue me from my tower, but because he reminded me I don't need that.

You don't seem like the kind of person who needs rescuing.

He even told me. He believed it, so why didn't I?

Because I never know if it matches, if it *fits*. If my mood matches the moment, whether what I feel is true or not – and whether I can even tell the difference.

The memory of the library at Fallowmill crowds into my head, pushing everything else out. The orderly rows of books, all lined up and locked behind their wood and wire-mesh doors. Caged to keep them safe.

Who decides what safe means?

Me.

I do.

Me.

My head. My doors, my locks.

I keep my own keys.

I guess it's time I used them.

Seventeen

Charlie walks past my open bedroom door, carrying a basket full of laundry...then stops and takes two steps back to poke his head round the frame and stare at me.

"Flora?"

"Hmmm?" I half-lift my head from my pillow.

"What are you doing?"

"Looking at dresses." I turn my phone screen around to face him.

"Yes, fine, but...you're on your phone." He dumps the basket on the floor and a load of rolled-up socks bounce out.

"Well, yeah. How else am I supposed to look?" I sit up, swinging my legs over the side of the bed.

"Right. I mean, yes. Exactly. I was just...surprised." He eyes me thoughtfully. "So you're looking for a dress for the party?"

"I can't exactly wear my pinafore dress, can I? And nothing else is, you know, a dress?" I survey the wasteland of my wardrobe. I've not really bothered too much about clothes since I came here. There's never been any point. Mostly I wear the same stuff all the time: T-shirts and denim shorts or jeans, and I steal Charlie's old jumpers if I need one. And there's always my uniform… But none of them will do for the party.

The set-up has already started – a fleet of big white vans with *Angelo Events* written in neat silver lettering on the sides streamed up the drive yesterday afternoon, ready to start unloading for "the greatest moment in the hotel's history" according to Barney. The funny thing is, the most important thing in the hotel's history – the *house's* history – happened a hundred years ago… But to me, it feels like it's happening now too, and I want to tell everyone. I want to show them the world as it was when Albie stood in the gardens at dawn, when Iris whispered his name into the water at Fallowmill, when George Harbutt cut his name into the beam in the glasshouse. I want to tell them that they lived. That they were *here*.

And that so are we. So am *I*.

Which is why I need a dress.

The stairs creak as Charlie heads back downstairs, the un-emptied basket of clean laundry still in his hands. It sounds like he gets to the bottom just as Felix comes out of the kitchen.

"I thought you were putting that lot away? What's wrong?"

"She's in her room."

246

"And…?"

"Felix, she's on her phone."

"Doing what?"

"Scrolling through dresses."

There's a pause, then I can *hear* Felix smile.

"I told you."

"Look, this one's been posted in Britain too. Southampton – and it's uncensored." The uncensored letters are getting rarer again – either things changed in France, or Albie's luck getting them sent unread ran out. Some of them now are barely more than notes, little more than *I'm still alive*, scribbled on flimsy army-issue paper. Some are longer but almost all of those have long black bars of writing scratched out, redacted in heavy ink. How anyone could have got anything from the censored letters – anything at all – I don't know, but more and more, finding one that isn't feels like hitting gold.

"There must have been someone else from his unit on leave. Southampton had lots of troops coming and going through it – whoever it was probably posted it as soon as he got off the boat."

"Albie doesn't say anything about where they are, though. There's nothing, you know, confidential – he's not that stupid."

Hal takes a long swig from the bottle of water sitting

between us on the attic floor, carefully twisting the cap back on. "It wasn't just military stuff they weren't allowed to talk about. The longer the war went on, the worse it got – but nobody wanted people at home to realize just how bad."

"Nobody?"

"Politicians, mostly. They'd spent the first couple of months of the war saying it would all be over by the first Christmas, remember? Now we're in…what, 1916?"

I check the date and nod. August 1916.

"Exactly." Hal's eyes flick from me to the letter.

There's no escape from it. Even in the rear trenches, the guns and shells clatter and rattle like trains, constantly. They are our birdsong and our church bells, our heartbeats and our lullabies, summoning us to duty or death or both. The sounds are in our heads and under our skins. The men joke that if a chap should break his leg in the trench, the sound of whistles and machine guns would pour out of the bone.

The war is not what we thought it would be. I daren't say what any of us imagined, but I know none of us could have pictured this in the worst of all our nightmares. Sleep here is both a friend and an enemy – a release from the mud and the rot and the stench, but an open door to every fear that each of us buries in our bellies during the waking minutes of every day. Death walks among us, over the top and on the field and in the trench, and every soldier here knows His hand could fall on our shoulder next. And, oh, the guns, Iris. The guns. Like a thousand armies marching across the roof of the world, they clatter and they boom and they shriek. And the mud, churning like an ocean of despair between us and them — and we aim to kill them and they aim to kill us, and for what?

I could lie to you. I could tell you it is easy. But that would be almost as great a lie as if I were to tell you that I did not miss you more with every passing moment, and you made me swear that I would never lie. So instead, I shall speak of happier truths: that I have made good friends, brothers, among the men and the other officers. Bill spends most of his time teaching that ridiculous dog he adopted to do tricks. No one quite knows whether getting it to play dead when he shouts "Bang" is the greatest or very worst idea any man has ever had. Dougie Marton took a hit in the shoulder from some shrapnel — a

Blighty, we call it. Not enough to lose the arm, thank God, but enough to send him home. He should be back in the village by autumn, and I will try my best to send word with him.

Know this: I love you. I am yours – all that is left of me at the end of this is yours. All that I ever was or will be or might have been. And I will do everything I can, everything in my power to come back to you.

"He'd been at the Somme a month." Hal squints as he tries to remember the right dates.

"But he's still alive! He's okay, right?" I slap my palm down beside the letter as though I can somehow pull Albie out of it, out of the past and into the present. As though I can save him.

Hal stares gloomily at the remaining letters from this, the last of the trunks from this period of Hopwood's history. We've checked all the others – there's only this one left, and the pile of papers that came out of it is very small.

I grab his hand as he reaches for the next letter. "Let's stop."

"You want to stop? Now?"

"Yes." I nod. "Yes, I do. Just for today. Just…give him a little longer."

Give *this* a little longer, because I feel more and more like me again with every day I spend up here. And with every day I spend with Hal, the less I want him to finish his project. Because what happens when he does and leaves? What happens to us? To me?

Hal follows my gaze to the few remaining pages. "You know it doesn't change anything."

I know that – but I can't tell him that it's not just Albie I want to have longer with. So I sigh and change the subject. "Either way, we've got to stop because I'm not even meant to be up here right now – I've got to meet Mira downstairs in a minute. We're getting the bus into Bath. And I'll see you tonight at the party…"

He opens his mouth to say something, and then closes it again.

"How's the car, by the way?" I scrape together our notebooks and pens – the skeleton of the story he'll take back to his grandfather – tucking them to one side.

"Oh. It's good. Well. It's nearly dry, so it's a start?"

"Sorry. About flooding it."

"Nah." He waves a hand. "I shouldn't have driven into a river."

"It was a ford."

"That," he says, unfolding his crossed legs and jumping up in one fast motion, "was a river and nothing you can do or say will convince me otherwise."

"Nothing?" I put my hands on my hips.

"*Nothing.*" In a moment, he has wrapped his arms around me, knocking my hands aside and pulling me closer.

251

I breathe him in, feeling the warmth of him as he rests his head against mine, feeling the rise and fall of his chest as he breathes. His heart, pounding against mine.

I don't want to pull away from him. I don't want to let go of him.

When we turn over the last page of that stack, I have to.

He leans even further into me, the two of us taking up the same space in the attic, in the world. The thought of how much I'll miss him, miss *this*, when he leaves is like someone reaching into my chest and taking hold of everything inside and twisting.

Not just because I really do like him, but because I like the version of me I've become since he arrived. The old me. And however much I try not to be, I'm scared that when he leaves, he'll take *that* me with him.

Gently, he slips a finger underneath my chin and turns my face towards his.

"You do know, don't you?"

"What?"

"That when I came here, I only planned to stay until I found a name. That was all I needed." He hesitates, and I can actually feel his ears reddening. "All I *thought* I needed." His words cut through everything, slicing clean through the rising noise in my head, the rising doubt. "I stayed *because of you*."

And he catches my face between both of his palms and draws me to him again; his lips on mine and mine on his until everything else – the rest of the world, the ghosts and the living, all the clocks and calendars and all the time they keep – flares brightly, then flickers out.

Eighteen

"You still want to go to Bath? Not Bristol? We could have gone to Cabot Circus!" Mira drops the loose change for her fare into the bus driver's hand, then yanks her ticket out of the machine and pinballs off the seats along the aisle until she gets to an empty double.

"Like either of us could afford something there." After a bit of rummaging around in my bag, I manage to dig out the right cash and grab my ticket, dropping into the seat next to Mira as the bus starts moving with a lurch. We only just made it to the stop on time – and that was only because Mira came barging into the attic and dragged me out. That's the thing about Hal – when I'm with him, time seems to have no meaning.

Except the stack of pages is so small, and however much he says he's stayed because of me (has he? Did he mean that?) he can't stay for ever. He has a life away from here – one he'll have to go back to. One I'm not part of.

Mira elbows me – hard. "Hey! Stop it."

"What? I wasn't doing anything!"

"You were. You were thinking." She nods. "You were thinking about *him*, weren't you? Your face does this... thing...when it's him."

"It does not! Hang on – a 'thing'?"

She just nods again, infuriatingly.

The little bus bumps its way out of the village, climbing up from the valley and out onto the top of the next hill. Mira flicks through a shopping list of dresses she wants to look at in town, skipping between pages and maps on her phone, planning the afternoon like it's a military campaign.

"And there goes my phone signal," she sighs. "Give me your phone?"

"I don't think my signal's any better," I say, unlocking it and handing it over. She jabs at the screen...and misses the icon she was going for, hitting the one next to it. The screen immediately fills with a scroll of photos, each one more perfect than the last. Perfect people with perfect hair and perfect faces and clothes, all in perfect places living perfect lives with perfect friends.

"You have an Instagram account?" Mira stares at my phone. "You never told me!"

I shake my head. I want to ask for my phone back – or for her to at least close the app – but my lips have glued themselves together and my tongue is stone in my mouth. I watch her swipe over to my profile page – and frown when she finds a completely empty grid. "Where are all the photos?"

"I deleted them." I force my voice to work, to say the easiest thing, and reach for the phone before she asks any other questions… But it's too late. I've been caught.

"Why?"

If I close my eyes, I can do it. Mira may be my best friend, but there are things I haven't been able to tell even her. Things I keep in the darkest, softest corners of my memory. "It's complicated."

"I'm listening."

"When I was…ill, you know? I wanted to…disappear."

"Disappear?" I can *feel* her looking at me.

"Everything was so hard. I just wanted it to *stop. I wanted to stop.*"

Silence, except for the bus engine and tinny distorted grime leaking from the headphones of the guy three seats in front of us.

Then she understands. "*Oh.*" It's less of a word than a breath – but at least I can't see her face. I don't *want* to see.

She'll be different around you now. She can't not be after that – not even Mira. She'll think you're weak or weird or looking for attention. Freaky Flora, right? Just like everyone else thought.

Doesn't matter anyway. She'll forget all about you when she gets to college.

But then, from somewhere behind the voices inside my

256

mind comes another one. Quieter, gentle, but clear like a bell.

And you let her in anyway. Well done.

And even though I can't see Mira's face, I feel her hand close around mine, holding it tight.

"I don't think you should delete it, Flora. Take down the photos, by all means. Temporarily deactivate it if you must. But keep the account."

"Why? I don't want it any more. I don't need it. I don't…"

"Need anything?" Sanjay leans back in his chair. "Come on. We've talked about this kind of language."

"I don't care."

"I know."

We sit in silence, him in his chair and me in mine. He waits. He always waits. It drives me crazy. Crazier.

I fold my arms. He knows I'm not going to break first.

"Our brains," Sanjay says at last, leaning forward in his chair again and putting his hands together on his knee, "are the windows through which we perceive the wider world. Not," and he holds up a hand, because he knows I'm going to say it, "the eyes. No, Flora, listen. Our eyes take in the information, but they don't process it. We see with our eyes, but we don't perceive with them. That's what our brains are for. So, if you picture yourself as standing behind a window, looking out, then the glass between you and the world is your brain. With me so far?"

"Sort of."

"And just like glass, our brains – or the way they show us the world – can be tinted or obscured, changing the way we see things. Sometimes, the glass gets smeared up and it makes things look distorted, or prevents us from seeing them altogether." He presses his hands together, almost like he's praying. *"Glass can be cleaned, Flora. Just because you can't see through the window now doesn't mean you never will."*

I only glare at him. He doesn't know anything.

"Everything is temporary," he says. "Even this."

I kept the account. I didn't understand why my therapist was so fussed about one stupid social media account – but now I think I get it. It was about the future. It didn't matter what I did with it – all that mattered was that I believed there was one. That I might want one.

When I open my eyes, Mira is still holding my hand, watching me.

"I'm okay."

"You are. I know." She lets go, and throws her arm around my shoulders, rocking me alongside her. "But whenever you aren't, even if I'm not here, you'll call me? Yes? You promise?"

"You don't want that. I mean, thank you, but—"

"No. No 'but'. And no, I don't want you to *not* be okay – but if you aren't, I want to be there."

Something has stuck in my throat. I don't know what it

is or how it got there, but it feels like it's the size of a fist. "Even if you're going away?"

She shakes her head. "I'm going to college. Not the moon."

The last hill before Bath drops away, and the little city spreads out along the river valley, its honey-coloured buildings shining like possibility as the bus bounces down towards it.

"No. No. Nope. Maybe – oh, no. Definitely no." Mira grabs the dress hangers out of my hands and, one by one, tosses them all over the nearest rack. It's so like it used to be, like *I* used to be, but different. Better? Not sure. But it's something.

"What's wrong with this one?" I lunge for my favourite from the pile, a dark blue one.

She just gives me a withering look. "You are kidding me, yes?"

"Fine." I drop onto the padded bench in the middle of the changing-room waiting area. "So what do you suggest? I told you leaving it until the day of the party was dodgy."

"And I told you we should have gone to Bristol, but here we are! Never mind. I have an idea." She ditches the last of the dresses and scoops up the bag with her dress in it. The very first one she tried on, made from gorgeous green lace. Twenty-three attempts later, I'm still dressless. "Come on."

"Maybe it's me and dresses. Maybe we're just not meant to be."

She tows me out of the shop and along the busy main street. "Shhhh. This way."

"Mira, can we not just…" She yanks me down a narrow side street, then another – and finally into a tiny lopsided courtyard. "Where are we going?"

"I told you. I have an idea." And she gives me a shove towards the back of the courtyard.

"Would you stop shoving…*oh*." Because there, in a shop window hidden away from the street, is a dress. A *perfect* dress. Such a pale blue that it's almost grey, and soft enough to look like it could fly; it's floor-length and chiffony, and there are rows of tiny pearls sewn around the edges of the neck and the arms.

"Oh." I look at the shop sign. "But it's a vintage shop – I'll never be able to afford it!"

Mira grins. "Don't you see the tag? It's half price."

I spin back around so fast I almost fall over on the uneven cobbles of the courtyard. "It is? Oh my god. It is. And it's my size. How is that possible?"

"It's a sign."

"I don't believe in signs. Or coincidences," I mutter. This is enough to make Mira snort with laughter.

"Then let's say *I* do."

As she propels me through the door, I spot the little framed notice.

*Supplier of authentic period clothing to
TV and film productions including
Downton Abbey.*

I picture Felix's face when I tell him.

Maybe it *is* a sign after all…

Inside, the shop is tiny and nothing like the ones we've been in already. Each piece of clothing is carefully hung and labelled with a brown cardboard tag: heavy woollen suits, a black-and-white dress that looks like it was meant for dancing all night in a smoky jazz club, a duffle coat, a pair of trousers that shimmer under the light like water. Hats and old leather suitcases sit on antique luggage racks above the rails, and below the clothes, neat pairs of shoes sit side by side. Mira spots what look like cowboy boots and lunges for them – leaving me to face the woman who has appeared behind the counter.

"Can I help you?"

"The…um…dress in the window. Is it really half price?"

She looks me up and down and narrows her eyes. "You're interested in that one?"

Mira emerges from underneath a fake-fur coat waving a cowboy boot. "She is. She really, really is."

The woman's face softens and she actually smiles at me. "Good. It's my favourite, and it's been stuck here for ever. Would you like to try it on? It should fit you perfectly."

"Please." I clamp my hands together in front of me so

she can't see me shaking as she edges past to reach the window.

"I told you," Mira whispers. "A sign. It's been waiting for you."

"Don't be stupid."

But when the owner lifts the dress out of the window and swirls it around in front of me, it feels like maybe Mira's right after all. Maybe it *has* been waiting.

"It's not the most valuable piece we've ever had in, but I think it's one of the prettiest. Based on a pattern from 1912, I believe – altered, of course. You'd never have had a neckline like that, or the cross-ruching on the front, but the idea's still there." She holds it out to me. "The changing room's through the curtain there. I'll be right here if you need anything – sometimes the fastenings can stick on these ones, so just call."

A pattern from 1912? Okay. That's so much a sign it's almost spooky.

The little changing room is hidden behind a heavy red velvet curtain, and everything is softly lit by warm white bulbs all around the full-length mirror. Another mirror, just about as tall as I am and mounted in a wooden frame, is tucked into the far corner of the room along with a deep red velvet armchair.

"How are you getting on in there?"

"Good, thanks!"

I'm not about to say that I'm just standing here, staring.

Hooking the hanger over the top of the mirror, I shrug my T-shirt off and drop it on the floor along with my shorts and kick off my trainers. The dress slides over my shoulders like it was cut for me, sitting perfectly. It even fastens without a single hiccup. When I pull back the curtain and step out into the shop, Mira lets out a squeak, then beams.

"Yes. *That* one."

I smooth the skirt down.

"I think we have a match, don't you?" says the owner, nodding.

I turn, letting the fabric flare and fall – and when I catch sight of myself in the mirror behind me, just for once the Flora reflected in the glass agrees.

Nineteen

"How can you two still not be ready?" Charlie's howl from the bottom of the stairs is as loud as if he was standing in front of my wardrobe.

"Because we know you hate waiting?" I shout back. Mira laughs, sticking one more grip into her hair to hold it in place, piled up on top of her head. Downstairs, Charlie swears, but Felix laughs too.

"Anyone would think you didn't have a party to get to! The pair of you, downstairs in two minutes – or you're walking across the deer park."

"What do you think?" Mira puts one hand on her hip and pats her hair. The green dress and her red lipstick look amazing. And so glamorous that they're completely out of place in my cramped little bedroom.

"You look like…I don't know. A film star or something."

"Good. Film star will do." She flashes me a grin and grabs the tiny red clutch bag she brought with her. When I asked where she'd got it, she looked embarrassed – and said she'd *made* it.

"You made it?"

"Does it look so bad?"

"No! It looks brilliant. You should make some more and sell them. People would totally buy them."

She picked at the seam along the top, but I think I was only telling her what she already knew. Just like I know that, actually, what she needs is to leave here. However much I might hate her going, fashion is where she's meant to be.

Mira rests her free hand on the doorknob. "Okay. Are we good?"

"Yes. I think so." I don't only mean that we're ready to go downstairs. The mirror on the inside of my wardrobe door is a lot smaller than the one in the shop changing room, but the Flora there looks the same as she did earlier. The dress still fits like it was made for me, like it's been waiting all this time. Like this Flora has been waiting all this time.

And the dress even goes with the one pair of heels I already own.

"See? Like it was meant to be. Like I said," Mira says approvingly over my shoulder.

Charlie and Felix are downstairs, Felix twirling the key of the Land Rover around his finger and Charlie staring at his watch and grumbling. My brother looks surprisingly neat in his suit, and even Felix (less neat, but still smarter than usual in a grey waistcoat, his tattoos of leaves and twisting vines clearly on show below rolled-up shirtsleeves) could pass for someone who belongs around actual people and not trees. As we come down the stairs, Felix nudges Charlie and whispers something in his ear, and Charlie beams.

"About time," he mutters, shaking his sleeve back down over his watch. "Better get going." But the inside of his words and the outside don't match. "I like your dress," he says as he holds the front door open, watching Felix help Mira into the back of the Land Rover. Her shoe slips as she climbs in and she laughs, with Felix pretending to shove her in – and it really hits me how much I'll miss her.

"Thank you."

The inside of my words don't match the outside either. On the outside, I'm saying thank you for the compliment, because that's what we're meant to do. On the inside, though, there's so much I need to thank him for – and I don't think I can ever say it all out loud.

Felix gives me a wink as he helps me clamber into the back of the Land Rover – which just for once, doesn't even smell like a farm.

As we cross the deer park, Hopwood appears in flashes through the trees, the windows glowing and strings of lights criss-crossing the lawns and terraces. It looks like something out of a fairy tale, and the closer we get, the more magical it becomes. Flaming torches are fixed into metal posts along the hedges and on top of the tower in the middle of the maze. As we pull into the staff car park, tiny white lights glitter in the topiary shapes and around the stone urns in the flower borders.

"Look at this place!" Mira breathes, craning her neck to be able to see it all at once. "I never thought it could look this way!"

I didn't either, not really. We've had all kinds of parties here before – weddings or birthdays or…things people have parties for – but the Hopwood has never looked this beautiful for any of them. It feels as if it's under an enchantment.

Inside, the wooden staircase we spend so long every day cleaning is completely lost underneath the ivy and white roses wound all around the banisters and the lanterns perched at the side of each step. Giant vases of white roses and green eucalyptus branches intertwined with tiny glittering lights have appeared on every available flat surface. Through the open doors, the main lawn has sprouted an avenue of silver birches, their delicate branches also draped with little white bulbs lighting the way to a huge marquee in the middle of the grass, overlooking the lake and the maze. Lanterns line every path, flames dancing in their glass cages and casting flickering shadows on the gravel as people wander up and down with glasses in their hands. Barney moves from group to group, shaking hands and making small talk. A flash near the reception desk means the photographer is already at work, and all through the crowd I can see people I recognize – other members of staff, all looking a tiny bit awkward out of uniform. We're not used to *being* the guests.

But no matter where I look, no matter how many knots of guests I pass, I can't find him.

Hal's not here.

The lobby is crowded and loud. People laughing, the clatter of glasses on trays, the piano in the bar, music from the marquee outside drifting in on the warm night air…

So loud.

And Hal's not here.

He should be here – he said he'd be here. He asked me to be here.

I don't know what's pounding harder – my heart or my head, which suddenly feels like it might split open. The world has taken on strange outlines, as though everyone is lit from behind. I edge my way through the crowded space and lean on the end of the banister, trying to control my breathing. Where did Mira go? She was right here, and then…

"Flora."

Only one person says my name like that.

The noisy room is suddenly silent and the air feels like water, heavy and slow – I have to push against it to turn around and it takes an eternity.

And there he is, two steps from the bottom of the staircase.

"Hal."

His hair is swept back from his face and he's wearing a white shirt and dark blue suit. And when he smiles at me, the room glows brighter than ever. How can he be so much himself? How can he always be the same person, the whole of himself? What does that feel like, and how can someone who finds that so easy ever understand someone like me? But then in the attic, when he spoke to Barney and was somebody so different, that wasn't a Hal I recognized. That wasn't the Hal who kissed me on the bridge or on my doorstep. It wasn't the Hal who laughed when we sat on the roof of his car. How can he carry this other self inside, and never be bothered by it? How can Mira come to work day after day after day and never mention that what she really wants, where she really belongs, is somewhere and something else – something she's working towards in secret, even though it's hard and she's tired? How can Charlie think all the things I overheard him saying to Felix and never let me see how much he worries?

Suddenly the world shifts and mirrors itself and knits back together – and there I am, left standing in the middle of the echoes of what I thought I knew.

Everyone is divided. *Everyone* has different people, different pieces of themselves, inside. Hal, Charlie, Felix, Mira – even Barney. If everyone is on their own roller-coaster, looking through their own personal panes of glass…then we're all kind of in it together. And if we're all in it together, maybe other people *will* understand, and I can just...be. No more worrying about whether I'm too fast or too slow, or how I explain *me*.

Maybe *he'll* understand.

Someone says my name, just on the edge of my hearing, and I turn. It takes me a moment to see them in the press of people. Three girls about my age gathered around one of the side tables and holding glasses, two wearing dresses just like ones Mira tossed aside and one wearing a jumpsuit. They look familiar, but I can't place them.

The girl in the jumpsuit shakes her head, smiling. "I told you – it's definitely Flora. I can't believe she's actually *here*."

The one on the left, in a taupe dress, frowns. "My cousin said they gave her loads of pills. Probably shock therapy. He was there when she, you know, *freaked out*."

They're talking about me like I'm some kind of exhibit. They obviously don't know I can hear them, or how loud their voices are.

Maybe they just don't care.

A horrible, cold sensation claws up the inside of my stomach.

This is everything I've been afraid of.

The one in the middle, the one wearing a long navy blue dress embroidered with little gold suns, gives her a playful push. "You don't know what you're talking about. Your cousin doesn't either." Her voice sails across the room on bladed wings. "So what do you think they *actually* did

270

to her? Do you reckon they had to put her in one of those padded rooms?"

She lifts her glass to her lips, tilts her head back to drain her drink…and sees me looking straight at her. I watch her eyes widen, see her dig her elbow into Taupe Dress's side, but it's already too late.

The glow around the world sharpens, deepens. Panic pinpricks up and down my spine and my heart moves from a jog to a flat-out sprint.

Everything I've been trying to tell myself is a lie.

Faces turned to stare out of the bus window as Mr Parkins takes for ever to cross the road.

I used to go to school with them. They know.

They're talking about the Incident.

About Crazy Flora, Freaky Flora, Mad Flora.

And standing right behind me on the stairs, Hal has heard every single word.

Twenty

Barging past them, I make a break for the door. If I can get to the door, through the door, out into the big wide outside, then I can let everything in my head out. Somehow.

Hal calls my name – I hear it, but I don't stop. Not even for him. Not now, not this time. My name follows me to the open door, but it doesn't catch me, and outside in the blue-pink of the evening, the gold of the candle lanterns and the green of the lawns, it won't find me. I can taste the scent of the grass as I run across it, away from the hotel, from history, from Hal…away from my name, away from *me*.

Ahead, the entrance to the hedge maze is flanked by tall flaming torches, the pathways glowing with yet more lanterns, but none of the party guests have ventured this far out and the maze is silent and still.

Into the labyrinth, right hand on the hedge and keep it there…turn, turn, turn…and my brain starts to settle as the quiet and the rhythm of the maze takes over. I've always loved this part of the gardens. When Charlie first got his job here I would try to find my way to the centre before he could – I never won. And after…after I broke, this was one of the places I found the pieces of myself, walking in the cool of the towering hedges, because a maze is just another puzzle.

"You're okay. You're okay. You're okay."

The branches bounce my voice back to me at every turn, all the way to the heart of the maze and its fairy-tale tower – built as a folly long before the house was a hotel. Following the path through the maze, sidestepping lanterns and dead ends, means following the people who lived here before me, before any of us. It brings my edges back into focus and into reach.

The tower, like the rest of the maze, has been lit with lanterns – its little stone windows glow from the inside. Just like Sanjay taught me, I count the steps up the spiral staircase. I put all of myself into the tips of my fingers on the rough stone walls, letting them ground me, draw me back to earth even as I climb. By the time I reach the top and step out onto the platform of the round roof to lean on the low wall, the hammering in my brain has fallen silent and the world is quiet.

Except for my name, which floats up from somewhere below me, drifting between yet another pair of flaming torches that loom above my head, and lands at my feet like a feather.

"Flora!"

Not Mira. Not Charlie. Not Barney.

Hal.

Hal is in my head. It doesn't matter where I go, or what I do, I can't outrun him.

"Flora? Are you there?"

He isn't in my head.

He's *here*.

Somewhere…

Peering down into the maze, I can't see any movement.

No. I must have imagined it…

"Flora! Over here!"

At the very edge of the maze, all the way back at the entrance, I see him. His hair and the white of his shirt gleaming in the torchlight. He's waving.

"Are you okay? How do I get to you?"

How do you get to me?

How does anyone?

Why would you even want to?

I can't let him. He'll only see what they see – and then he'll never want to look at me again.

I lean a little further over the wall and shout back to him, my voice carrying on the still air. "You don't."

"What's wrong?" His voice has rough edges when it's raised, and my tightly-knotted heart shakes itself loose inside my ribs.

I ignore it. "I just need…"

What? What do I need? To be normal? To not have this *thing* in my head? This part of me that talks too fast and feels too much and can't bear to wait for the world, moving and thinking a million times slower than I am, to catch up? From the outside, it probably looks obnoxious. Like *I'm* obnoxious.

How can I tell him what it's like when it's too fast even to feel it coming? It's shiny and bright and it flashes like a fairground ride, making the world whistle and spin. From outside, maybe it doesn't even look so bad.

But like a fairground ride, all you can do is hold on tight, and hope that when the mania has burned itself out, it hasn't taken all of you with it; that there's something left that you can salvage…that there's time before the bipolar pendulum swings the other way, dragging you back into the dark where everything is cold and empty.

What do I need?

To not feel like I'm faulty, I guess.

To feel like what I am is enough.

I'd almost convinced myself that that might even be true – that maybe he would think so. Stupid me. How could he? How could *anyone*?

"I just needed…to be on my own for a bit."

"Can I come in?"

"Into the maze?"

"That's the idea."

"You'll never get through to the middle."

"Try me."

He stops, and there's silence. A long silence. Has he turned around and gone back to the hotel? However much I crane my neck, I can't see. The light is starting to fade just a little too fast, and the shadows of the maze pathways are thickening. If he's not careful, he'll be in there all night.

"Hal?"

"What?" His answer comes from deep in the hedges.

"What are you doing?"

"Getting lost, apparently."

"Hal!"

"What now?" He sounds more frustrated than he did a minute ago. "Oh, you're kidding. How can this be *another* dead end?"

I cup my hands around my mouth to make my voice carry better. "HAL!"

"WHAT?"

"Pick up a lantern."

"Unless it's got a map on the bottom, I don't see how that'll help!"

"Just do it, will you?"

A corner of the maze brightens as a glow that wasn't there a moment ago flickers into life.

"Flora? Are you still there? I can't figure out which way to go…"

"Hang on." I can't quite see where he is – I'm not high enough.

I look along the wall to the right of me.

The torches on the roof of the tower are always here – they don't get lit very often, but they're a permanent fixture bolted to the wall and the floor.

They're *sturdy*.

I peer down over the wall. It's not so very high…

Okay, so it's *quite* high.

But you know what? I'll be fine.

I kick off my shoes and wrap one hand around the metal torch post closest to me, pulling the loose skirt of my dress aside with the other.

One.

Two.

Three.

I climb up onto the top of the wall…and there he is, down in the bottom corner of the maze. Going entirely the wrong way. Again.

"Hal!" I let the hem of my skirt drop back down, holding onto the pole with both hands. The ground actually looks a lot further away than I thought. "I see you!"

"Which way?" The glow of his lantern moves right… then doubles back on itself to the left.

"Keep going – straight ahead, past the next two turns." The light stops moving. I can just about see the top of his head from here, looking left, right, straight ahead. "Okay?"

I picture myself down in the maze, following the path to

the heart of it. "Left. Turn left." The candle moves again, following my directions to the next set of possible turns.

"Hal?"

"Yep."

"Why are you coming after me?"

"Because…" He tails off. Or at least, I don't hear him say anything. After a pause, he says it. "Because I had to."

"I don't need you to rescue me," I shout.

"That's not what I meant. And anyway, I was kind of hoping you'd rescue me?" he calls back. His face shines in the lantern light.

"Turn right. Then right again." I watch the candle moving, watch the light of it glittering off his hair, watch the blue of his suited shoulders lightening and darkening as he moves through the maze until he's only a few turns away.

"Straight on, then right."

I loosen my grip on the post and jump down from the wall to the roof, just as he emerges from the last turn of the hedge into the clearing at the heart of it. He looks up at me, standing on the tower, and I look down at him, and I can feel where our gazes meet. It pushes the breath out of my body, steals a beat from my heart. It makes my hands tremble.

And none of that is bad – not this time, not like it has been before.

He sets the lantern on the bench in front of the tower

278

and puts both his hands in his pockets…and he doesn't once look away from me.

He's in my head.

He's in my head and I can feel his voice brushing against the inside of my mind and it feels warm and welcome… and safe.

He's in my head and he is real – and he's waiting for me to come down from the tower.

Carrying my shoes, I walk out of the tower doorway and into the little square at the heart of the maze. The lanterns at the edges cast little golden pools of light all around us. "You heard what they were saying, didn't you?"

"It's none of my business what they were saying."

"You still heard it though, right?"

He looks uncomfortable for a second. "Look, if you want to talk about it…"

"No. Maybe. No. It'll sound crazy." It *is* crazy. "Maybe later. I just needed to get out for a minute – seeing them, it brought back…stuff I'd rather not deal with right now. That's all."

"You're sure?"

"I'm okay. Really. You don't have to, you know…wait with me, or whatever." I wave an arm in the general direction of the hotel.

He doesn't move. "The way you ran…" He stops abruptly, swallows the words that were already on his tongue, and then half-smiles. "People only run like that when they know they're never going to get away from something. Like they know it's tied to them. I know a bit about running away. I mean, I know what it's like to feel like you have to, like it's the only thing you can do, even if in the end it doesn't make any difference," he says, his eyes on the ground between us. "Can I tell you a secret?" He takes half a step towards me, closing the distance between us to almost nothing. I can smell the scent of him and feel the warmth of his face almost against mine as he leans closer; feel his breath move my hair as he lowers his voice and whispers into my ear, "I'm kind of afraid of the dark."

He leans away again, scanning my face as though he's waiting for me to laugh or to tell him he must be kidding, right...? But he wasn't kidding. He meant it. Whatever memories of his are hiding in the darkness, they frighten him.

He's afraid of the dark, but he followed me out into it.

He walked me all the way home through the deer park.

With one hand I pick up the lantern from the bench, and with the other I take his hand, weaving my fingers through his – and I look into the future with my eyes wide open.

"Me too. But I guess if we stick together, we'll be okay."

He smiles at me, closes his hand around mine.

And together we walk into the darkness of the maze.

* * *

He doesn't pull his hand away when we come back out onto the lawns. If anything, he knits his fingers more tightly through mine. Ahead of us, light streams from the ground-floor windows of the hotel, from the library, the bar, the restaurant. The terrace shines with candles and torches. Faint voices and piano music drift from the marquee.

"Your boss knows how to throw a party." Hal swings our hands back and forth as we walk.

"He does."

The evening has got cooler, and quickly. And while my dress is extremely pretty and extremely half-price, it's also extremely not warm. It doesn't help that there are large damp patches in the middle of the back where I panic-sweated through it. Goosebumps parade up and down my bare arms…and Hal spots them.

"You're cold?"

"No." I try to suppress a shiver. "Hang on, wait – no…" Because he's started to take off his suit jacket. "Don't do that."

"Why not?"

"Because that's ridiculous. People don't actually do that. Not real people at real parties."

He makes a dismissive sound as he drapes his jacket – carefully, gently – over my shoulders. The lining still carries the echo of him – the warmth of his body, the shape of his shoulders…

"Want me to take it back?" He arches an eyebrow at me,

281

and I shake my head, sliding my arms into the sleeves.

"Now you've gone to all that trouble…"

He laughs quietly, and reaches for my hand again.

How did this happen? How did this guy who came from nowhere hardly any time ago end up here – with me wearing his jacket and holding his hand, knowing what it's like to be kissed by him and to kiss him back?

Does my mood match the moment?

Right now, I feel like if I'd stepped off the roof of that tower, I really would have flown. So yes, actually I think it does.

But as we skirt the side of the hotel, his arm finding its way around my shoulders, drawing me into him, something doesn't seem right. Something, somehow, is out of place. The gentle chatter on the terrace drops away, but I can still hear voices. In fact, I can hear shouting. I speed up – but suddenly he's ahead of me as I gather up the fabric of my skirt, taking the steps to the terrace two at a time. With every pace, Hal draws further and further ahead in front of me, focused on the voices coming from inside.

"Hal?"

He makes a "wait" movement with his hand and, with a burst of speed, he darts up the steps ahead and vanishes through the doors from the terrace into the bar.

"What's happening?" Mira darts between two bar tables as I follow him and grabs my arm. "Where's Hal going?"

"I don't know." He's already disappeared from the bar

282

into the lobby beyond. And now people are stopping mid-conversation, glasses still raised, turning towards the doorway, to the bottom of the main stairs, to the source of the noise.

As I step out of the bar and into the lobby, a ring of guests – spectators now – has formed around the edges of the space, all watching the bottom of the stairs where two men are…what? Talking? No. One is talking, quietly, rapidly. The other is holding the end of the banister, one foot on the bottom step, and shouting.

"No. No, I will *not* calm down!"

"You're *making* a *scene*."

The quieter man is maybe in his early fifties and chilly-looking, all points and edges with short, dark hair. His face is thin – *everything* about him is thin and narrow, his forefinger sharp as he jabs it towards the other, older man, who must be in his seventies. They seem to know each other…there's something in the tilt of their heads, the line of their chins and cheeks that says family. But clutching onto the banister like it's holding him up, there's a vagueness about the older man, something missing in the look he gives the other. He just keeps staring hopefully up the stairs.

"Where's Barney?" No sooner have I said it than I see him, adjusting his tie and putting his manager-face back on as he moves through the clusters of guests with a whispered, "Excuse me, excuse me…"

283

And then I see Hal, walking straight over to the bottom of the staircase. Neither of the two men have noticed him; the older man keeps looking up the stairs, still holding onto the banister.

"I just want to go to my room."

"*How* many times do I have to tell you? You don't *have* a room here." The dark-haired man's voice has as many edges as the rest of him, all of them jagged. "We're leaving." He reaches his hand towards the arm of the older man… who stares at it in horror.

In turn, a hand settles on the dark-haired man's shoulder. "Dad. Don't."

Dad?

Hal drops his hand as the dark-haired man turns to glare at him. But he doesn't move away – instead, he steps between the two men.

Dad?

Mira nudges me hard in the side. I ignore her.

"Henry."

Henry?

Of course. Hal is short for Henry.

Sharp Pointy Man is Hal's father.

"Grandpa? Pa?" Hal has turned his back on his father and is talking to the older man gently, calmly, his hand resting on his elbow. "It's me."

The older man looks straight through him. "I just want to go to my room."

This is Pa. This is who it's all been for. I hadn't even thought about the fact they might be here too, but I suppose it makes sense. They're in the hotel business. But why didn't Hal tell me they were coming? Didn't he want them to know about how I've been helping him? Or did he just not want them to know about *me*?

Hal's dad snorts and, impatiently, Hal rounds on him.

"What's your problem? He's just confused."

"He's an old man. That's my problem."

Hal opens his mouth to say something – then blinks, thinking better of it. Which is when Barney finally makes it to the bottom of the stairs, clapping his hands once and raising his voice in a breezy, confident way. "It's all right, everyone. Everything's fine. Please carry on with your evening… I think we're about to have some more music down in the marquee, so if you'd like to make your way across the terrace?" He makes vague shooing motions with his arms and pretty much everyone takes the hint.

Except us. Mira and me.

We stay. Even if we do take a step or two back so it's a bit less obvious we haven't left. But it means I see Barney's smile fade just a little as he tips back on the heels of his shoes and spins to face the three men at the bottom of the stairs. Hal still has his hand on his grandfather's arm and his body between the two of them. Barney looks them all up and down.

"Eddie."

"Barney."

What did Barney call Hal's father before? "A grade-A, weaponized arse"? Right now, that looks like a pretty generous description.

"What seems to be the trouble?"

"My father." A long, weary sigh. "As you can probably see."

Hal interrupts. "He's just having one of his turns. He'll be all right in a minute." His father swats him away like a fly. Hal leans towards his grandfather, who is still shaking his head and murmuring quietly to himself. At least he seems calmer. Outside, the piano has started playing again. "He'll be all right."

"Come on," says Mira. "We should go."

"No, you go. I'll just…hang around here for a minute and make sure everything's okay." I don't exactly know what I can do, but walking away feels like it would be wrong.

Hal's father is still talking loudly, saying that Pa doesn't have a room.

"Why don't you give him yours, Dad? I mean, you're probably just going to sit up all night in the bar anyway, right?" For one awful moment, Hal's voice is as sharp and pointy as his father's, the hollows of his cheeks flushing livid red. Barney, trying very hard to find somewhere else to put his attention, spots me and closes his eyes as if he's trying to clear his head.

My heart cracks for Hal, for his grandfather. At first, I really did think his trying to track Albie down with nothing more than half a house name was insane…but seeing the two of them – the *three* of them – together like this, I understand.

"I wasn't planning to stay. Neither of us were." Each word that comes out of Hal's father's mouth is a shard of ice.

Barney has stepped forward again. "I'm sure we can manage something – let me speak to my staff. If you'd care to wait in the bar, Mr Waverley? Perhaps I can get you something to drink." The question is aimed past Hal's father, straight at his grandfather. A smile, a welcoming gesture. Barney knows what he's doing, and cautiously, Pa nods.

"That would be very kind." His face shifts, and so does Hal's – with relief. Whatever happened, it's over.

Except as Barney leads the way to the bar, with Pa just behind, Hal's father's hand snaps out and locks tightly around his son's arm.

"Why haven't you answered your phone? Or returned my calls?"

"I've been busy."

"*Busy.*"

I make myself invisible, just like I do on any normal day here. But I can't leave. Eddie Waverley's voice is hard and cutting, and watching them from the other side of one of the huge flower arrangements, I see exactly what anyone else would. A furious man in an expensive suit and tie hissing at his son; wanting to shout but not wanting anyone to know, bringing him to heel like a badly behaved puppy. I see Hal, turning his face away, his jaw set hard and an angry flush to his cheeks, his hands pressed deep into his pockets and his shoulders locked and tense.

Then I see something else, something more. Something that happens so quickly, it takes a moment before I understand what it was.

Movement. Hal's father first, reaching forward as if to grab Hal's shirt, right below the neck…and Hal, moving faster than I've ever seen, his whole body twisting away. His hand slapping his father's down – and then his arm outstretched, keeping him at bay. A warning finger held out and pressed so hard against his father's tie, right over his heart, that the fabric dimples around it.

I slip into the doorway of the library, pulling it almost closed behind me, before Hal can know that I've seen.

What I've seen.

Their voices seep through the door.

"I'm not bankrolling this stupid obsession of yours a moment longer. You're coming home. With me. You can put all this…energy into the office."

"It's not an obsession. And it's not stupid! It's for Pa…"

"'It's for Pa,'" his father mimics him, then makes a disgusted sound. "Pack your things."

"No."

"I'm sorry? What did you say to me?"

"I said no."

Deep inside my chest, my heart aches for him. It aches and it burns and it hurts. I want to throw the door open and run to him, but I can't. After what feels like an hour, he clears his throat. "We had a deal, remember? You agreed. Besides, the room's paid up front for another couple of days. Non-refundable," he adds. "If I check out now, it's money wasted. And I know how you feel about that, *Dad*." His voice is full of prickles, of sharp pleats and creases. Not like the Hal I know at all.

His father snorts. "Oh, I think we can swallow the price of a couple of nights' bed and breakfast, don't you?" There's the click of shoes on the floor as he starts to walk away – and then Hal calls out after him.

"You promised. You promised me that I would get to finish this."

"I beg your pardon?" It's low. Dangerous. Vicious. He's turning around, going back over to where Hal's still standing his ground.

"When you said I couldn't go to university, did I make a fuss? No. But you and me, we had a deal."

"Are you *out* of your *mind*? I—"

"I get to finish this, and then you get me. No complaints. I come and work for the company, doing what you tell me. I'll do whatever you want. That's it. No more research, no more history. I'll never even mention university again –

289

not once. But I do have this. You agreed." I hear the breath Hal takes, deep and ragged. "Isn't that the thing you pride yourself on? Being a man of your word? So *be* one."

The silence between them pulls so tight that it could cut through flesh and bone. Then:

"Fine." The answer should be a relief, but it feels like a death sentence. "You can stay until then. Finish off whatever it is you've been doing. And then I want you home. It's time you grew up and acted the way I expect my son to. And by the way, don't think I'll be paying for the repairs on that little toy of yours. It can stay in the garage for a while, I think. Perhaps it's time you actually appreciated just how much I do for you."

Another swish, and more clicking. I peer around the door just in time to see him stalking away into the bar – leaving Hal standing in the shadow of the staircase alone, absently rubbing the forefinger on his right hand.

"You heard all that, didn't you?" he says hoarsely, his head barely turning towards the library door.

"It's none of my business."

"You still heard, though."

Our conversation from earlier, turned on its head.

I open the door and step out into the lobby, reaching for him. He pulls away.

This is why he never mentioned they'd be at the party. He wasn't trying to hide me from them; he was trying to hide them – *this* – from me.

"So that was your grandfather?" I try. "Pa."

"That's him."

"And your dad."

"Yep."

"I get it."

"You don't. But thanks." He sighs. It hurts my heart. "Look, you should probably find Mira or your brother. I've got to go...be me."

It feels like a whole new pane of glass has slid down between us.

"I'll see you tomorrow?" I'm almost afraid to ask.

"Yeah. I guess we might as well finish that stack of papers off. Maybe I can show some to Pa before we leave. He'd like that." He sniffs. "Goodnight, Flora."

But the mood and the moment don't match.

What he says is "goodnight". What he means is "goodbye".

And when Charlie and Felix have found me and near-bundled me, still shrouded in Hal's jacket, into the Land Rover, and we pull around the side of the Hopwood, I crane my neck to look – and I find him. Sitting alone in the library, his shoulders hunched and his head in his hands. All I see is a flash, enough to know it's him, and then he's lost to the darkness.

Twenty-one

The hotel feels like it's still half-asleep when I walk in through the staff entrance the morning after the party. The usually rowdy kitchen is relatively quiet – instead of yelling at each other over the noise of the ovens and fans and the clatter of pans, everyone seems to be whispering. I guess most of the kitchen staff put in an appearance at the party last night too. The staff break room's not much better – a couple of the housekeeping staff are in there, and everything has the volume turned down. Even Mira.

I perch on the arm of the chair she's slumped in, her sunglasses pulled down over her eyes.

"Morning!"

"OH MY GOD!" She actually twitches – and slides half-out of the chair. "Don't do that," she groans, pulling herself back into the seat.

"You were asleep."

"Resting my eyes."

"Good night?"

"Where did you go? I looked for you…after the stairs."

She knows I'll know what she means.

"Home. Charlie and Felix needed to get back, and I didn't…"

I didn't what? Didn't want to stay after that conversation with Hal? Didn't feel like being at a party? Maybe.

"I didn't want to walk back in the dark," I finish.

Mira doesn't believe me, but she nods anyway.

"How is he this morning? After the thing with his grandfather?"

"Hal? I'm not sure."

The truth is, on any other morning lately I wouldn't have come down here first. But this morning…I don't know. I've never heard him sound like that before – so *cold*. In that moment, the Hal I had almost convinced myself I could tell anything to was gone.

And after seeing the girls from school…Well.

It took me for ever to remember their names, but I did. Eventually. Lying on my bed, staring up at nothing.

Emily, Yaz and Clare.

I used to take maths with Emily. I sat at the desk across the aisle from Yaz in English, and Clare was in the year below me. I didn't exactly know them *well*, but it was only a year ago – and they looked at me like I was some kind of monster. Just like I was afraid anyone would if they knew, if they'd seen me when I was bad. And then I did the worst possible thing – ran away. Because that's what mad, freaky Flora does, isn't it? She runs away. Oh look, there she goes again.

I have *got* to stop running *away*. I need to run towards.

Towards what?

No idea.

But there must be something. Maybe it doesn't even matter what it is, just that I know it's out there.

See, Sanjay? I did get it. It just took me a year to understand it.

"Go find him. He'll be going soon, no?"

"I guess so. A couple of days, maybe." I wonder whether I should tell her everything I overheard.

"And then it's finished?"

"Finished?" Something stabs at my insides. Finished. Yes. It'll be finished. How can it be anything but finished after he leaves here? That conversation made the bargain he has with his father pretty clear – and I can't imagine there's a place for someone like me in Hal's life if his father's in charge of it. All I have of Hal is what's left of Albie's letters. And the worst thing is, that's all Hal has left of himself too.

He's traded his future for someone else's past...and I think, if I was ever going to fall in love with somebody, that might be the kind of thing that would make me do it.

Maybe?

I don't know.

I don't even know what love feels like, I don't think. I always thought it would be like the mania: bright and sparkling, like cut glass. Brilliant and sharp. But this... isn't. It's the sound of him laughing on the roof of the car, the warmth of his jacket around me. The smudges of dust on his nose.

Is it really so easy? So little and so big at the same time?

Either way, soon all those things will be gone and only the traces in my memory will be left, ready to be wiped away by the next twist of my brain.

Mira's still watching me, waiting. "I said, the research will be finished." She blinks at me over her sunglasses. "What did you think I meant?"

"Oh. Nothing." I try to sound casual. I don't quite manage it. Mira makes a loud "Mmmmm" of disbelief. "Anyway, there's still some stuff to sort through – we haven't quite figured out what happened, but I think we're getting to the end."

Of Albie.

Of us...whatever "us" is.

All we have left is stolen time.

"Look, I should get going. He'll be waiting for me. I'll catch up with you later?" Maybe by then I'll have more of a handle on all this. Even if I don't, maybe I'll tell her anyway, because she's right – whether she's at Hopwood or in Bristol, Mira's always here for the stuff that matters. Even if she's hungover.

And I think this matters. I think it matters a lot.

"Later? Sure. If I live so long," she mutters, and slouches even further back into her chair. I can still hear her groaning and muttering to herself as the break-room door swings shut behind me.

Sitting on the old Chesterfield under the window in the lobby is Hal. And beside him is his grandfather. They must be waiting for a car to pick Pa up. A jacket I don't recognize is folded neatly over the arm of the sofa, which reminds me that I still have Hal's jacket from last night hanging on the handle of my wardrobe door. He's swapped his clothes from the party for grey jeans and a dark T-shirt, but I catch myself studying his face for any hint of his father. There's nothing. In fact, watching him sitting beside his grandfather, leaning in to hear what the older man is saying and smiling as he replies, makes me see him even more clearly. He runs his hands back through his hair – and then suddenly he looks right at me in that way he always does, as though he can feel me watching him. Maybe he could. His smile widens and brightens, and he tilts his head to one side… and then his grandfather looks over at me too and even from here I can see his eyes are as sharp as anything.

"We were just talking about you." Hal jumps up as I reach the sofa. "He really did leave last night, by the way," he adds – meaning his father. "Don't worry."

"I wasn't."

I was. But.

He eyes me warily, then nods and gestures to his grandfather. "Flora, I'd like you to meet Pa – Marcus Waverley. Pa, this is Flora."

His grandfather stands slowly, as though he's off-balance, and looks me up and down, breaking into a broad smile. "Flora." He holds out a hand.

"Mr Waverley." I take it and he closes both his hands around mine, laughing.

"Marcus, please. 'Mr Waverley' makes me feel old. Older, anyway," he adds, nudging Hal. "Hal's been telling me all about you."

I nod, keeping my mouth shut. It's the only way I can guarantee I won't spend the rest of the day worrying whether what I said was *actually* stupid or just felt it.

Marcus lets go of my hands, waving at the lobby in general. "Well, I must say your staff are doing a beautiful job of…"

Hal's cheeks slowly fade up to scarlet. I shake my head and try to keep my own face from doing the same. "Sorry, but I think Hal's promoted me. I *am* the staff. I work in housekeeping."

This only seems to confuse Marcus for a split second, because then he shrugs and smiles even more warmly. "In that case, I'm very impressed. I know a little about keeping a hotel looking smart – yes, Hal, I do," he interrupts himself, as Hal tries to say something, then carries on smoothly, "and it's harder work than most people think. So good for you. And it's nice to finally see my grandson getting along so well with someone his own age. His father never saw the point of friends, I can tell you…"

"Pa, Flora doesn't need to know my life story right now." Hal steps neatly between us in an uncanny echo of the way he separated his father and grandfather last night.

I swear Pa actually chuckles, resting his hand on Hal's shoulder. From outside there's the sound of a car horn.

"That must be my driver," he says, turning to check through the window, where a smart blue car has pulled up outside the door. "No, no, you don't need to walk me out, Hal. I'm sure you have more interesting things to do with your time, and I'm not that decrepit yet." He drops his hand from Hal's shoulder and moves towards the door – then stops and turns back to me. "It was a pleasure to meet you, Flora. I hope our paths cross again soon."

Watching him walk out to the car and climb into the back seat as the driver holds the door, I find myself hoping exactly the same thing. And as the car disappears down the drive, I turn to Hal.

"Did you tell him about Albie?"

"No. Not yet. I decided I want to tell him all of it at once." He tucks his hands into his back pockets as the car finally vanishes from view. "Thanks for not bringing it up."

"I wouldn't. I mean, it's your thing, isn't it? Yours and his."

Anyone who saw the way Hal and his grandfather spoke to each other would have got it – why he's been so determined to do this, and what it means.

"Ah, I think it's yours too now, don't you?" He turns away from the window. "Look, about last night. My father…"

"No. You don't have to apologize."

"I do, though. He did kill the party mood a bit."

"You really, really don't. You never have to apologize for something somebody else does. And anyway, if that's how he talks to your grandfather, he's a bit of a dick, isn't he? You definitely don't apologize for other people when they're being dicks."

Hal chokes back a laugh. "He's like that pretty much all the time."

"Then he's obviously a full-time dick." I scoop up a napkin, crumpled and dropped by the side of the sofa, sticking it in my pocket.

He tugs at his hair and lets out a growl of frustration. "I just didn't want you to see all that. The Waverley family drama, you know? It's not…it's not what I want to be. I try not to be… Like him, I mean." Running out of words, his eyes search for mine and lock onto them like a lifebelt.

"I know." I slip my hand into his. His fingers close so tightly around mine that pins and needles prick my fingertips. "I like your grandfather, though."

"You do?" He visibly brightens.

"You can tell the two of you are related."

"Everyone always says that. I don't get it," he says, shrugging. "We don't look that similar, do we? Please say no," he adds in a whisper.

"Not like that. But there's something. It's hard to explain. It's just that, seeing the two of you sitting together, you sort of...*go*. Does that make sense?"

It makes no sense. But it's what I mean – that there's something about them that matches. Inside.

"I think so. Like you and your brother. You look alike."

"We do? That's unfortunate for one of us."

"I didn't... You have the same nose, is what I meant. Same eyes."

"Luckily for him, we've got different brains, though."

"Sorry?" Hal frowns, confused.

"Nothing."

I can't believe I said that. Of *all* the things I could have said...

"Come on. We should get up to the attic. Albie's waiting – and didn't you say you wanted to tell Pa the whole story?"

But as we head for the attic, all I can hear is ticking. In my head, a clock has started counting down the hours until he has to leave.

* * *

"Do you recognize this writing? I don't think we've seen it before."

Hal slides the letter he's reading across to me. It definitely looks different from any of the other pages we've read – where Albie's writing is heavy and looping, Iris's is sharper and more hesitant, but this is something new. It's narrow and the loops are thinner, the letters taller, and it's written in pencil pressed heavily into the paper. All the other letters have been in ink.

"Where was it?" I start scanning the first couple of lines. It's not like there are many places it could have come from – the stack is so small now that I can practically count the sheets from here.

"It was just in there with the rest."

He shifts in his spot on the floor, waiting for me to read. Halfway down the page, I look up – and he's watching me. Still waiting.

"You've read it?"

He nods.

"And?"

His eyes flick down to the floor.

He stopped seeming himself, you see. At first, we thought he were tired – time's a funny thing here, and no matter how much a man sleeps (if he _can_ sleep) he's still as bone-tired when he opens his eyes as he were when he shut 'em. But with the Lieutenant, there's something as isn't right. Most times, he stares into the wall or the mud. Rats have run right over his boots and all he does is stare at them. Sometimes he talks about the birds at home, to himself, over and over. That worsened after he were trapped in a shell hole. The man with him - you'll know it now, Charlie Brewer - took a bad hit, and he were a goner. The Lieutenant were there the whole time, held his hand, talked to him about the swifts because he knew he loved 'em. He were pinned down by guns and shellfire, in there with Charlie's body for two days, half-dead himself. When they found him, scouts tried to make him come away, and he said he wouldn't. Not until they brought a stretcher to bring Charlie back to our trenches. The Lieutenant wouldn't leave him, not even for himself.

I suppose you'd be wondering why I'd tell you that, seeing as we've never met more'n to pass the time of day. Or why I'd wait to write you till now when I'm back, and not send straightaways from France. It's like this: they read our letters home you see, over there. Some of the men say it's because of spying, but more of us think it's because they don't want everyone to know what it's really like. Once this war is over, I can't think of a single man who's seen it who will ever want to speak of it again. George said they call it the war to end all wars, and by Christ (if you'll pardon me) I hope that's so.

But you need to know - knowing as I do about you and the Lieutenant - that he's not in his right mind. Not since

Charlie. It's what we call the collywobbles. And I don't want to fright you - he's not so bad that he won't follow orders, they can't court-martial him just yet - but I've seen it happen a dozen times already. I know it's hard with your place, but the family need to know, and I can't tell them. Maybe you can get word to someone in the house, someone they would give an ear to? Tell them Master Albie is the bravest Lieutenant we have on the whole of the Western Front and not a soul would doubt it, but the war has cracked something inside him. There's no shame in it, no weakness. The opposite, to tell the truth. It's just that he's our Lieutenant, and he's been looking out for us since the minute we got on the boat at Southampton, and now it's our turn to look out for him, as it were.

    You've a fine man in Albie Holmwood, Iris. And God willing, he'll be home with you soon.

    Dougie Marton.

"That's the Dougie Marton in Albie's letter, isn't it? From the village. He said he got…what was it?"

Hal screws his eyes shut, trying to remember. "A Blighty. I looked it up – it was what they called it when they had to be sent home for treatment."

"So now he's home – and he sent this?" I pat the letter. "What does it mean?"

"I think it means Albie's got shell shock."

"That's like PTSD, isn't it? There was something about

it at Fallowmill," I add, before he can ask any questions.

"Lots of soldiers suffered from it, especially at the Somme." He fumbles his phone out of his pocket and taps something into the browser. "There's more about it here." He holds it out to me, but I already know what it's going to tell me. A deep breath – and then the bomb I knew was coming. "Albie had a mental breakdown." He sighs.

The bars across the windows, the locks on the doors at Fallowmill flash before my eyes.

Locks and bars. Barbed wire and trenches. No war as complete and no prison as secure as your own mind. Nowhere harder to escape from. And whatever happened to him after that, he never came home.

We already know how the story ends.

Twenty-two

There are only two pieces of paper left. That's it. Nothing else left in the attic is from the same period. Hal has carefully noted it all down and retied the strings that held the stacks and bundles together as we found them. The last two pages sit there in front of the crates, face down.

I press a finger into the middle of the knot Hal's tying. "What happens now?"

"I don't know. We pack them back up, I guess. And they stay here."

"You're just going to leave them here?"

I only realize I'm not actually talking about the letters after I've said it.

"I can't take them with me. What am I going to do with them?"

Maybe I wasn't talking about the letters, but I really, really hope he is.

"And anyway, they probably belong to somebody. Albie's family – or the hotel."

Relief washes over me. He did mean the letters.

Relief…and hope.

"Maybe that could be the next thing. We could try and track them down? His family, I mean."

There has to be something I can suggest. Anything that gives us more time.

Anything for there to be a future. It doesn't even matter what it is.

I don't think he's listening, but I try anyway. "Maybe there are hospital records somewhere. Maybe he…"

Maybe what? He ended up somewhere like Fallowmill after all?

You've seen those bars. If that's what happened to him, would you really want to know?

"Hmm, what?" Hal looks up from scribbling something in his notebook.

"Oh, nothing. Just an idea, but it doesn't matter."

"Sure?"

"Yeah, it's fine."

I eyeball the pages. They look so innocent while we can't see what's written on them.

All right, Year Eleven. Settle down. You have exactly one and a half hours, and you may turn your exam papers over… now.

Out of the corner of my eye, I'm sure I can see something

fluttering. Sheets of paper, thrown up in the air and falling again.

Falling...

He takes a deep breath. "I guess this is it. Are you ready?"

Ready to find out what happened, or to let go?

"Are you?"

"No. Yes. Fnnnph." He makes a sad noise in the back of his throat. "It's just...I've been doing this for so long, planning it, researching it...I'm not sure what I'll do now."

He's lying. He knows, and – just like me – he doesn't want to face it.

Just like me, he's afraid of it. But here we are.

"Okay." He draws his shoulders up almost to his ears, then lets out a long, long sigh. "Okay."

He stretches towards the pieces of paper – then stops. His hand reaches for me, and his fingers curl through mine and hold them tightly.

"Together," he says.

And I don't know whether it's because he can't do it on his own, or because he doesn't want to, but we turn the page together.

The handwriting is neat and clear – but smudged in places.

"It's from a nurse," he says. "Look, it's signed Sister something. Alice? Agnes?"

"Agnes, I think. Why's a nurse writing to Iris?"

"It wouldn't be to Iris, remember. Too risky." The top's

too smudgy to read. "I reckon it must be to Albie's family."

My heart crawls up into my mouth. "He's not…? Is he?" I can't bear to look.

Hal's eyes skim down to the end of the page and straight back to the top again, reading and rereading, trying to see past the smudges and gaps.

"No," he says after an eternity. "He's in hospital. Kind of. A 'casualty clearing station', they call it. See here?" He points at a line I can't even read. His finger shakes. "Lieutenant Albert Holmwood…damage to the lungs and neurasthenic breakdown."

"What's that?"

"It's what they called shell shock when officers had it. It was on that site I pulled up…" He starts to fumble for his phone. "You want to read it?"

I shake my head. "I really don't."

"It looks like Dougie was right when he said in his letter Albie wasn't doing so well."

"But what's the thing about his lungs?" I squint at the page, trying to make anything else out, but it might as well be written in German.

Hal shakes his head sadly. "Gas."

"Gas?" A foggy memory of an English lesson one rainy afternoon a lifetime ago swims up through my mind – a poem about coughing and masks and a gas attack. A war poem. He must have been caught in a gas attack.

Hal frowns at the page. "Hang on."

"What?"

"This says…" He gulps and looks up at me again, his eyes locking onto mine. "This says they're going to send him home as soon as he's able to travel."

"It can't!"

"It does – right here." He bangs his fingertip down on the paper so hard that he almost tears it. "See?"

I can't see it – not at all. Maybe it's because the paper's too old, too fragile, too smudgy…or maybe it's me. Maybe my mind's too fogged up to focus. Maybe my eyes are. I don't know.

I reach for the last page. It's a hundred miles away and it's right in front of me. It's a hundred years ago and it's now.

All the colour drains from Hal's face as his hand moves in slow motion, reaching for me, for the last piece of the puzzle, for the past.

"Together."

We turn the page over, and somewhere very far away and very near all at once, a bell rings.

It's a simple scrap of pinkish paper, yellowed by time. A telegram, sent all the way from August 1916. Some of the words are missing where the typed message strips have fallen off and been lost.

The missing words don't change the story.

```
Deeply regret…LT. Al…Holmwood…recently…
injuries rec'd…shell attack on casualty
```

`clearing station…missing.`
`Presumed dead.`

Albie never made it home.

All the air is sucked from the room. I hear it go with a loud hiss, carrying something I'd only just found away with it. Hal's lips are moving, but no sound comes out. Shadows press in on the edges of the world, on the edges of my vision, and everything starts to blur.

It's over. Everything. It's *over*.

"I…I need…I just need…"

My heart thuds against my ribs so hard I'm afraid it'll shatter them.

"I'll…I'm going to…" The words stick to the roof of my mouth, to my tongue. They clog up my throat. The air in here is choking me and I have to get out. I have to. If I don't, I'll suffocate. "I have to go. Sorry. I have to."

I do what I do best.

I run away.

I move feet that feel like they belong to someone else; move them towards the door, towards the stairs and down. Down and down and out…the corridors blurring, everything blurring…and then I'm outside on the front drive, the air clean in my lungs…and even then I can't stop. I keep going, round the hotel and past the terrace, through the gardens and out, down, further and further until I reach the glasshouse. Gravel ricochets off the glass as I pull the door open. The air inside is humid and warm. Soft. Safe.

"Charlie?" My voice is swallowed by the benches full of tiny plants. "Charlie!"

There's no answer, but a noise from the far end of the space, in a sheltered corner behind tall plant support frames, means someone's there.

"Charlie? Is that you?"

I thread between the benches full of delicate plants, eyes on the corner, trying not to run.

"Charlie!"

Suddenly he sticks his head out from behind a frame, a piece of string between his teeth and a pair of earphones around his neck. I'm so close that I almost crash into him. He twitches as I swerve, only just missing the tomato plants he's tying to the supports.

He picks the string out from between his teeth and drapes it over the end of a frame. "Bloody hell, Flora. You nearly gave me a heart attack. What's the matter?"

My head is pounding, my heart is pounding, my mind and body are screaming at me to run away as fast as I can and to drop to the ground with my arms around my head all at once. The air is too thin and too thick and I can't get enough of it into my lungs, and I *can't*.

"Okay. Okay. You're okay. You're okay." My brother's hands press on my shoulders, rooting me to the spot.

"You're having a panic attack. Breathe."

How can something as simple as breathing suddenly be so hard? It's *breathing*. But I can't remember how to do it – at least, not right. The air comes in gasps and hiccups and black spots prickle across my vision.

"Listen to me, Flora. You're safe. You've done this before. You know what it is. Don't fight it – let it pass."

But all I want to do is fight. How can I not?

Charlie's voice is low and soft. "Listen to my voice. Can you hear me? What else can you hear? The birds outside? Hear them?"

Somewhere, very far away, the swifts are screeching mid-flight.

When swifts die, they fall; one moment freewheeling, crashing to earth the next.

High to nothing in a heartbeat.

Do they know they're falling, or are they just…gone?

I shake my head, hard. Charlie's grip on my shoulders tightens.

"Stop. Flora. Stop. You can do this. You're safe. I promise you're safe. You're in the glasshouse, with me – can you smell the tomato leaves? And where the soil's damp from the watering pipe?"

Slowly, slowly, the world comes back into focus. The air becomes itself again, neither thick nor thin but just plain old boring air, and the horror behind my eyes fades into the dark.

I can smell the tomatoes. I can smell the wet earth. I can hear the birds wheeling above, chattering outside. I can feel Charlie's hands on my shoulders, and slowly, slowly, the pressure inside my skull eases away to nothing.

"See? You're okay. It was just a panic attack. That's all." He bends his knees a little, drops his face level with mine. "Better?"

I nod, because I can't put the words together. I just had a panic attack.

In front of Hal.

I couldn't stop it; I didn't even see it coming. One minute I was fine, the next I thought I was going to *die*.

I lean into my brother's shoulder. It feels reassuringly solid and real as another tidal wave of panic crashes over me.

"Can you take me home?"

Twenty-three

Albie is dead, but he still follows me into my sleep, along with his letters. His words so full of both love and fear at once. And…what did Dougie call it? "The collywobbles"?

There's no shame in it, no weakness. The opposite, to tell the truth.

Is that really true? Maybe it was for Albie, after everything he went through. But what about me? What excuse do I have?

I am not Albie Holmwood. He is not Flora Sutherland. His life and mine couldn't be more different, and even if we had somehow found ourselves in the same time and the same world, we would never have met… *But…*

My heart hurts for him.

Our last session; me sitting in the plastic chair like always, Sanjay sitting in the cushioned chair next to his desk, his notepad on his lap.

"What if I get bad again? How will I know?"

"You might not."

"I might not. So I might completely freak out at any point and there's no warning, no anything?"

"The brain doesn't work like that, Flora."

"But you just said…"

"I just said you might not know. A condition like yours can be unpredictable. You might go years without having another manic episode, or another depressive one – you might never have one again. Or it could be a regular repeating cycle. Until we're further down the line, there's no way to be sure – and you might not be in a position to recognize it until afterwards. That's why it's important you have this."

He hands me a folder. It contains only one page, printed in clear black ink on soft yellow paper. A checklist, with tick boxes alongside it. My name at the top, followed by a question.

Are you experiencing (or have you recently experienced) any of the following symptoms?

And there they all are, in black-and-white – or black-and-yellow, anyway.

Racing thoughts, heightened senses, seeing things, hearing things, talking too fast, panic attacks, flights of ideas and disorganized thinking.

Tick, tick, ticky ticky tick.

A score of several positive responses, experienced continuously over a period of time, may indicate the onset of a bipolar episode. Please advise your next of kin as

315

discussed in your relapse-prevention plan, and arrange an appointment with your mental health professional as soon as possible.

"So this is it? For ever? I have this…thing, and it could just jump up and bite me whenever it feels like it?" I wave the sheet at him.

Sanjay half-smiles. "That's a very negative mindset, Flora. We've talked about that."

"Well, this doesn't look very bloody positive, does it?" I roll my eyes…then, seeing his raised eyebrow, add a muttered, *"Sorry."*

"There's always the chance of relapse, but there's also the possibility of what I call a reactive episode. Not a relapse as such, but…think of it as an echo, if you like, of this. A ghost."

"And if I get one of those?"

"Then we'll deal with it if and when it comes."

"If I know it's happened," I grumble, sticking the sheet back in the folder.

"You should have a little more faith in yourself, Flora, and in the people around you. Your brother, his partner, your friends… All of them are there for you, but you have to let them in. You have to be honest with them. Even if you can't see clearly, they can."

What did Iris think when she read those letters, saw him coming apart through his words, just the same as we have?

I love you. I am yours – all that is left of me at the end of this is yours. All that I ever was or will be or might have been.

When he talks about coming back, he doesn't just mean from France.

He knew.

He knew he was coming undone.

Would he ever have recovered from the shell shock? Or would he have faced a future somewhere like Fallowmill; almost able to see his home through the bars on the windows? So near to normal, but so far away from it?

How would he have lived, if he'd lived?

Albie is dead, but I can feel him in my head and under my skin anyway. He walks through my mind – officer's cap pushed back on his head and trailing the smell of smoke and cordite – and wherever he walks the world flashes white and black. He leads me through the woods, through the deer park and through the open doors of Hopwood – but where the lobby should be is a huge and empty landscape, a road stretching ahead of me and, on either side of it, two different worlds. One is dark, the trees all black and twisted, bent double as though weighed down by the heavy black sky. The other is bright, so bright that looking at it almost blinds me. Someone calls my name, first from the dark and then from the light, and they call me over and over until the sound hammers on my brain and makes my ears bleed…and even though I start running, however hard and fast I run I can't outrun the voice because

317

it's my own. Both of my siren-sides screaming at me to come to them, to step off the road as it gets narrower, narrower, narrower…

And at the point when I can't run any more, when the voices – my own voice, echoing through every piece of me – are too much, the road snaps up in front of me, up and up until it blots out the sky; it folds around me, blocking every possible escape…and I am in the attic. The attic at Hopwood, but there's nobody here and the space is bare. The door is open, but as I run for it, knowing with all my heart that I have to get out, it slams, and there's the terrible grinding sound of a key turning for ever in a lock. I try the handle, I kick at the door – but there isn't a door there now, and there never was. It's just a wall.

I run to the window and reach it just as the bars slam down across it. In the gardens below, I can see my friends, my family, *myself*, all looking up at the attic. At me. And one by one they turn and walk away…and I am alone.

You have to let them in. You have to be honest with them.

When I wake to the sound of swifts and the touch of gold-yellow sunlight filling my room, my bed sheets soaked in sweat and tangled around me, I know it with absolute certainty.

I have to tell Hal. Today. Before he leaves.

What do I have to lose?

Except my mind. Same as usual.

I can't keep running from this part of me, locking it away. I have to take hold of it before it takes hold of me. I keep my own keys.

Albie didn't have a choice. He didn't have a chance. It happened *to* him.

This *is* me. Part of me. I can't cut it out or wash it away.

I have to live with it. I can manage it, sure, but it's not going anywhere soon.

I might as well get used to living with *all* of me.

There's a knock on my bedroom door and, as usual, Charlie opens it and walks straight in before I can answer, carrying a steaming mug. He seems to think of knocking as more of a last-second warning that he's coming in, rather than a way of checking it's okay.

I pull my sheets up over my head.

"You're awake," he says, and I can hear him putting the mug on my bedside table. "How are you feeling?"

"Nggggh." My mouth feels like someone wiped it with an old sock – a side-effect of the sedative I took after Charlie had to half-carry me through the front door, when I couldn't stop shaking and couldn't stop crying and I couldn't shut the floodgates that had opened somewhere in between my head and my heart and let everything I've been trying to keep safely locked inside *out*. All the life I could have had, and all the fear I *have* had. All the times

319

I've made myself step back, stay small and safe...

Who decides what safe is?

I do.

"Here's your phone, by the way. I had to come in and take it after you went to sleep – it kept buzzing."

I yank the sheet down from my face.

"What?"

"Here." Charlie holds my phone out, and it's all I can do not to snatch it from him. "We were worried it would wake you up." He picks the mug back up again and hands it to me. I take it, and put it straight back on the table, cupping my phone – the same phone that for so long has made me feel even more alone. No messages, no calls. Nothing.

And now...this.

Missed calls, texts, messages...

So many of them.

Hal, over and over again.

Mira.

Are you OK? Hal said you ran off – he's looking for you. Call me?

Hal again. And again. And then:

I'm coming over.

Charlie watches me scrolling through them, one after another, and nods.

"You were asleep. I told them you weren't feeling well. Mira understood."

"You didn't tell Hal about me...?"

"No! It's not up to me to tell him. But you should."

"I know." I drop my phone onto the bed next to me. "I'm going to – this morning."

"Good idea." He taps both his hands on his knees. "You can come right down."

"Sorry?"

"He's waiting downstairs."

"He's downstairs?"

"Yes, Flora."

"Here?"

"Yes, Flora."

"Now?"

"Shall I just write it on a piece of paper and hold it up for you? It'll save us all a lot of time…"

"No. No no nonononono…" I fight my way out from the tangle of my bed. "He can't be here. Not now! I don't know what to say, how to… He can't see me like…"

I run a hand back through my hair. It feels like a bad night's sleep. In the mirror, my face manages to be both pale *and* flushed at once, which is an achievement. The whole look is finished off beautifully by dark purple shadows under my eyes. I sigh at my brother. "This is not how I'm supposed to look for this." I grab a hairbrush and start forcing it through the tangled mess on top of my head.

"Look for what?"

"I mean, I actually *look* like a crazy person. If you were going to ask someone, 'Hey, what does a crazy person look

like?' they would point to this." I wave the hairbrush at…
well, all of me, really. "I can't tell him looking like this."

"Mmmm."

"What does that mean? You don't think I should?"

"I absolutely think you should. You can be quite a…"

"Quite a *what*, Charlie?"

In the mirror, his reflection chooses his words carefully.
"Challenge. I was going to say, challenge."

"Right."

"It's not always easy to live with, you know. So yes, if you
think he's…going to be around for a while…then he should
know what he's getting into."

I stare at him in the mirror. "But he's leaving. He's *not*
going to be around at all, is he?"

"There's leaving, and there's *leaving*," says my utterly
infuriating brother.

"But his dad, and…" I run out of oxygen. The tiny flame
flickering in my heart has used it all up, burning brighter
by the second. "I'll never see him again after this."

Charlie mutters something under his breath, something
I don't quite catch. It could be "I doubt that", but maybe
that's just what I want to hear.

Either way, as he picks up my slightly crumpled (but
mostly clean) hoodie from the floor and hands it to me, he
looks at me kindly. "Well, if that's true, you don't have
anything to lose, do you?"

He turns to go.

"Charlie!"

My brother stops when I call him and looks back around.

"What if…" I drop my voice to a whisper – the house is small and Hal is right downstairs. "What if he really does just think I'm crazy? Properly crazy." I wait for Charlie to say something comforting. He doesn't. "*Does* he think I'm crazy?"

"He thinks you're you. Whatever label you go and stick on yourself." Charlie moves back towards the door – but before he walks out of it, he turns back with one last parting shot. "Does it occur to you that he might actually *like* you for who that is?"

The stairs creak under his feet as he goes back down, leaving me alone with that thought.

I've been so afraid that Hal would see the parts of me that I try to hide from the world, the parts I try to brush over and camouflage, the imperfections I can never change or mend – but maybe he saw them anyway. Maybe he just saw them as being part of the grand Flora experience and… maybe he didn't think it was weird. Maybe to him, it's just…me.

He might actually like you for who that is…

I guess there's only one way to find out.

Taking one last (hopeless) look in the mirror, I venture out onto the landing, pulling my hood close around my neck.

It's not that I'm cold, exactly – the weather's too warm for that – but I feel somehow exposed, like a layer of skin has been peeled away. When I peer around the banister at the top of the stairs, I can only see the top of his head, his hair glinting copper in the front room as he talks to Felix about something. Their voices are too low for me to hear anything more than a soft mumble – of course, they're talking quietly so they don't disturb me, aren't they? Charlie's gone out through the kitchen, and there's a clattering sound from beyond the back door. There's birdsong and sunshine out there, and somehow that makes it feel like completely the wrong day to talk about a nervous breakdown.

It's never the right day to talk about a nervous breakdown. And anyway, we're not talking about a nervous breakdown. We're talking about me.

I look at the back of Hal's head, nodding at something Felix has said.

Me. A walking, talking nervous breakdown.

An overfull ford that floods the engine, and my brother has come and towed me out.

He thinks you're you.

He might actually like you for who that is…

I lean further out, putting too much weight on the rail, and it squeaks. Below me on the sofa, Felix's head moves just a little, because he recognizes the sound even if Hal doesn't. There's a pause, then he says something to Hal before getting up and pushing his sleeves to his elbows. He makes it to the front door, which is already standing open to let in the warm air from outside, before he glances back across the room and up at the top of the stairs. At me.

And just before he steps out through the door, he winks.

I step down onto the next stair, hoping it will creak and Hal will know I'm there, and I won't have to announce myself – but just for once, the stairs are completely silent. So I give up and clear my throat quietly.

"Hal?"

He turns and sees me.

What does he see? Who?

His face lights up and he jumps to his feet, almost tripping over Felix's stacked tool catalogues as he tries to edge around the sofa, his eyes never leaving me.

"You're up!"

"Charlie says you've been waiting." I pick at an imaginary scratch on the banister with my fingernail. "You didn't have to…"

"I wanted to make sure you were okay. I was worried."

"Worried? About me?"

"Well, yeah. That Albie…that what we'd read had upset you. Or maybe it was about the party, or…"

He stops again and runs a hand through his hair, brushing it out of his eyes. His cheeks, meanwhile, turn a furious shade of red. Hal has absolutely no filter when it comes to his feelings – or does he? Because when I remember how he stared down his father, remember the way Hal slapped his hand away, I wonder whether that's strictly true.

Maybe it's just when it comes to his feelings for *me*...?

"It's not about you going," I mumble, and a frown flickers across his forehead. Just for a second.

"Oh. Right. Well, good. That's good. I'm..." He shakes his head and lets out something like a growl. "But, you know, way to make a guy feel *special*."

"I mean, it is, yes, obviously it's that too, but...there's more to it than that." I stop picking at the banister. "It's complicated."

The stairs have never felt so long, so steep. There are so many things I need to say, but all I want to do is feel his arms wrap around me and to rest my head on his shoulder.

The clattering outside the back door gets louder. Charlie starts singing what I think might be a song from *Moana*, louder than he probably means to. I cannot have this conversation to a soundtrack of Disney classics – least of all one performed by my big brother.

"Sorry. It's his favourite. Do you maybe want to come up?" I jerk my head back towards my room.

Through the kitchen, Charlie goes for a high note and misses by a full nautical mile.

"I'll come up," says Hal.

Whatever he thinks when he walks into my room, Hal's face carefully doesn't show any of it. I see him take in the open window – the mirror of the one in the attic, now I think about it, facing back towards the house – and the beams. The wonky walls with their old white paint and my battered posters. The narrow bed with its white metal frame, tucked under the eaves; the beams that criss-cross the ceiling. I spot the small heap of clothes next to my wardrobe – the ones that haven't made it to the laundry basket yet – and wonder whether I can somehow position myself in front of it, or steer him around the room so he can't see it… And right in the middle of me thinking all this, his eyes sweep across the room and he looks right at my dress from the party, its hanger hooked over a nail that sticks out of one of the beams.

"You have no idea how amazing you looked in that," he says quietly. It hangs there, silently. It almost feels like I'm standing in the room with my own ghost – the ghost of the me I *could* be. If I let myself.

You can't tell him. He won't understand. He'll think you're crazy.

What if all this being determined to tell him, to be "you" is wrong? What if you're just going manic again? You're not brave, remember. You're just mental.

I take a deep breath and, with every fibre of my being, tell my brain to shut. The. Hell. Up.

Just for once, it listens.

Hal, oblivious (thankfully) to everything going on in my head while I try to guess what's going on in his, has sat down on the edge of my bed.

327

"Do you want to talk about it?" he says, his head lowered, looking up at me from behind his fringe.

"Not really." I lean back against the window sill. "But I probably need to."

I'm not sure there's a breath in the world deep enough, a moment long enough for me to be ready. But maybe being ready – waiting to be perfect, waiting for the moment to be perfect – is overrated.

Everything is imperfect. Everyone. That's nothing to be ashamed of or afraid of – it just *is*.

And if I'm imperfect, just like everybody else, what does that make me?

Normal. It makes me *normal*.

And when they have something to say, normal people just…talk. So I talk.

"Yesterday, in the attic, I had a panic attack."

"I figured. Not that it was that, exactly, but that there was, you know, something." There's no question in his voice. No surprise, no judgement, no nothing. Just Hal.

"And at the party, when I kind of…ran out of there too? And you came looking for me?"

I have to stop running away.

"You had one then?"

"No. Yes. I thought I was going to – or not exactly, but…" I stop, and rub my hands over my face, hard. This is so much more difficult than I was hoping, and there's just no easy way to do it.

I should just say it.

Keep my own keys. Open the doors, take down the bars.

"Okay. So. I have a thing. In my head. You've probably noticed."

Doing great so far, Flora.

Why, thank you, Flora.

"And the thing in my head…it's…it makes me act… weird. Sometimes. Not all the time. It's a condition. You know? It's. Umm. It's just…" I stop and look at him, as though that's going to help. "Are you with me so far?"

He looks about as puzzled as I'd expect. "Maybe?"

"I should start at the beginning. I was at school and there was…an incident."

"An incident."

"Yes."

"What kind of incident?"

Papers thrown in the air, fluttering down around me.

Head pounding, heart racing.

Letters, stories…

Sweat-soaked school shirt.

Exam papers.

Answer papers. Show your workings, five marks, ten marks, twenty marks.

Someone shouting. Running footsteps.

Paper fluttering like wings as it falls.

And nothing.

"I had an episode at school, during the exams. I…messed

things up. Not just for me, but for other people. The doctor said it was probably brought on by stress; that maybe it – my condition – had been there all along, and it had just never shown up before. People usually get their first…" I try and think of another word, but there really isn't one. "…episode somewhere in their teens. And with the stress of the exams…" I hold up my hands weakly. "Ta-da."

"What happened?"

"Oh, everyone got their grades adjusted because of 'a disturbance in the exam room'. It was fine in the end – for them, anyway. They got better grades *and* a story to tell."

"I meant, what about you?"

"I became the story." I drum on the window sill – and then stop, because this is exactly the kind of thing that makes people think I'm weird, isn't it? Tuning out, skipping around the conversation. Moving on too fast.

"You haven't gone back?"

"I couldn't. I mean, they would have let me, but *I* couldn't. Would you want to go back for resits, knowing everyone would be remembering the last time they saw you? What you did? Making jokes about how you were completely loopy?"

"Didn't your friends stick up for you?"

Did they put her in one of those padded rooms?

"Friends?" I don't want it to sound bitter, so I pick my words carefully. "It's funny how quickly people forget that they ever knew you when they think you're mad."

He frowns, but it's a different kind of frown to the one I've seen before. It's a sad frown. "So you left?"

"I came here and started doing this." I shrug. "I started doing a hospitality apprenticeship, so I didn't have to go back. Charlie was already here, and I started working with Mira, and she was really cool – she *is* really cool. And she and Barney knew, because Charlie had warned them about his loopy little sister…and they never cared." I drop onto the side of the bed next to him – and it's only when I've been sitting there for a moment that I realize I'm waiting for him to move, to flinch or edge away. He doesn't. All he does is look at his knees.

It feels like hours before he speaks. Days, even. A hundred years have passed and I'm still waiting for him to say something – anything. To get up and leave, to look at me differently…

I'm not sure which would be worse.

"You didn't have to keep it secret, you know. You could have said something." His voice is warm and soft, and I want to climb into it. It feels safe there. I pull the edge of my blanket up from my bed and around my shoulders instead – it feels like the next best thing.

"It's not the kind of thing you usually tell people you've only just met. 'Hi, I'm Flora – oh, and by the way, I'm mad.'"

"You could have told me." His eyes suddenly lift up from staring at his knees and move to my face, searching it – for what? "You know, like Albie was saying Iris made him promise to always tell her the truth?"

"That was different." The blanket slips, and I tug it a little more closely around my shoulders. "And this isn't the kind of thing you just *say* to someone you like."

"What, in case you scare them off?" He laughs.

"Maybe," I say quietly, and he stops laughing. He looks at me – really looks at me – for a minute, and then he reaches for the edge of the blanket closest to him, peels it back and wraps it over his shoulders too. We sit there, side by side, the blanket across our backs like a shield.

"Do you have to take any medication?"

"I did, for a bit. To start with." I shrug. "I've been off it a while now, though. I wanted to try and manage without, if I can. And then I know that if I need it – if I get...bad again, it's there. But nothing's guaranteed. I just have to try and work at it. All the time."

"It sounds lonely," he says.

"It is." A loose thread tickles the side of my leg, and I pull it away, stretching it out between my fingers and twisting it until it doubles back on itself over and over again, knotting into a tiny ball. I drop it on the floor. "You know why it's called bipolar disorder?" I can't look at him. I can't. If I look at him, I won't say it. It feels like I'm peeling back the lid of my heart and letting someone else see inside, see all my secrets and my fears – the sharp edges that cut; the cold little black ball, no bigger than the ball of thread

I just dropped, that I carry around with me all the time. "It's because if I was a compass, there'd be no east and no west. No sunrise or sunset. Just me, in the dark, with my needle spinning from pole to pole. And both poles are just as hostile, and both poles can kill you."

He doesn't say anything. There isn't much to say, is there?

So I carry on.

"It's like, you know how people say nobody ever died from sadness? It's not true. People do die from it. It eats them up from the inside and there's just the shell of them left – whatever armour they covered themselves with, however thick a skin they grew, that's all there is. It hurts all the time, and they just want it to stop. And it doesn't matter whether you call it depression or something else – it all means the same thing, and that's what it does to you."

I take a deep breath, and now it isn't just Hal waiting – it's the room, the house, the *world*. Waiting for me to say the things I've never said before – not to Charlie, not to Sanjay, not even to myself, late at night when my thoughts have been racing and my mind has been raging and I've wondered if it's possible to die of thinking too fast and too much.

"And then there's the other bit. You know how sometimes you hear a song, and it's a song you love and it makes you want to jump up and dance, and you feel like if you don't, you'll just explode? It's that feeling. That's what I mean.

333

The kind where you think you can do *anything*. Like you're somehow invincible. Except you forget that you're not *actually* invincible. Most of the time, it's fine – the world's just that little bit more in focus, a bit brighter. But then, sometimes…"

I know he's trying to follow. I know he wants to and I know he's listening – but how can I make what's inside my head make sense to him when it barely does to *me* half the time?

"I'm not explaining it properly. I'm sorry. It's hard. How about this? There was a girl in the waiting room at my therapist's office. She was there to see one of the other therapists every week, just the same time as me, and sometimes we'd talk. She had this scar, all the way down here." I trace my finger down the side of his chest, from just below his shoulder, halfway down to his hip and back up again. "When she had a manic episode, she'd stabbed herself in the heart – or tried to. The scar was from the surgery to save her. She didn't know why she did it, and she didn't even remember doing it. She was doing okay when I met her. She was nice. I liked her. But she had this scar to remind her, every day, that she can't always trust her own mind. And I'm scared – all the time – that the same thing could happen to me one day. That my mind could do that too, and that I wouldn't even know. Because you don't. I'm fine most of the time, but how would I know if I wasn't? All the time, I'm between those two places, with both of them pulling me in different directions, and me just trying to stay where I am. *Who* I am."

My finger is still pressed against his chest, and gently – the way someone might handle dynamite – he closes his hand around mine and holds it in his.

And that's just it. I don't want to be treated like I might explode at any moment, leaving everyone around me broken too. I don't want him to be *careful*. I don't want him to look at me and see someone who mustn't be shaken or jarred, who mustn't be upset. I want him to see *me*.

"I didn't say anything before because…well, because I didn't want you to see *that* and not me. I thought I was fine, and I didn't want it to be an issue."

"It isn't," he says quietly. His eyes seem sad, and there are things under his voice, things he's not saying. I guess he wants to let me say all mine first.

"It is. It becomes an 'issue'. I become an 'issue'. And I'm not an issue. Issues don't have dreams or things they're scared of. Or dirty laundry on their floor or, you know, a *life*."

He squeezes my hand, just once, and lets go, slipping out from under the blanket and walking over to the window; leaning on the sill, his back to me, he stares out at the park, the gardens, all the way to the house.

"It was Albie's letters, wasn't it? I knew they bothered you. I should have asked or said something."

"Why? You didn't know. It was my head, not yours."

335

"But that's what it was, right? It was the stuff about shell shock?"

"A bit. But it's more than that. It's bigger."

Bigger. Darker. Scarier.

More complicated.

But for once, it's not just black-and-white – it's a hundred different kinds of grey.

"I'm sorry," he says, and his voice is thicker than usual, and he has to stop and clear his throat. "I'm sorry," he says again, "that you have to deal with all that." He turns around to face the room, face me, and his cheeks are flushed. "And I'm sorry that you have to live with it…" The red in his cheeks deepens by three shades. "But if you…I mean, I…aaagggh." He groans, and runs his hands back through his hair. "You don't have to deal with it by yourself, is what I'm saying."

But before I can say anything, his expression shifts. Something in his face changes, first to confusion…then to complete amazement as he stares at a spot on the sloping ceiling.

"Flora."

"What?"

"Flora, come here."

"What?"

"Come *here*!" He waves an arm at me, and I untangle myself from the folds of blanket.

"What? Is there a spider? Because I hate to break it to you, but I always get Mira to—"

He turns me round, then lifts his arm up and around me, pointing to a spot where two beams meet just above our heads. The wood is old and cracked, and covered in scratches and dents and holes made by everyone else who's ever lived here.

"I don't get it…"

But suddenly I do – and the second I see it, I wonder how the hell I ever missed it, because it's *right* there.

They are right there.

The scratches on the beam in my ceiling rearrange themselves, as if by magic, into two pairs of letters. *Initials.*

I spin back around to face Hal so quickly that our faces almost collide.

IC and *AH*.

Iris and Albie.

The letters might as well be written in fire, they blaze out at us so brightly. How have I never seen them before?

They were here. Both of them.

And they have been all along.

Twenty-four

We sit in the dappled shade of the apple tree in the cottage garden, listening to the breeze in the leaves above us. Charlie and Felix have both disappeared, even though I know neither of them are working today. Leaning against the tree, Hal has his head tipped back against the bark, his eyes closed. Stretched out on the grass beside him, I twist my face towards him. "What do we do now?"

He doesn't answer. At first, I don't think he's heard me, but then he opens his eyes and they search for mine. "I don't know."

"At least now you have the whole story to take back to your grandfather." I sit up, brushing bits of grass and leaf out of my hair. Hal smiles and plucks a stray daisy out of it, holding it for me to take.

"It's going to blow his mind," he says. "I can't believe we found him," he adds quietly.

"*You* found him. I just came along for the ride."

He has that look again – the complicated one that I recognize now. The one that's all about how much he loves his grandfather, and how afraid he is.

Love and fear. Funny how often those two seem to go together – like light and dark, sunshine and shadows.

"You're worried that you're going to lose him, aren't you? Pa." I shuffle around so I'm sitting cross-legged, facing him. "He'll still be there – he'll always be there. Nobody ever really goes and nobody's ever completely lost – look at Albie. He's not been around in over a hundred years, but he's here *now*. Because of you."

"Because of Pa." He slips his hand out of mine and rubs the back of it across his eyes. "I really wanted to tell him that Albie had a family. It was the thing Pa always said – he wished he'd asked more questions about that soldier, because then he could have found his family and told them that he was remembered. That he left a mark on the world."

I think of the initials carved into my ceiling, still there after all these years; as much of a memorial as the initials cut into the post in the glasshouse. "He did."

"But there wasn't anything else about Iris. What do you think happened to her?"

"I don't know – maybe there's something else about her somewhere? I guess she wouldn't have stayed, even if the house wasn't sold. Not after that. I mean…would you?"

"What, stay? Knowing he wasn't coming back? Probably not." Hal stares up into the tree as though the answer's hidden up in the leaves. "Maybe she married somebody else."

"I hope so." I peer up into the tree with him. Blue patches flicker through the shifting green. "It'd be kind of sad if she didn't. If she spent her whole life just waiting for Albie, even though she knew he was never coming back."

Overhead, a buzzard soars and the swifts dance, just like they always have.

"You're leaving tomorrow." My voice wobbles, but I don't think he hears.

"I have to. My father was pretty clear on that one."

"I wish you could stay."

"I do too." He sighs. "But this is what he does. He likes to show everyone how much power he's got over them. When I was a kid, he'd remind me that I didn't actually own anything. That everything that was 'mine' was actually his. The clothes I was wearing, my room, my stuff. None of it really belonged to *me*. I used to be afraid that one day he'd turn around and take it all away because I wasn't good enough or smart enough or enough like him. It wasn't about the stuff, you know? It was more that in his eyes – in the world I grew up in – *things* were power. They *are* power. I'd look around my room, or the house, or even in the mirror, and I'd realize that I had nothing – it was all his and he was in control of it all. Including me."

He's showing me inside his heart, the place where he carries all the things he's afraid of. The place where he thinks he'll never be smart enough, brave enough, good enough.

Where he thinks he'll never be *enough*.

He won't meet my gaze, won't look me in the eye, as though he's ashamed. As though saying this somehow makes him weak instead of strong; as though I'll see him differently now.

That, I do know something about.

I shuffle closer, leaning my forehead against his and looking straight at him. "If your father can't see who you are, he's the one missing out. *I* see. And it doesn't matter what he thinks. It doesn't matter what he wants you to be – you're you, and that's enough. *You're* enough. But if you don't believe that, nobody else is going to – so start, okay?"

He blinks, and the world flickers.

All I can hear is his breathing, soft and low and close to me; close enough to feel his breath warm on my lips.

"Besides, there's already one of your dad in the world, and that's plenty. Personally, I'd like there to be more Hal in the world."

Inside me, something aches. Because this can't last. Because he's leaving and, whether I like it or not, I think I need to find my own balance; my own place.

I know I ran away to Hopwood. I can't run away to Hal, however much I want to. And he can't run away here.

I have to go.

Somewhere in my head and my heart, *I have to go*

341

becomes *I have to let go* and I understand what I have to do next.

No safety net. Nothing to catch me if I fall.

Maybe I'll come crashing down to earth, maybe I won't. But I don't have only one chance. I have a whole lifetime.

"Was it worth it?" I ask him, and I'm afraid of every answer he could give.

"Absolutely," he says. Suddenly his eyes are ablaze, and they lock onto mine and hold them, and his hands are in my hair and his lips are on mine… And I close my eyes, because just for now, here, this – *he* – one last time, is enough.

His bags are packed, and the sky is still streaked with flashes of early-dawn purple as we stand on the gravel in front of the Hopwood, waiting for the taxi that will come and take him away.

Away from me.

Neither of us has said it, but neither of us needs to. This is still a goodbye. It can't be anything else, however I look at it. I don't know where I'm going next – all I know is that it's not here. I came to Hopwood because I needed to feel safe. And now…?

I wrap my arms around myself, trying to shake off the early morning chill. There's a dampness in the air that feels like autumn is trying to remind us it's only just around the corner. Far down the sweep of the sloping drive in the distance, there's the sound of a car. Feeling me shiver, Hal slips an arm around me and pulls me closer, one hand rubbing my back and his face nudging against mine.

"You okay?"

"I'll be fine in a minute."

If I pull him close enough, will it slow the car at the gates?

No. Like Sanjay told me once, everything is temporary. Even this.

Somewhere near – far too near – there's the hoot of a car horn.

"It's here," he says, pulling me even closer. "I have to go."

I have to go.

The taxi makes the last turn of the drive, breaking free of the shadows and out onto the sweep of the gravel. Its tyres crunch on the stones, chewing up the last few moments before I have to let Hal go.

He turns to face me, his hands cupping my cheeks in his palms and drawing me to him. His kiss is soft – like he's already pulling away and there's a veil slipping between us. We already said goodbye, already said everything, because we both knew this is how it would feel. And even though I want to hold him here, keep his lips on mine, I let him go.

He has to go.

I have to go.

With one smooth motion, he slides something into my hand and steps away from me – his eyes still on mine – and then he turns and opens the car door, dropping onto the seat along with his bags. The door closes and all I can see in the tinted glass of the window is my own reflection, standing in front of the Hopwood, my hand raised in goodbye.

I look down at the piece of paper pressed into my palm; unfold it once, twice, and open it out...and there it is.

My map.

The map I drew, standing by the road, the very first time we met.

He kept it.

He kept it.

A hair ribbon, a letter, a map.

A way out of the maze.

I watch the car creep forward; watch it turn, watch the rear lights disappear into the shadows of the drive until it's gone. Until he's gone. And when he is, I watch the daylight move across the lawn, watch the lines of the terrace and the gardens form in sharp shadows. I watch until the sun finally edges around the trees and bathes the whole of the front of the hotel in warm golden light – and I stand there, letting it wash over me, soaking in it, until someone whistles from behind me and calls my name.

When I turn around, Philippe is standing by the corner of the building, right by the staff entrance, wearing his checked chef's trousers and white jacket with the neck hanging open.

"You want some breakfast? I need a guinea pig for this brioche I've been working on!"

He doesn't. Philippe can make brioche with his eyes closed and one hand tied behind his back because that's his job – but he's trying to make sure that even when I move out of the sunlight, it stays with me.

"Sure," I say. And with one last look at the emptiness of the drive, I head for the staff entrance, shutting the ache that ripples out from my heart behind a door and turning the last key I have left.

Twenty-five

With Hal gone, the world shifts back to how it was – or at least *almost* how it was. Because even though I'm back on the cleaning shifts with Mira, something is different.

Me.

I'm different.

Or perhaps I'm the same; the same as I was *before*. Before The Incident. Before…everything.

After that morning, when he steered me down the steps and into the noise and life of the kitchens, Philippe and I started to talk a lot more. I mean, that wasn't exactly hard, given how much we *didn't* talk before, but any time I'm on my break and he's around, we actually sit together. He tells me about his family, about growing up in the corner of Brittany in France where he's from, and about how he really wants to ask Libby from the kitchens out but is convinced she'll say no. Other times, he's mostly asking me to test whatever new recipe he's come up with. I don't know why we weren't friends sooner – especially when one day, he tells me how he was diagnosed as bipolar II four years ago.

Mira gets her place on the fashion course, and suddenly she's happier than I've ever seen her. The funny thing is, I'm actually glad – even though it means she's one step closer to leaving. Because even though it took some time, I understand now – that's where she's supposed to be, and like Charlie said, there's leaving and there's *leaving*, and she's only leaving. She'll still be there, because she's Mira. And she's my friend.

As we're getting our stuff from our lockers one afternoon, she whacks my arm with a rolled-up newspaper.

"Ouch! What was that for?" I rub my elbow.

"Page fifteen. In the adverts."

I skim the page – it's mostly ads for part-time jobs, things like leafleting, casual work…except for the one at the very bottom.

"Isn't that the dress shop?"

"It's a sign."

"It's not a sign. It's an advert."

"For a job. Yes. You could do that."

"I couldn't."

"You could – and when you're not working, you could go back to studying."

My mouth drops open. I actually feel it, like I'm in a cartoon.

Mira rolls her eyes. "We all saw you while *he* was here." Like always, she's careful not to call him by name. I'm grateful, because however much I want to be okay without him here, however much I want to be doing this for me, there hasn't been a single day since he left that I haven't thought about him. Every time I knock on the door of room fifteen, part of me hopes he'll answer. I've picked up my phone so many times, almost calling him or messaging him...and it's only at the last second, as I've gone to type his name into the contact box, that I've stopped myself.

But then he hasn't called me either. Of course he hasn't.

It's better that way, right?

Yes. And no. I don't know.

"And what am I supposed to study, wise one?" I ask her, half-laughing as we push through the door into the service corridor.

"History. Obviously." She slides her sunglasses down over her eyes, stepping out of the staff door and onto the drive into the late September sun.

"Oh, *obviously*."

I try to brush it off, but the thought itches inside my brain the whole walk home, like something trying to put down roots. I could, I guess. I mean, it's not like I don't know anything about it...or like I don't have something I want to find.

Some*one*.

Because ever since Hal left, I've been looking for Iris.

348

I've combed through every single case in the attics – even the ones we checked already – looking for the tiniest clue. I started to look for her online…but even trying to register on some of the sites that might help nearly gave me a panic attack. When I emailed the British Library, I could practically hear them laughing at me over the internet. I even went back to Fallowmill. Nothing. So I stood in the grotto while Charlie and Felix walked around the gardens, and I tried to hear her voice, just like I'd heard Albie's in his letters… Still nothing.

I kick the front door of the cottage shut behind me and drop my bag in the corner of the front room. Flattening the newspaper on the makeshift table made of Felix's stacked catalogues, I draw a big red ring around the advert for the vintage shop. I mean, I did like it there. And maybe Mira's right – maybe it is a sign after all.

"Flora?" Charlie's voice sounds wrong. Too far away.

"Yeah – where are you?" I shout back.

"Up in the attic. Hang on…" There's some distant thumping far above my head, and then the clatter of feet on a ladder before he appears at the top of the stairs, brushing dust from his hair.

"Why the hell are you up in the attic?"

Even the word "attic" makes something under my skin shimmer. It makes me think of *him*.

"I need to clear some kit out of the sheds. Thought I might stick it up here for the winter." He rubs at his hair again, and a little grey cloud floats down the stairs. "How was your shift?"

"Yeah, fine. I—" And I stop. Because there's something in the corner of the room that shouldn't be there. Something I haven't seen before. A small suitcase, thick with dust. "What's that?"

He follows my gaze. "I found it up there. Thought you might be interested."

"You found it in our attic?"

"Mmm." He clomps downstairs, shedding cobwebs and dust with every step.

He picks the suitcase up and carries it into the kitchen, setting it down on the table with a dusty thump. It sits there, its clasp rusted and its leather cracked.

My stomach turns over on itself.

Faint against the dirt-aged leather, there are two initials embossed on the front of the case.

AH

Albert Holmwood. *Can* it be? Is that too much of a coincidence? Or is it a sign – a sign that he, that the house, is still calling?

"It was in our attic?"

The front door slams, followed by two hollow-sounding clonks as Felix kicks off his boots.

"Hello? Anyone in?"

"In the kitchen!" Charlie reaches into the fridge for a beer, knocking the cap off and slamming the door. He takes a swig, then holds it out for Felix, who strolls in and takes it gratefully.

"Cheers. What's this then?" he asks, pointing at the case.

"We don't know," Charlie tells him, his voice hushed.

Albie's suitcase… Not in the big-house attic. In ours.

Their initials. Their place. His case.

It can't be.

It's too much to hope for.

My heart hammers on the inside of my ribs like it's trying to crack them open, break the bars, smash its way free as I try the latches on the case.

They stick at first, and for a horrible moment I'm sure the case is locked…but then they snap open, and all three of us breathe out again.

"Well?" It's Felix who asks first, before I've barely even got the lid open.

"Hang on, would you?" I stop and glare at him. Charlie laughs and puts an arm around Felix's shoulders, ruffling his hair in the process.

The lid of the case catches, the hinges protesting loudly as I lift it. At one point, there's a horrible cracking noise and I freeze.

"There's no point just stopping now, is there?" says Charlie. "Do you want me to do it?"

"No!" It's louder than I meant it to be. More protective, my hands instinctively splaying across Albie's initials.

"Okay then. Just…open the case."

I swing the lid all the way open, resting it back on the table, and the three of us peer in.

"More papers. Of course."

There's something different about these ones – as though instead of being piled into the crates and chests simply to get them out of the way, these were placed here on purpose. Deliberately, carefully.

I take out the first pile, tied together with dusty brown string.

"And? Is it to do with Ha— Uh, *his* project?" Charlie corrects himself. And then, unable to wait, he grabs the first papers, flipping the top sheets forward and peering at the ones behind.

"Charlie!" I reach for them, but he twists away, back towards Felix.

"Hang on a minute, I'm looking!" He studies them, his eyes skipping along the lines of typewritten text on each page, nodding and chewing on his bottom lip as he goes. "Mmm. Mmm-hmm. Oh…"

"What? What does 'oh' mean? *What?*"

He glances up at me and half-grins, slipping one sheet out from the middle of the bundle.

"Here. This one. You'll want to read this."

…Can confirm that we have released to our client the documents held for him in the event of his return…

352

"Who's the client?"

"You tell me." Charlie nods at the paper, and I skip forward a couple of lines.

...No wish to contest or delay the sale of Holmwood House. As the sole remaining member of the family, all funds are to be...

In the event of his return.

My hands are shaking so hard that I almost tear the paper as I turn it over to look for a date.

October 1919.

It can't be.

It *has* to be.

I look up at Charlie. He sighs.

"All right, all right. Let's get it out on the table."

I sit on the floor with my back against the sofa, my phone lying in front of me.

Like I have been for the last hour.

"You know they only work if you actually touch them, don't you?"

"Thanks, Charlie. I'll remember that."

"Make the call. The longer you sit here..."

"Just...give me a minute! Please?" I snap at him.

"Fine, fine. Have it your way," he mutters, holding up

his hands and wandering off back into the kitchen.

I stare at my phone some more.

What if I call and he can't answer?

What if I call and he doesn't?

What if I call and he doesn't care?

What if I call and he doesn't even remember who I am?

Worse, what if I call and he doesn't *want* to remember? What if he looks at his phone and sees my name and thinks to himself, *it's the crazy girl*, and – like other people – he flicks me away and out into the darkness.

What if…what if…

What if I'm holding the last piece of the puzzle; the piece we never even knew was missing?

What if I run towards, instead of away?

I pick up my phone and dial.

The number rings twice, then goes to voicemail. Instantly, I hang up.

Okay. Let's try that again.

I hit redial.

Ring-ring…voicemail.

Redial.

Ring-ring…voicemail.

This time, I listen to the greeting. It sounds strange – like him, but not him, as though I'm listening to someone doing an impersonation of him. Like he's doing an impersonation of *himself*. And then there's a beep and I realize I'm now basically leaving a heavy-breathing message on his voicemail and that's not good – so I blurt out the first thing that comes into my head.

"Hal, it's me. Flora. From the hotel. Hopwood Home. Obviously. Listen, there's a case. A suitcase. And stuff. And it's him, it's really him, and you're not here, and I need to tell you… Call me back, okay? Call me. It's Flora. Obviously. Hi. Call me."

I hang up again to find both Charlie and Felix staring at me over their shared bottle of beer.

"What?"

"And he can actually understand all that, can he?" says Charlie pointedly.

I give him what I hope is the sort of look that can turn a man to stone.

And then my phone rings – too fast for him to have even listened to my message.

"Flora?" The voice on the other end makes me ache for him. "You *called*."

This isn't voicemail Hal. It's real Hal. My Hal. And hearing him again, so near and far away, rips open the door I've tried to close, and I don't care.

"We were wrong."

"What? Sorry, I don't—"

"We were wrong! We never knew how the story ended. We only *thought* we did."

My phone pressed to my ear so tightly I'm half-afraid I'll crack the screen, I duck back into the kitchen, shooing my brother and Felix out. I stand in front of the table and I take a deep breath of air that tastes of the past, of dust and secrets…and I tell him. I can hear him listening – I can practically see his eyes widening, see the flush in the hollows of his cheeks as the pieces we never imagined we'd find click into place, one after another in a final rush.

When he speaks at last, it's in a whisper; his voice hoarse with disbelief. "He survived?"

"He survived and he *came back*. It's all here, in his solicitor's letters. They made him speak to doctors, everything. There's a big file with all this stuff in."

"Three years? He stayed out there for three years?"

"No, only one. The casualty station was hit by a shell – that's why they thought he was dead, but he wasn't! He says he was brought back to Britain in 1917, by…" I check the scrawled note I made earlier. "A doctor from Edinburgh who he says basically adopted him. He says, 'He made me myself again.'"

"But what about his family? They'd already had the telegram that said he'd been killed."

"Right, and – are you ready for this? – because of the shell shock and the trauma, he didn't remember who he was. Not until the start of 1919. By then his father had died, and his mother had packed up the house and moved to a flat in London. She died a couple of months later. So when he got better, and he tried to write, there was nobody here and nowhere to send the messages on to. There's a note –

the solicitor thinks they must have got lost when there was a fire at the village post office. He's figured it all out for us. If only we'd found this case *first*…"

"Where was it?

"In the attic."

"How did we miss it? I thought we—"

"Not the Hopwood attic. *Our* attic. *Here.* At my house. Charlie found it this afternoon."

"Oh my god. I mean…" There's a long silence, and something like a chair creaking under sudden weight. "Wow."

"You want the rest?"

"There's more?"

"There's more."

"Should I come back? I should come back…"

"But your dad…?"

"I'll handle my father. I need to come back. I want to."

"No! I mean…yes, but listen. I need to tell you this now, because if I don't, I think my head's going to explode." My mind is racing…but it's not the free-fall whirling I'm used to, the kind I dread more than anything, where everything is shining and cold and ready to consume me. It's something else. "He wrote to his family – when he remembered who they were – and nothing. While that was happening, the house was put up for sale, it's all going through…and he turns up at the gate one day out of the blue. Finds it all locked up, so he goes to the family solicitor, who basically

357

thinks he's seen a ghost. So they go through everything to prove he is who he says he is, and he is, and they offer to cancel the sale, help him reclaim the estate…"

"There's a 'but' coming, isn't there?"

"Kind of? He's just not interested. All he cares about is Iris."

Hal doesn't say anything. I know he's just waiting for me to tell him the rest – but now I'm not sure if I can. My throat closes up and the words are going to choke me if I try and get them out. Because after all this time, after everything he's been through, Albie is still thinking about Iris.

"But she's gone." It takes everything I have to keep my voice steady.

When I pieced this together, half an hour ago, it felt like someone had put a heavy rock on my chest and leaned on it. What must it have felt like for *him*, all those years ago? Finding his way back to her, only to realize he was chasing a memory.

"What happened?"

"She was offered another job, in Yorkshire."

"When the house was shut up?"

"Yes. And she must have married, because there's something here about Albie specifically telling Faraday – that's the solicitor – not to let her know what's happened or that he's back. 'After she waited four years and mourned the man she loved and let him go, how can he come back from the dead?'"

358

Hal groans softly. I know exactly how he feels – my heart hurt when I turned over that note and read it, read between the lines and saw what it really meant.

But there's more. There's more, and I have to tell him.

"There's another photo of him in the bundle – a proper one. It says *France, 1916* on the back in his handwriting. It looks like it was taken at the same time as the one we found – the one of the group of them. But you can see his face better in this one."

Felix turns the picture over. He blinks at it, eyes wide, and hands it to Charlie without a word. Charlie takes it, blows out a long breath and shakes his head...and passes it straight over to me.

"Hal...what was your great-great-grandfather's name? The one who started the family business? Do you know it?"

Something in the set of his jaw, the way he looks straight into the camera. Something familiar about the half-smile – even though he's on the front line and in the middle of hell.

How did we not guess it already? Coincidence on coincidence on coincidence...the house wanting us to know.

"Of course I do – it's on everything round here. The company logo is the founder's signature. Why?"

"Just tell me."

Say it.

There's nothing but silence on the line. Does he know what I'm asking him? Has he figured it out? Has he followed the story all the way to the end – and further?

Eventually, he speaks. "Bertie. His name was Bertie Waverley."

I take a deep breath. "The last letter from Albie – or the last one in this case, anyway – is about the money from the sale of the house. His parents were both dead, and Faraday somehow managed to get the sale through – I don't know, there's loads of stuff about it, and I don't understand *any* of it. But Albie's writing to say he's received the money, and he says he's met a girl and thinks he might settle down and get married. Leave the past behind, make a clean break. But there's something in the letter you need to hear."

"What?"

I know he's figured it out. He's just waiting for me to fill in the gap.

"First up, he says he's changed his name, asks Faraday to only ever use his new one now. And he says, 'You asked what I might do with the remaining proceeds from the sale. I have it in mind to open…to open an hotel.'"

Silence.

Something in the eyes; the way they hold the camera's gaze. The freckles across his face, clear even under the age-spotting on the photograph. A family resemblance that has somehow travelled down through time.

"He changed his name, Hal. Albie Holmwood came home in 1919 and sold the house and *changed his name* and got married and opened a hotel. Albert Holmwood died.

And Bertie Waverley was born – Waverley after the station in Edinburgh. Because of the doctor. *That's* why he disappears, not because he died. He actually lived! Albie was your grandfather's grandfather – I'm sure he was. Albie – this Albie, our Albie – he was your great-great-grandfather."

Bareheaded, holding his uniform cap in the hand resting on his knee. And if the photograph was in colour, his hair would be the colour of copper in the sunlight.

"Hal...I think you're a Holmwood. This isn't just his story. It's *yours.*"

Twenty-six

The first of the autumn leaves are starting to fall as I straighten the sign on the library door for what feels like the fifteenth time.

Closed for private function.

"What time did he say they'd be arriving?" Barney sticks his head out from behind the door, checking his watch.

"About two o'clock." I straighten the sign yet again. Why won't it hang properly? Barney nods and disappears back into the library to put the finishing touches to the set-up in there. Ever since I walked into his office and told him he wasn't going to believe what that research project had turned up, he's been counting down the hours until Hal comes back almost as impatiently as I have.

Almost.

With Charlie's help – and Mira's and Felix's – I've sorted through the little suitcase and pulled some of the other letters and papers back down from the Hopwood attic.

Predictably, Hal left them all in such perfect order that even I could figure it out. I wonder whether he's ever thought about a career in housekeeping?

There is the first letter – the warning from Jane that she won't help Iris ruin her life or her reputation. There are their secret notes, passed between them with the help of GH, George Harbutt, the gardener who lived in my house and gave them a safe place to meet. There is Albie's letter of goodbye, the photo of him with the other soldiers awkwardly arranged in the garden of a French farmhouse. There is Dougie's letter, the nurse's letter, the telegram. There are all the solicitor's papers, the newspaper clippings…the solution to the riddle. The final piece. And there, at the very end of the table, tucked into a silver frame borrowed from the suite upstairs and propped up so he can survey it all, is Albie's portrait.

There is a whole life – two whole lives – laid out before us. Both the person that Albie was and the person he became.

The sound of shoes squeaking on the wooden floor of the lobby makes me look up to see Mira moving at the special walking-very-quickly-but-definitely-not-running speed every hotel staff member develops here. There's a huge grin on her face as she hurries over to the library door.

"They're here!" She grabs my arm and tows me away from the library towards the wide lobby windows overlooking the drive.

A sleek silver car – an old convertible – sweeps into the drive and crunches across the gravel, and even at this distance the sunlight flashes on red hair and my heart skips.

Hal is driving, and next to him in the passenger seat is his grandfather.

The car swings around, and pulls up to the exact spot where the squashed-frog car parked that very first day.

It takes a *lot* not to throw myself through the open door and out onto the drive – but instead I wait and I watch.

I watch Hal jumping out of the car, his sunglasses catching the light, then darting around to open the other door. I watch him holding his arm out to his grandfather to help him – and his grandfather teasingly pushing it away, then taking it after all. He gets out of the car slowly, and then the two of them stand there, side by side, looking up at the front of the house, hands raised to shield their eyes from the low autumn sun.

The Holmwoods – because that's who they are underneath – have finally come home.

What does that feel like, knowing that in another life, this could have been theirs? That it *would* have been theirs? They're not just looking at a building – at the stone and the shining windows and the slate roof – they're looking at a chapter in their history. One neither of them knew they would ever read.

Hal lowers his hand and, even without being able to see

his eyes, I know he's looking at me. I can *feel* his gaze on me. And to me *that* feels like coming home, after a long time away.

Together, they walk slowly across the gravel – Pa in a dark blue suit and pale pink shirt, Hal in black, his hair swept back from his face and his eyes still on me behind the glass pane of the window. He leans his head closer to his grandfather, says something to him, and they both smile, and now that I know what I'm looking for I can see Albie in both of them. They're bringing him home with them.

By the time they reach the entrance, everyone has run to the lobby – confusing nearby guests, who all crane to look out of the window, expecting somebody famous. Why else would the manager of the hotel be holding the door open for these two men? Why else would so many of the staff be waiting?

Every second of it feels like a homecoming. One that's a hundred years overdue.

When his grandfather stops to speak to Barney, Hal doesn't. He turns his head to say something to them both and then walks right on, only stopping when he reaches me.

"Hello," he says, and his voice fills my head and my heart and drives away all the shadows.

"Hello."

The world melts away as we stand there, a breath apart from each other.

"Are you ready?" Hal slips his hand into mine, pulling me closer to him.

"Are *you*?"

His grandfather is waiting at the library door, laughing with Barney as they chat about hotels, about the weather – about small-talk things that are nowhere near as big as this. He watches us as we walk across the lobby, and I can see more than Albie in him. I can see him in Hal and Hal in him.

"You must be Flora," he says, holding out a hand when we reach him; taking mine in his and folding both his hands around it. "My grandson has told me a lot about you."

"I am. And you should know, Hal talks about you a lot," I tell him, glancing back at Hal. He's fidgeting nervously with the edge of his sleeve. His eyes are careful, his whole face cautious – does he think I won't know what to say or what to do? I lean closer, dropping my voice to a whisper. "We met before – you won't remember, it was only for a minute…"

"Ah, yes. We did. Hal told me. I'm afraid I don't – you'll have to forgive me. My memory…" He shakes his head, but his eyes glitter. "It isn't quite what it was." His hands are still clasped around mine, warm and dry, surprisingly soft. "But he also tells me that you've solved our family puzzle."

"Me? No, I just helped. It was mostly Hal."

"Bollocks it was," snorts Hal – and then clamps his hand over his mouth, turning red. "Sorry, Pa."

But his grandfather just laughs. "Perhaps you'd like to show us what you've found…"

Barney opens the library door.

We talk him through all of it. The house, the war, the names…everything. He stops when he sees the portrait, and his fingers grab for the edge of the table as though he needs to steady himself. Behind him, Hal looks at me, then at him.

"That's him all right," he says after a long pause, studying the photo. "That's my grandfather – your great-great-grandfather, Hal." He presses a hand to his chest. "I never knew. All my childhood he told me that story, and he never once let me know it was him."

"Maybe it wasn't," I say quietly. "Maybe Albie Holmwood really did die in the war, as far as he was concerned. Or maybe talking about it like it happened to someone else was the only way he could talk about it at all? Maybe he was trying to protect himself."

"Protect himself from his memories, you mean?" Pa blinks, turning his head ever so slightly towards me. "Yes, perhaps…I think we could all understand that." He reaches a hand towards the photo frame, his outstretched fingers almost touching the glass. "Extraordinary," Pa mutters, shaking his head. "I never knew." He takes the picture in his hands, lifting it up and looking into it, at the face of his own grandfather – familiar and a stranger, and a puzzle solved.

He sets the picture down, reaching into the pocket of his jacket without ever taking his eyes off the frame, and pulls out another photo – smaller, and with creases across it. In it, a little boy is sitting on the floor in front of a much older man – his grandfather. The man's face is wrinkled, heavier with age – but still clearly recognizable as Albie, or Bertie, or whatever label he had chosen to wear. "My grandfather," says Pa, nodding…and then, resting a finger on the boy's face, "and myself."

He lays the photo down on the table in front of the other picture, and eases himself down into the nearest chair.

I clear my throat and reach for the Hopwood Home folder on the table. "There was one more letter. It was in the top of the case." I open the folder and pull out an envelope. "And it's never been opened." I hold it out to Pa. "It's addressed to Iris, but we thought perhaps you might want it."

"Never been opened," he says quietly. When he takes it, his hands shake – they shake so hard that he almost drops it again. He turns the envelope over in his hands, running a finger along the writing on the front – a gesture so familiar because I've seen Hal do it on every single letter we read.

Albie, Pa, Hal.

All of them are here.

"I can't think of a better time or a better place to open it, can you?" He looks around for something to open it with.

Hal's there, already beside him. "Are you sure?"

"Quite sure. Here. Now. I don't suppose anyone has a... ah, thank you." He smiles as Barney hands him a silver letter-opener. "I don't think my eyes will be up to it, I'm afraid," he says – but I don't think that's true. "Hal, would you?"

"Of course, Pa."

Hal slides the letter from the envelope – the last letter, for the last time.

This is how the story ends.

My dearest Iris,

Faraday tells me you are married to a good man, that you have built a new life for yourself in Yorkshire, and that you are happy. He also tells me that you are expecting a child. You may wonder why I have never tried to find you, and the truth is that for so long, I was so very lost that I could not even find myself. I believe the man who went to war died there for a time, and it was only with love and care from others that he began to come alive again. By then, you had – and rightly,

for I wish you nothing but happiness –
taken a different path from the one we
imagined we would walk. Should you one
day read this, I hope you will allow me to
congratulate you and to give both you and
your family, however large or small it may be,
my most sincere and heartfelt hopes for the
future.

Among the papers you left with Faraday,
I found an instruction that should either I or
any of my belongings return, any letters of
yours that survived the war should be burned.
Per your request, I have burned the greater
part of those few I had managed to keep with
me – all but the most precious, and I hope that
you will trust and permit me to keep these
small tokens for myself as a reminder not just
of you, but of who I once was. As for mine to
you, I leave them – as you have – here, where
they belong. Should you ever choose to claim
them, they will be waiting for you.

I wish you well, my Iris. May your path
hold nothing but joy.

Ever yours,
AH.

The library is absolutely silent as Albie's last words fade

away. Shaking his head, Hal places the envelope on the folder.

"I can't believe it was in your attic. How did that happen?" He reaches for me, his fingers twisting through mine; both our hands locked together as he pulls me away from the table to the relative safety of the bookshelves and Barney offers round glasses of champagne from a tray that has magically appeared.

"I don't know – I guess it just ended up getting put up there at some point. Maybe Albie couldn't get back into the main house, but he could get to the estate cottage, and he wanted to just leave everything behind, start over? Or maybe it's because that was *their* place?"

Charlie clears his throat loudly. Everyone's turning to look at him, and I realize he's waiting to say something.

"Actually, there's one more thing," he says – and then I see Felix and Philippe carrying something in from the lobby. A box, and what looks like a big book.

No. Not a big book. An album. An old photo album.

One of our old photo albums.

"What's going on?" Hal's breath is warm in my ear.

"I don't know." I shake my head and pull a face at Charlie. He pretends he hasn't seen me, but he can't hide the twitch of a smile at the side of his mouth.

My brother is up to something,

"If I can have your attention for just a minute," he says, clearly enjoying himself, "there's one more thing we need to do." He takes the box from Felix with one hand, reaching into it with the other. "And that's to introduce you to Iris."

What?

He lifts a frame out of the box and sets it down on the table, right next to Albie's. It's very small, the picture so dark that I can't even see it from here.

"While we were sorting everything back into the case, we found a pocket where Albie had put a photograph of her – probably the one he took with him to France – and this." He drops the box and moves his hands apart, and suddenly he's holding what looks like a piece of blue-grey string, plaited and tied into a loop. A string or...

"Is that the ribbon?" Hal whispers to me, and I can feel his heart beating against my shoulder as we turn to look at each other. "Her hair ribbon, from the dance?"

"He kept it all that time – and then he left it here."

Oh, my heart. He came back and he left it here, along with all the other pieces of them. Where they belonged.

"Do you want to know what she looked like?" Hal nudges me forward and before he's even finished speaking I'm across the floor and straining to see past everybody else who has crowded around the table to see her face in the frame.

There she is – the picture darkened by age, but clear enough. Long dark hair pinned back, dark eyes and wide lips. She's pretty, and seeing their photos side by side, the two of them reunited after all this time, I can picture the two of them dancing, laughing, smiling, walking through the gardens and the corridors. I can picture the life they could – *should* – have had.

"What's the album for?" I point to the book as Philippe passes it to Charlie.

"Oh, that's the best part," he says, thumbing through the pages. He stops about halfway through, holding it closed against his chest with his finger tucked between the covers to mark the page. "I thought she looked familiar, so we did a little digging to get to the bottom of this once and for all. Come take a look."

He opens it, turning it to face outwards.

On the left-hand page is another photograph, almost as old, held in place by ornate cardboard corners. It's a picture of a family: a man, a woman and two young children – one a baby in the woman's arms, one little more than a toddler. The adults are both looking at the camera – but I can only see *her*.

It's the same person.

It's Iris.

And that's my grandmother's old photo album.

My mouth moves, but no sound comes out. My hand tightens around Hal's, but I can't move.

What is my grandmother doing with a photo of Iris?

"This," Charlie says, pointing to the man in the picture, "is Jack Clark. He came from Yorkshire, fought in the Great

War and afterwards he went back to the village where he was born. He met a girl who'd moved there to work, and they married and had a family. This –" he taps the picture again, this time pointing at the toddler – "is Sibyl Clark. She grew up, married a man called Alec Downing and had a daughter, Emily."

Oh my god.

The world spins and the air in the room thins.

Hal is already staring at me, already there too.

"That's not possible. It's just not. How?"

Emily Downing was my grandmother.

Which means Iris Campbell, our Iris, Albie's Iris…was my great-great-grandmother.

Iris and Albie, Flora and Hal.

Not just their story.

Ours.

Hal's mouth is open and his eyes are wide – and everyone is suddenly talking all at once…and I have to check, but yes, the noise is definitely outside my head and not inside it. It's not me.

Coincidence on coincidence on coincidence.

When there's that many, it starts to feel like maybe it's something else.

All the pieces that had to move, all the stars that had to align; all the paths that had to cross, to join, to meet…

All to find them, out in the dark; to find *us*.

"Are you okay?" Hal's voice cuts through the rest of the

noise. Of course it does, because he's in my head. But when I look at him, he's as pale as I feel.

I just point at the door. It's all I can manage.

He glances back over his shoulder at his grandfather, who's dabbing his eyes with a handkerchief and now busily examining the photo album with Charlie and Felix. "I think maybe that's a really good idea. Come on."

His hand and mine entwined, his past and mine entwined, we slip out of the library, out through the quiet lobby and into the gardens and, without saying it or even really thinking it, we head for the maze, one hand on the hedge, letting it lead us further and further into the heart of it.

Their photos, their letters, didn't tell their story – they needed us to finish it. Not to end it, but to complete it. To bring together all the parts and all the pieces of it – of *them*. To solve the puzzle that was each of them and both of them. And solving that meant I got to solve me too. Or to start to, at least.

One hand on the hedge, one hand in Hal's.

Maybe it takes a lifetime to solve a person, maybe more. It took more than that to solve Albie. Maybe we're not even *meant* to be solved in the end. There are no right or wrong answers. We are not simply one thing or another; not two halves that never quite touch. We are not written in the binary code of ones and zeroes, on or off, up or down, black or white. Manic or depressed.

Maybe we're all the whole of a compass, complete – and we deserve to be remembered that way.

Him, them…

Me.

And that? That's enough. How could it not be?

I let my hand drop from the hedge. I don't need to keep it there any longer.

Hal looks nervous. "We're not going to get lost, are we?"

I shake my head and lace my fingers more tightly through his, pulling him closer.

"It'll be okay," I say. "I think I know where I'm going now."

The End

Author's note

I never intended to learn so much about the First World War. I never intended to write about it at all, really. I set out to write a story about a girl with a history...and then real history came and got involved. It does that.

The Pieces of Ourselves started as an idea about a girl running away, colliding with a boy running towards, and how that meeting might change them both. In Hal's case, it's the past he's running towards, hiding from his present in it. Flora, meanwhile, is running from her past self – or an image of it that she needs to learn to see more clearly.

I've been in Flora's position, and I know how it feels. I have tried to draw from some of my own experiences in writing her. That's why she means so much to me, and why it was so important to tell her story with honesty and with hope – because there is always room for both.

I have no experience of war (and definitely not of the

First World War) to draw from, so for Albie's story I have relied on reading and research. I read a lot about shell shock – which we would now broadly recognize as a kind of PTSD – its effects…and its so-called treatments, which were for the vast majority of patients ineffective or even downright cruel. As someone who has needed a little help and support with their mental health several times over the years, it was hard and often heartbreaking reading. The condition was not well understood, and many never received the right kind of help, or any at all.

But today, for those of us – like Flora, like myself and like so many others – who need a similar sort of understanding from time to time, we are much more likely to find it. Every conversation we have about mental health helps to normalize it, to increase our knowledge of it. Most of all, there is help – which can now come in a wide range of forms.

Flora's mental health is not her story: it affects her story, but it's only one small part of it. She's so much more than just that. We all are.

Acknowledgements

Many people have contributed to this book and made it possible – some in small or surprising ways, others in much bigger, more obvious ones. But without them, it simply would not exist.

My deepest thanks go to my editor at Usborne: Stephanie King, who with her patience, careful reading and feedback, her support and her guidance, has taken Flora's story and turned it into something far better than I could ever have imagined. Whenever I got lost in the middle of it all, the light at the end of the tunnel was always Stephanie, waving a flare. If this book has a heart, it is hers.

Rebecca Hill, who listened to what was at first a very vague idea and helped to shape it into something that could honestly be called a story worth telling.

Juliet Mushens – for knowing exactly what's needed and when, always. Liza DeBlock, for a level of admin efficiency that shows the rest of us up. (Or me, anyway.)

Stevie Hopwood, for unending enthusiasm and ideas. The Hopwood couldn't have been named after a better person.

Sarah Stewart for her copyediting skills, and Anne Finnis and Gareth Collinson for their eagle-eyed proofreading.

Sarah Cronin for interior design, and Will Steele for a gorgeous cover.

All the team at Usborne for all their work in turning ideas into actual books on shelves.

Gemma Varnom, whose messages and emotional support made all the difference when things got the better of me. Without her kindness and generosity of spirit, writing this book would have been a much colder and darker experience.

My family, who have lived inside this book almost as much as I have over the last few years – and now know more about both the First World War and its aftermath than I imagine they ever expected to.

Dale Dennehy, Garden & Park Manager of Dyrham Park National Trust property near Bath, who gave me a guided tour of the grounds as part of a research trip for a different book. That one never quite happened, but what I learned during that visit planted a seed that grew into a different story: this one.

I read a lot of books about the Somme and the life of a soldier in the First World War, but the one I found myself returning to was by John Lewis-Stempel, *Where Poppies Blow: The British Soldier, Nature, The Great War*, with its deeply moving, human perspective on life on the Western Front.

Although the Hopwood Home hotel and Hopwood-in-the-Hollows are fictional (as are Fallowmill and other houses mentioned in the book), the concept of the Thankful Village is real. The loss of life after the First World War was so extreme, so widespread, that towns and villages whose sons all returned from the war were the exception and not the rule.

A real-world version of the pillar in the glasshouse where the gardeners carved their initials can be found in the Thunderbox Room of the Lost Gardens of Heligan in Cornwall, where the garden staff signed their names on the wall before leaving to join the war. But wealth and privilege were no protection from grief either, and while the original owners of Hopwood Home are my own invention, their story was partly inspired by that of the Hoare family of Stourhead – now another National Trust property. Henry Hoare, their sole son and heir who died during the course of the Great War, lent his name to Hal – and it was only after I had written several drafts of the book that I realized one of the buildings in the Stourhead gardens is known as the Temple of Flora.

About the author

Maggie Harcourt is the critically-acclaimed author of *The Last Summer of Us*, *Unconventional* and *Theatrical*. As well as studying medieval literature at UCL, Maggie has variously worked as a PA, a hotel chambermaid and for a French chef before realizing her dreams and beginning to write full time. She lives in Bath with her family.

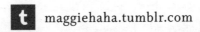 maggiehaha.tumblr.com

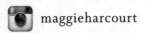 maggieharcourt

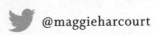 @maggieharcourt

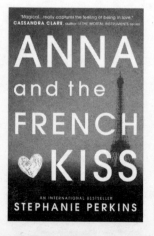